In Love We Trust

by Marnie L. Pehrson

Published by CES Business Consultants
CES Publishing
Printed in the United States of America

ISBN 0-9676162-5-5

To Marcia,
for taking a chance
on me and making this
such an enjoyable adventure!

Acknowledgments

Marcia Lynn McClure took a risk on me when I was a fledgling author, partnered with me on CleanRomanceclub.com, and introduced me to her loyal readers. That act of faith on her part led to the writing of these two ebooks and many others.

Through revisions and editorial suggestions made by my editor Julie Bellon and my faithful proofreaders, Betty Morton and Cathy Nattress, these two stories are combined for your reading convenience in print form. Any errors that survived are probably things I stuck back in when they weren't looking.

Thanks must also go to the loyal Clean Romance Club fans for encouraging me to keep writing. Last but not least, special thanks to my husband and six children who spent nights and weekends without their wife/mother so these two stories could be put into print.

Chapter 1

Mandy Gates jogged through the park, her cross trainers slapping the wet pavement as the rain drizzled down her cheeks and arms. Her drenched chestnut hair, pulled back in a pony tail swayed back and forth with each step she took. Faintly through the Saturday morning mist, she could discern the headlights of an approaching automobile. As the beams broke through the fog and the car passed her, the driver waved and Mandy returned the greeting.

Again alone on the road, Mandy chuckled to herself as she pondered upon park etiquette. Anywhere else in town, you'd pass someone without acknowledgement, but in the Chickamauga Battlefield there was this unspoken rule. You always wave at joggers, walkers or bikers in the park - to refuse to do so would be just plain rude. Where would be your Southern hospitality to pass a jogger and not wave? Or to jog by a car and not acknowledge the driver?

Perhaps it was the old South which the park symbolized – those days gone by when people knew all their neighbors, looked out for each other, cooked boat loads of fried chicken, corn on the cob, mashed potatoes and gravy and showed respect with a string of "yes ma'am's and no sirs."

Lost in her thoughts of how much society had changed since her grandmother's time, Mandy rounded the corner and came upon a rider dressed in full Confederate uniform atop a beautiful auburn bay. Mandy came to an abrupt halt and the rider, being just as surprised to see a young woman in front of him, pulled the reins and the horse pranced about for a moment or two and stopped.

"Mornin', Ma'am," he greeted in a rich deep Southern drawl as he tipped his hat and nodded. His dark brown eyes twinkled in the early morning light and dimples appeared on his unshaven cheeks, the day's beard growth matching his short-cropped hair.

"Good morning," her eyes caught his and then traveled over his gray uniform.

"Sorry to startle you, Ma'am," he smiled and pulled a toothpick from his lips.

"So you're a re-enactor?" Mandy stated the obvious.

"Yes, Ma'am, my regiment's just right up here at Widow Glenn's," he pointed his toothpick in the direction in which he had been traveling. Just as he did so, a flash of lightning cracked, followed by an immediate roll of deafening thunder. Mandy flinched and looked up at the dark gray clouds in the direction of the lightning bolt.

"You really shouldn't be joggin' out in this, Ma'am," he pointed his toothpick at her and then toward the sky from which plummeted a sheet of rain. "Here!" he tossed his toothpick aside and stretched out his hand to her.

"What?" she looked at him puzzled.

He shook his palm, "Come on. Let me give you a ride to shelter."

Mandy hesitated and then another lightning bolt struck with an instant earth-shaking rumble. She placed her soaked palm in his, and he pulled her into the saddle behind him in one powerful swoop. Immediately the stranger nudged his horse's ribs and the animal bolted off the main road and into the woods. With the sudden jolt, Mandy grabbed the stranger's waist holding onto the scratchy wool uniform and leaned her head against his broad shoulders as the horse leapt over fallen tree trunks and darted amidst the lush green forest. The rain continued to pour, the lightning to flash and the thunder to rumble. Mandy found her heart racing – not from the jogging she'd been doing prior to meeting the stranger in the middle of the road –

but from the sheer exhilaration of finding herself on the back of a horse with a Civil War soldier in a thunderstorm.

Her imagination, already aroused by her previous thoughts, needed no nudging to leap into a daydream that she was a maiden in distress being rescued by a gallant southern gentleman. When the horse approached a small shed, the stranger leapt from the horse, tied it to a tree, put his hands on Mandy's waist and lifted her with the same ease he would lift a small child from the horse's back. Grasping her hand, he guided her to the small shelter. It wasn't more than a lean-to – three sides and an angular roof made of old boards.

Just as they stepped under the shelter, lightning struck a nearby tree and it fell in a deafening crash not fifty feet in front of the structure. The nervous horse whinnied and pranced. Without thought, Mandy clasped her arms around the soldier's uniformed waist and buried her head in his broad, wool-clad shoulder. His gentle hand patted her back.

"It's all right," he whispered in a low comforting tone. Noting her shivering shoulders, the man removed his wool coat and draped it over Mandy's soaked navy t-shirt. She looked down at herself – her rain drenched cross trainers, crew socks and spandex running shorts cut to her thighs. The Confederate soldier's coat draped over her floppy Blood Assurance t-shirt gave her the feeling her modern reality was slipping into the historical past.

The rain continued to pour, but the delay between lightning and thunder increased, indicating that the storm was moving away from the area. Mandy retrieved her arms from around the stranger and extended her hand to him, "I'm Mandy Gates."

"Bronson Reilly," the re-enactor appeared to be in his late twenties and evidently worked out at a gym, for with his coat removed his white shirt refused to mask his muscular form.

"So are you re-enacting the Battle of Chickamauga?" she felt drawn to his big brown eyes and would have looked up into them longer, but forced herself to divert her gaze.

"Preparing for it. It's not for another month or so – September 18-21st," he replied.

"That's right, I forgot," she looked out at the rain splattering on the leaves.

"It's starting to lighten up. I'll give you a ride back to your car," he offered.

"That's okay, maybe just a lift back to where you found me."

He stepped out from under the lean-to, untied the horse and motioned for her to join him. He helped her atop the animal and climbed into the saddle in front of her. Since the rain had become only a slight drizzle, he took the horse at an easy gait back to the main road to where he'd found her. Then stopping at the side of the road, he inquired, "Are you sure you don't want me to take you to your car?"

"My car's not in the park. I live over in a neighborhood just outside of it."

"Then a ride home?" he offered.

Mandy could just see herself riding up on the back of a Confederate soldier's horse and having nosey Mrs. Wallington quizzing her for weeks. Her neighbor constantly coaxed her to find herself a husband, settle down and have a family. At twenty-six, Mandy was satisfied with teaching history and math at the local middle school and had little interest in getting involved with anyone. She'd seen too many people she cared about fall victim to doomed relationships. She wouldn't be joining their ranks.

"No thanks, just let me off over here at Delores Lane, and I'll jog the rest of the way. I don't wanna hold you up."

"It's no trouble, Ma'am," he offered again.

"Really, just let me off down here at Delores. I'll be fine. I don't live far from here."

The horse trotted onward and when they reached her road, he stopped and put out his arm to help her descend.

"Thank you so much for the ride, Mr. Reilly," she pulled his coat from her shoulders and handed it to him.

"You're most welcome, Mrs. – is it Mrs. Gates?" He slipped his arms into the coat.

"Miss – Miss Gates," she started to back away from the horse and its handsome rider.

"Enjoy your day," he smiled and tipped his hat.

"You too, thanks again!" she called as she turned to jog away.

~*~

The rhythmic cadence of the windshield wipers carried Mandy's mind back to the previous Saturday morning. Her unusual encounter with the re-enactor had been surreal. The whole event – his gallant rescue and polite demeanor – made her feel as if she had stepped back in time. Even now, amidst the Monday morning mist, she could still catch the faint scent of his wet wool uniform.

She turned into the school parking lot, drove around to the teacher's side and stepped out of her car. As she did so, her friend Jan Griffin waved as she too emerged from her car and opened her umbrella.

"Hi!" Mandy waved as she quickly pressed the button on her keys to lock the door and made a run toward the building.

Jan smiled and came toward her. "Where's your umbrella?" she inquired, extending hers to cover both of them. Jan adjusted her satchel on her shoulder.

"I keep losing them, so I quit buying them," Mandy replied as the two teachers stepped under the awning and Mandy opened the door. Jan shook the rain from her umbrella and closed it.

"How was your weekend?" Jan asked as she raked a hand through her sandy blonde hair.

The image of Bronson Reilly astride his horse flashed into Mandy's mind. "Great . . . it was . . . great," Mandy felt the smile creeping onto her face. She bit her lip to hold it back.

Jan stopped walking down the corridor and put her hand on Mandy's arm. "What happened?"

"Nothing really," Mandy knew her face looked like a teenager with a silly crush on the cutest boy in class.

"You met someone," Jan stated with one raised eyebrow.

5

Mandy looked around the corridor, making sure no other teachers were within earshot. "I don't know that you could call it *meeting someone*. Come on, I'll tell you about it in my classroom."

Jan followed Mandy to her room and waited for her to unlock the door. They stepped inside and Mandy set her satchel on the desk, began retrieving items from it, and arranging them on her desk.

Jan leaned against the other side of it, her curious eyes following Mandy's movements. "So? Are you going to tell me," she prompted and looked at her wristwatch. "I do have work to do."

Mandy glanced at her friend and wondered how to begin. Her reaction had been rather silly, really. Perhaps she was making too big of a deal out of it, but her chance meeting with the re-enactor felt significant. She walked across the classroom, shut the door, and turned to her friend.

Approaching Jan, Mandy began telling her the story. She started with her jog and suddenly meeting Bronson Reilly atop his horse. Finally, she concluded, "It was like I'd stepped back into the past. I would have thought I was there if I hadn't looked down to see my t-shirt and shorts!"

"Wow!" Jan whispered. "So are you going to see him again?"

Mandy shrugged, "I doubt it."

"You should've let him give you a ride back to your house. Then he'd know how to find you again," Jan rose from her perch on Mandy's desk and prepared to leave.

"Nah, it's better this way – a fond memory – without really getting to know him and finding out he's a loser like all the other men I've known."

"All men are *not* losers," Jan scolded. "Just look at my Kevin. He's a gem."

"Yeah, well, they broke the mold when they made Kevin," Mandy winked with a smile. "He was the last one."

Jan shook her head, "You're crazy, you know that?" Mandy did not reply. "Well, I better get to work. Try to keep your nose out of the clouds and don't forget the faculty meeting at ten."

"I'll be there," Mandy said as she stepped behind her desk and pulled out her chair.

Jan left and Mandy sat down. The week before school started was always a blurring whirlwind of activity. The open house would be Thursday night, and she had so much preparation to do before then. She pushed her romantic thoughts aside and set to work.

Chapter 2

The second Friday in August, after the first full week of school, Mandy awoke to her alarm. She rolled over and jammed the snooze button, burying her head in her pillow. Closing her eyes, she willed her mind to continue the dream she'd been having. She was running on the rainy battlefield in a flowing dress, straight into the arms of her Confederate soldier. As she lay there, trying to continue the dream, her history teacher's imagination carried the scene into an outlandish Civil War tale in which he not only rescued her from a thunderstorm, but also from dangerous villains. She'd envisioned such a scene several times over the last couple weeks, and it always culminated in an ardent encounter with her irresistible rescuer.

The alarm rang once more and she forced herself out of bed, into the shower and prepared for work. After a quick breakfast, Mandy stepped out of her small two-bedroom home and locked the door.

"Ready for the weekend, Mandy?" Mrs. Wallington's kind elderly voice wafted through the air as she peeked over her rose bushes to greet her youthful neighbor.

"Yes, I am! It's been a long first week of school," Mandy flashed a grin and went to the garage to retrieve her bike. She lived close enough to the middle school that whenever the weather cooperated, she preferred riding to driving.

"You going out tonight?" Mrs. Wallington's voice was filled with hope for the hopeless.

"No, ma'am. I'm renting a movie and kicking back in my PJ's with some popcorn." Mandy climbed aboard her bike.

9

"Too pooped to party – eh?" the silver-haired woman's eyes followed Mandy to the edge of the driveway.

"You could say that," Mandy waved over her shoulder, "Have a good day, Mrs. Wallington."

"You too, dear!" the woman called and returned to her pruning.

Mandy rode to the school, locked her bike, scurried into the building, and up the steps to her classroom.

"Morning, Mandy!" Jan poked her head inside Mandy's classroom.

"Hi Jan!" Mandy greeted.

"Don't forget about the change with fifth period today." The seventh grade English teacher ran a hand through her sandy-blond hair.

"That's right . . . the historian's coming today," Mandy muttered under her breath as she shuffled papers on her desk and then lifted her eyes back to the doorway. "Thanks for the reminder!" Jan waved and disappeared down the hallway as students began trickling into Mandy's room.

Grateful that it was Friday, Mandy sailed through her day looking forward to a relaxing weekend. The first week of school always took more energy to remember names and get to know new students. Mandy had learned that the rules she put into effect that first week would set the tone for the remainder of the school year. Seventh graders, still in the spit-ball and food-fight stage of life, were hard enough to handle even with well-defined rules. After four years of teaching, Mandy had learned that it was easier to be strict and then lighten up as the year progressed than to attempt the reverse. She felt satisfied with the level of respect her students showed her and expected a good year as a result.

By the time fifth period rolled around, both the students and the teachers were ready for the weekend. Jubilant that they were to obtain a reprieve from their typical last class of the day, the excited youth chattered as they entered the auditorium. Mandy took her place at the back of the room where it would be her task to keep rowdy youngsters in line.

Soon the principal appeared at the front of the auditorium, called the group to order and introduced their guest speaker – a local Civil War historian who would be showing them a collection of artifacts and memorabilia and sharing what it would have been like to live through the war. Mandy's ears perked up, and she motioned for two chattering teenage boys in the row ahead of her to be quiet. They were talking so loudly, she couldn't even hear the man's name announced. She knew from the last faculty meeting that a historian would be addressing the seventh graders, but the principal hadn't specified the Civil Ward period.

Mandy pulled the pen from behind her ear and prepared to take notes on the yellow legal pad in front of her. When she looked up next it was to see Bronson Reilly striding to the podium in his re-enactor's uniform. Mandy's breath caught and her eyes opened wide as her palms began to perspire. The imagery of her dreams flooded into her mind. She closed her eyes and shook her head in an effort to drive away the thoughts. If only her pulse would stop drumming in her ears, she might be able to concentrate on what he was saying. It was something about the war, she knew that much – *yes what else would a Civil War historian be talking about?* she scolded herself.

Mandy knew that he must be an excellent speaker – not because she registered anything that he said – but because the children were laughing at the humor he sprinkled throughout his presentation. They sat spellbound by his stories and eagerly examined the artifacts he passed them.

All Mandy could do was notice his clean-shaven features. His brown almond-shaped eyes even met hers for an instant, and she looked down at her notepad. The next time she lifted her gaze, her eyes traveled the length of his broad shoulders. The deep intonation of his voice mesmerized her into another daydream of life in the 1860's. Before she knew it, she rode with him on the back of his horse through the Battlefield as bullets whizzed by them. He spurred his horse and took a sharp right through a thicket, under a low hanging limb, and over a fence.

Suddenly he stopped the horse and pulled her from its back, into a bunker where he shielded her protectively with his body as gunfire rent the air. He settled his rifle atop the rise and opened fire. A flurry of shots ensued. She lowered herself into the trench. Leaning her back against the embankment, she hunched lower as he continued to defend them against their assailants. Finally, silence prevailed. He slid down, leaning his back against the embankment beside her and resting his rifle across his knees. He gathered her in his arms, making sure that she remained unharmed.

Those brown eyes gazed into hers as he held her in his secure embrace. Mandy could feel the warmth of his breath on her lips and her mouth watered in anticipation of his kiss when . . .

"Mandy, are you gonna sit here all day?" Jan put her hand on Mandy's shoulder and nudged her. She looked around and nearly half of the students had already cleared the auditorium. Regaining her bearings, Mandy glanced up at Jan and then to the podium where Bronson stood talking with principal Boynton.

"Are you okay?" Jan asked.

"Oh, I'm sorry. I guess I was just in my own little world," Mandy released a nervous chuckle.

"I figured you'd be enraptured by that historian's facts and stories, but you don't look like you listened to a word he said." Jan pointed to Mandy's legal pad, which lacked her usual copious notes. Mandy rarely missed an opportunity to learn something that would help her in her career. She loved to learn little tidbits of history and make it come alive for her students, or discover a new way to teach math where her students could better understand it.

"Oh, I was enraptured enough," Mandy rose from her seat, gave her friend a playful smile, and put her back to the podium.

Jan looked from Mandy to Bronson and back. Her eyes widened with understanding. "You mean . . . "

"Uh huh," Mandy nodded affirmatively.

"*Your* re-enactor?" Jan breathed in hushed astonishment.

Mandy nodded again. "I need to get out of here," she whispered as her eyes searched for the best exit.

"Are you kidding? You can't let him leave without talking to him!"

"Oh, yes I can," she insisted and stepped past Jan to make her way out the back of the auditorium.

Jan shook her head with a sigh, returned to where she'd sat during the lecture, and gathered her notebook. When she reached the isle, Bronson stood in front of her.

"Mr. Reilly, I enjoyed your presentation," Jan smiled and extended her hand in greeting.

"Thank you, I'm glad you liked it," he nodded as he gave her a firm handshake.

"You really kept their attention. You should be a teacher," she added.

"Thanks," he smiled and still stood blocking her way.

"Can I help you with something?" she inquired.

"I noticed you were talking with Ms. Gates. Could you please tell me where her room is?"

Jan bit back a smile that threatened to burst from her lips. With a disinterested expression, she gave him the room number and directions. Thanking her, he shifted his crate of gear under his right arm and left.

Mandy stood at her desk gathering test papers to take home and grade over the weekend. She shoved them in her briefcase, flipped off the lights, shut the door, entered the hallway, descended the stairs, and exited the building to find her bicycle. Just as she left, Bronson arrived at room 243 and peered through the small rectangular window. Finding the room dark inside, he jiggled the locked doorknob, dropped his hand to his side, and left.

13

Chapter 3

Cara Richards slumped on her front porch steps, her head in her hands as tears rolled down her cheeks and her blonde hair fell in her face. Her head throbbed as she brushed the tears from her swollen eyes. Hearing the ticking of bicycle wheels approaching, she hurried to her feet, spun around and opened the screen door. Quickly shutting the door behind her, she stopped just inside the living room and her eyes fell to her protruding belly. Her baby boy would be born in only two more months and the thought of bringing him into the world in which she lived resurrected her tears.

I've got to get out of here for his sake she thought to herself and headed for her bedroom where she searched around for a suitcase. She pulled one from the closet, opened it on the bed, and crossed to the dresser. Her wedding photo caught her eye and she lifted it. In an instant, her mind transported back to that day over five years ago. It had been beautiful. Jason made her feel so loved and showered her with the attention she craved but had never received from anyone else. She could say that much for him - he gave her plenty of attention. Little did she know on her wedding day that when she vowed "for better or worse" that he would get the better of her and she would get the worst of him.

The last five years had been a roller coaster ride of fun and fear, passion and pain. He could make her feel like a million dollars or like a million knives had been stabbed in her back. Who was she kidding? She could never leave! He would just come after her. In her weakened state, he'd beg forgiveness, promise never to hurt her again and put on his irresistible charm. In an instant, she'd succumb, and she'd be right back where she started. To leave was just too much work for nothing.

She replaced the photo and put the suitcase away. *He promised that when the baby comes things will be different. Surely, he'll do better for his son* she quoted his lies and pretended that she believed them. *After all, Jason wants the baby. He was so excited when we found out I was expecting. Yes, it will be different once the baby's born.* Cara entered the bathroom, splashed some water on her face and went to the kitchen to start dinner.

When the doorbell rang, Cara's pulse quickened and her head jerked to read the time on the microwave. *Is Jason home already? Dinner isn't ready!* Then she realized just how foolish her reaction had been. Jason wouldn't ring the doorbell. She turned to the sink, washed the chicken batter from her hands, and dried them on a towel. When she opened the front door, she found Mandy standing in front of her with a loaf of freshly baked quick bread in her hands.

"Hi Cara! I got carried away and made too much bread so I thought you might like a loaf," Mandy cheerily stepped past Cara and entered the house without invitation.

"Thanks," Cara replied as Mandy headed for the kitchen with her loaf of pumpkin nut bread and set it on the round kitchen table. The last thing Cara needed with Jason due home any moment was Mandy chatting inside the house. Jason didn't let her have friends. He either drove them away with his violent temper or his well-crafted lies about Cara. But Mandy wouldn't take the hint. She'd moved in next door eighteen months earlier, and she wouldn't budge – not even when Jason played his mind games. She continued to appear at Cara's door with baked goods, an inspiring quote or just a comical story to cheer her day.

Cara trailed Mandy to the kitchen, "I really don't have time to chat now, Mandy. I need to finish dinner before Jason gets home."

She gave the microwave clock a nervous glance. "He should be here any minute." Mandy pulled out a kitchen chair and sat down.

"That's right, gotta have that food ready and waiting for Jason, don't you?" Mandy rolled her eyes, her voice dripping with sarcasm.

"He just likes his routine is all," Cara wondered why she defended the man who would never defend her.

Mandy bit her lip and nodded. Cara knew that look. Mandy was holding back a sarcastic comment about Jason. "Is there anything I can help you with before I go? Do you need help moving anything or reaching anything? You don't need to be straining yourself at this stage of the game."

Cara's eyes softened, "No, thank you. I really appreciate you asking though. The bread smells delicious." Cara lifted the cellophane-wrapped loaf to her nose. "This is more than enough. You're always so thoughtful."

"Ah, it was nothing." Mandy waved her hand, "Like I said, I got carried away and made too much." Cara followed Mandy's eyes as she looked around the immaculate house, which couldn't hide the tale-tale signs of abuse – a hole in the wall here, a crooked lamp glued back together there, and a chair missing a leg at the kitchen table. Cara turned her back to Mandy and closed her eyes, wincing at the memory of how that chair leg had been broken over her own back. She picked up the tongs and rotated a piece of chicken.

"I guess I'll be getting out of your hair," Mandy rose to her feet. "Holler if you need anything – okay?"

Cara nodded, "Thanks again, Mandy. I can't wait to try the bread."

As Mandy reached for the doorknob, she looked back over her shoulder. "I'll be home tonight. If you need me for anything, just come on over."

"I'll be fine," Cara's mouth turned up in a weak smile, and she shut the door behind her neighbor.

Something was brewing. Mandy could feel it. It had been a couple months since the last major "incident" at the Richards'. Every couple weeks there'd be some form of violent argument, but the major incidents could almost be timed like clockwork. Mandy remembered the last one vividly. It was that hot June evening when her central heat and air went out. She had the bedroom windows open to let in a bit of breeze. The yelling and screaming from next door woke her, and then there were the sirens and flashing lights that followed.

Standing on her front porch, she could hear Jason convincing the police officers that his wife had had a nightmare and that she just screamed out in her sleep. Cara had appeared at the door and agreed that it was just a nightmare – nothing more. In irritation, Mandy stood and watched the officers drive away. Jason shot her a deadly glare as she reentered her home. He made her sick. He had all the charm of a snake oil salesman, with the ability to convince almost anyone that somehow his petite pregnant wife "had it coming to her."

Mandy couldn't be fooled though. She'd watched her sister go through the same ordeal for nearly eight years. She knew the head games a spider like Jason Richards played. She also knew the predictable irrational behavior exhibited by a woman trapped within his web.

Mandy hated standing by and watching someone she cared about enslaved in bondage. Nothing was ever good enough for Jason. The house was never clean enough, his clothes never wrinkle-free enough, his food never prepared exactly to suit him. Anything that wasn't perfect was an excuse for a beating. Mandy despised the helplessness of knowing that no matter what hand of help she offered, Cara would never take it. An evening nearly a year ago, when Jason was out with his drinking buddies, Cara broke down and admitted to Mandy that she'd left him three times before. Each time he had convinced her to return. He was like a drug that she couldn't live without. As extreme was the horror, to that same extreme was the fantastic way he could make her feel.

No. Freedom would never come for Cara until she either hit rock bottom or ended up in the city morgue. The scary thing was that Mandy knew things had been quiet for too long. It was time. While there wasn't a cloud in the sky, she knew that another storm brewed on the horizon. She kicked a piece of gravel across the pavement and entered the house to cook her own dinner.

~*~

Mandy settled into her favorite recliner with a bowl of microwave popcorn and a couple rented movies. There was nothing like a good romantic comedy after a long week of school. She watched the first one and then popped in the second. Barely into the movie, she dozed off only to be awakened by the waling of sirens outside. Her pulse racing, she rose from the recliner, knocking the bowl from the chair arm and sending noisy kernels bouncing across the hardwood floor.

She pulled back the curtains and peered in the direction of the Richards' home. Two officers crouched behind their car with their firearms aimed at the front door.

"Come out with your hands up!" a voice shouted followed by a lamp that went crashing through the front window out into the yard.

"This ain't none of your business! This is between me and my wife!" Jason's slurred speech betrayed his intoxication.

Mandy darted to the kitchen, picked up the phone and dialed Mr. and Mrs. Kestler – Cara's parents. They were the only people Cara listened to when things got this bad – the only people who could possibly convince her to leave. The conversation was brief and soon they would be across town to be there for their daughter once more.

When Mandy returned to the window, Jason exited the house with his hands behind his sandy-blonde head. He came out claiming his innocence. An officer came behind him, pulled his arms behind his back and handcuffed him. Mandy waited for the officer to put Jason in the squad car, and ran next door to find Cara. Just as she reached the threshold, a second squad car arrived on the scene. When she entered the living room, Cara knelt in a crouched position holding her stomach.

"Cara!" Mandy exclaimed and ran to her side.

19

"My baby. He tried to kill the baby," came Cara's hysterical reply. Mandy scurried to the doorway and commanded the officers to call an ambulance and then returned to Cara's side to help her lie down on the couch. Cara curled in a fetal position while Mandy dampened a washcloth and began wiping her friend's brow.

"What happened? What did that monster do to you?" Mandy searched Cara's eyes.

"He kicked me in the stomach," Cara cried in obvious humiliation.

Mandy was not one to swear, but in this instance, a few choice adjectives for Jason came to mind and would have spilled from her lips had they not been stopped cold by the officer who stepped beside her. He knelt to check on Cara's condition. It took a second glance at the man's face before Mandy fully recognized Bronson Reilly kneeling next to her. She clamped her open mouth shut.

"We've called an ambulance and it should be here any second, Mrs. Richards," he gave her a comforting pat on the arm.

"Your parents are on their way too, honey. I called them," Mandy added.

"You shouldn't have done that! Mom gets so worried and Dad will go berserk," Cara began to protest.

"Mrs. Richards, you need to settle down and think about the baby. Relax and let us take care of your best interests," Bronson assured her.

Within moments, the ambulance arrived and began loading Cara onto a stretcher.

"I'm coming with you," Mandy stated emphatically.

"No, stay here and tell Mom and Dad where I am," Cara reached for Mandy's hand. Then, obviously assailed by another searing pain, Cara grabbed her abdomen and tightened her grip on Mandy's hand.

"We'll take her to Hutcheson," the paramedic stated as he and another man lifted the stretcher into the ambulance. Cara released Mandy's hand and the paramedics shut the ambulance door.

Mandy stood in the driveway with tears trickling down her cheeks watching the emergency vehicle drive away.

An officer stepped in front of her blocking her view. "Ma'am, you're the neighbor – right?"

"Yes."

"Would you mind answering a few questions for us?" the man inquired.

"I-uh," she glanced at Bronson who joined them. "I suppose."

Bronson interjected, "I'll wrap things up here. You two go ahead and book him." The officer nodded and returned to the squad car. Jason sat in the back seat arguing with the officer's partner in the front seat. It was then that Mandy noticed that Bronson didn't have a partner, instead there was a German shepherd panting in the front seat of his car.

Bronson put his hand around Mandy's upper arm and guided her back to her home.

"Maybe we could just go inside, and you can tell me a bit about Mr. and Mrs. Richards."

Mandy couldn't breathe. Where did this man keep coming from? Why did he keep cropping up in her life – whether it was in her dreams or her reality?

After offering Bronson a soda, Mandy sat across her kitchen table looking at the unbelievably handsome man. She found him entirely irresistible no matter the uniform he wore. Immediately, Mandy began berating herself for even thinking about what Bronson looked like while her friend was in the hospital. She needed to give him the answers he wanted and get to Cara's side as fast as possible.

Bronson began by asking her how long she'd lived next door to the Richards and what she knew of the couple's history. She answered him as honestly as she could. At this point, keeping secrets had become pointless.

"Does Mr. Richards have a drug problem?" Bronson asked.

"I don't know. I know he seems drunk quite a bit. But I don't know about drugs – why?"

"Just routine questions," Bronson waved his pencil and then made a note on the pad in front of him.

"What about Mrs. Richards? Does she use drugs?"

"Heavens, no!" Mandy exclaimed. "The woman's seven months pregnant!"

"That doesn't matter to some people." His somber eyes met hers, letting his statement sink in before he continued, "So you're sure she doesn't use drugs?"

"Positive. She doesn't even drink," Mandy insisted.

"Have you seen any suspicious visitors to the home?"

"I don't guess so, unless you count his loser friends," Mandy replied flippantly and rolled her eyes.

"Do you know their names?" he asked, letting his pencil hover over his notepad.

"No."

"Does he make any unusually large purchases?" he asked, not lifting his eyes from his writing.

Mandy's eyebrows furrowed as she glanced at the clock, "What does this have to do with him kicking his pregnant wife in the stomach? I mean, I hope you can understand that I need to go be with my friend right now."

He looked up at her once more, "I understand, Ms. Gates, but please bear with me. If you really want to help your friend, you'll allow me to ask you just a few more questions."

Her head nodded in agreement. She took a deep breath and exhaled.

"Have you seen him bring home anything particularly luxurious?" he waved his pencil as he spoke. "Extravagant purchases of any kind?"

"He sometimes brings Cara home jewelry and flowers when he's trying to win her back after one of his tirades."

"Anything else?" Officer Reilly asked as he jotted down her answers.

"He bought a top of the line speed boat last month. He keeps it at a slip at the lake. And he's always buying brand new cars. But he's a used car salesman, so maybe he's just getting a good deal?" Mandy shrugged.

Bronson nodded with understanding as he continued to write down the information. "Anything else?"

"I don't think so," Mandy shook her head.

"Okay, thank you, Miss Gates," Bronson rose from his chair and extended his hand to her. She shook it. "You've been very helpful," he added as he looked into her eyes. The combination of his touch and the magnetic quality of his eyes sent a thrill along Mandy's arms and caused an exhilarating shiver to ascend her spine.

"Thanks again for your help," he smiled and pulled a business card from his shirt pocket. "You'll call me if you think of anything else?"

Mandy took the card. "Sure." Just as Bronson reached the front door Mandy blurted, "I enjoyed your presentation at the school this morning."

He turned around to face her, thanked her for the compliment with a tip of his cap and left. She watched him go to his car, let his dog out, and the pair entered the Richards' home.

Just as Mandy stepped out her door to see what Bronson and the dog were doing sniffing around the neighbors', Cara's parents arrived. She quickly informed them that Cara had been taken to the hospital and that she would follow them in her car.

Within half an hour Cara's parents and Mandy were at the expecting woman's side. The doctors had been able to treat her and stop the initial stages of labor. A plan soon formulated that Cara would stay with her parents in Chattanooga. Fortunately, the baby was unharmed and by two in the morning, Cara was released to her parents' care. When Mandy arrived home, everything appeared locked and deserted next door. No sign remained of Bronson or his canine partner. Exhausted, she settled in for a well-deserved slumber.

Chapter 4

Saturday morning as she exited her home, Mandy opened her door to find Bronson waiting just outside. He wore jeans and a t-shirt this time, and again, she observed that he looked fantastic no matter what he wore.

"Hi!" he smiled, the dimples in his cheeks deepening.

"Oh, hello," Mandy muttered as she looked up into his irresistible brown eyes.

"It's my day off, but I was just over at the hospital to check on your friend, and they said she'd checked out. I thought I'd drop by and see what you knew. But if you're on your way out . . ."

"That's okay, come on in," she opened the door wider. "I was just going to the store. It can wait."

Bronson stepped inside the house. Mandy noticed that his large frame made her little house look even smaller.

"Have a seat," she pointed to a wingback chair in her living room. She crossed to the couch and sat down with her foot tucked under her.

Making himself comfortable in the wingback, Bronson listened to the latest news on Cara. Mandy had spoken with her already this morning, and she was feeling much better, resting at her parents' home.

"She says she won't go back this time, but she's said that before, so who knows." Mandy shrugged. "I hope she can finally break free of him this time – especially for the baby's sake," Mandy expressed with concern and a good bit of doubt.

"It's got to be hard watching a friend suffer," he observed.

"It is. It's really a helpless feeling. If only they would keep him locked up long enough to break whatever hold he has on her."

"That might be a possibility – not immediately but eventually," Bronson crossed his leg, resting his right ankle on his knee.

"Really? How's that? Cara's already said she won't press charges." Mandy leaned her elbow on the arm rest.

"There's more going on next door than abuse, Ms. Gates."

Mandy's eyebrows furrowed with a quizzical crinkle.

"I'm only telling you this 'cause you're her friend and neighbor and," Bronson added, "I could use your help."

"My help?" she questioned with obvious doubt.

"We have reason to believe that Jason Richards is a drug dealer. Earlier yesterday evening I received a tip from an anonymous informant claiming that Richards is dealing in crystal meth. When I heard the domestic disturbance call come through, I came by to see if it might open something up on the case."

"Good grief!" Mandy exclaimed. "I had no clue."

"He's quite a disturbing character on more than one level," Bronson leaned toward her, resting his elbows on his knees and lacing his fingers in front of him.

"So what do you need from me?" Mandy asked.

"I need somewhere to observe his comings and goings," he explained.

"You mean you want to use my house for a stake out?" she asked.

"Sort of like that . . . " His thumbs went round one another in what appeared to be a nervous gesture. "Except more like undercover."

"Undercover?" Mandy's voice rose in surprise.

"When I gave the captain my report after speaking with you last night, I mentioned to him that I had met you before. He suggested that I approach you about helping us."

"You mean, you want me to spy on him?" Mandy's stomach twirled in a nervous knot.

"Not really," Bronson took a deep breath and exhaled. She hardly knew the man, but it looked like whatever he was trying to say was making him nervous. He took a deep breath and exhaled slowly before continuing. "Ms. Gates, I'll be honest with you. I don't like using civilians for police business, but the opportunity in this instance is too tempting . . ." His eyes met hers, and she felt an odd sensation. He rushed on as if correcting himself, "Or I should say fortuitous."

"I don't understand," Mandy's eyebrows puckered with confusion, yet she felt hope rise within her - hope that whatever he was suggesting meant she'd be seeing more of him in the future.

Bronson scratched his head as if the action might stimulate his brain cells and allow him to say what needed to be said. He took another deep breath and let the words spill in one long string, "The captain wants me to ask you if you'd be willing to pretend I'm your brother so that I can have a cover for staying at your house for surveillance purposes." He raised his hand to stop her from saying anything just yet. "Now, if you don't feel comfortable with that or don't want to do it for any reason, I totally understand. This isn't something you have to do. It's just that it could take us some time to catch him in the act and the cover would help significantly."

"I just don't think it would work is all. My neighbors know I don't have a brother," Mandy replied.

"Hmm . . . then your boyfriend," he suggested.

Mandy's eyebrows rose in surprise. She could hardly believe her ears. Here this man she'd been daydreaming about was asking if he might pretend to be her boyfriend, stay at her house, and use her as a cover for surveillance!

"Take a few minutes to think about it," Bronson offered.

"I don't know. How often would you be here?" she asked.

"A lot."

"Would it be days? Evenings?" She hesitated and swallowed the nervous lump in her throat, "Nights?"

"Yes," he answered.

She could feel the butterflies in her stomach churning with even more intensity than before. Dreaming about the man was one thing, but having him in her house all the time was overwhelming. Then she thought of Mrs. Wallington. What in the world would Mrs. Wallington say? She certainly couldn't confide in the woman. The neighbor was a notorious gossip! Realizing the complexity of the situation, Mandy decided to proceed cautiously, "There could be a problem with that."

"What part do you have a problem with?" He leaned toward her, resting his elbows on his knees once more.

Mandy was afraid her intense attraction for him might cause her to agree to anything, but she stood her ground nonetheless. After all, she did have her principles. "Nights. I mean I have a reputation that I'd like to protect. I'm not the kind of person who has men staying at her house at night, and my neighbors know that. Not only do I feel uncomfortable with it, but also it's just not going to be believable."

Bronson nodded his head, but remained silent. She continued, "I take it your whole purpose for using the undercover angle is that you want it to look natural – right?"

Again he nodded.

"Well, it's not natural for me to have a man in my house all night," Mandy explained.

"I see. I can appreciate a person of integrity. We can probably work around that somehow." He rubbed his chin as if he were mulling. "Surely we can think of a way to keep surveillance at night without disrupting your world."

Ah, but he had already disrupted her world! He had no idea how much he had disrupted it, and it looked as if it was only going to continue. But Mandy kept her thoughts to herself. She wanted him to find a way to make this work.

"Could you tolerate my presence until oh, say, midnight or one?" he asked.

Tolerate his presence! She had to choke back a smile on that one. She coughed into her hand and determined to stick to her principles in spite of the great temptation to tell the man that he could move in and live there if he liked. "As you know, Lieutenant Reilly, I teach school. I go to bed around ten every night. On weekends it could be feasible, but through the week it isn't going to work."

"You don't have to stay up until I leave, I could let myself out," he suggested.

"But it's not believable that I would have someone here that late through the week," she reminded.

"Not even if you were in love?" his dimples appeared with his teasing smile, and she thought she might melt into a puddle of mush on the floor. Reining in her intense attraction for him, she forced herself to strengthened her resolve and stand her ground.

"Eleven tops on weekdays. One at the latest on Fridays and Saturdays. Take it or leave it," she negotiated in the most business-like tone she could muster.

"Fair enough. We'll have a surveillance team take care of nights from the street," he stood up and extended his hand to shake on the agreement. She stood as well and took his hand. Again, there was that unmistakable exhilarating shiver. What in the world had she just agreed to?

"When does it start?" she asked, her hand still in his.

"Immediately . . . if that's all right with you. Richards' mother just posted bail for him"

"Okay" she tried not to meet his gaze, for if she did, she knew she'd be completely undone. "Wait." She caught his eyes now, and he released her hand. "Jason probably saw you last night. Won't he recognize you?"

"I doubt it. He was preoccupied in an argument with the officer sitting in the squad car with him. Plus, he was completely wasted. I doubt he'd recognize me again even with my cap and uniform."

"Okay," she nodded, satisfied with his answer.

"There's one more thing I should let you know," he added. "I doubt there will be, but there could be danger involved. I will do everything in my power to put your safety first, but there's always a random element in these situations. Are you willing to take that risk?"

"If it'll put Jason behind bars and keep Cara and her baby free of him, I'm willing to risk it."

"Good. Thanks." His gaze traveled the room. "You care if I take a look around and find the best spot to set up?"

"Go right ahead. The spare bedroom has a window that faces the Richards'," she crossed in front of him and led him down the hallway toward the room. It held a twin bed, a night table with a lamp and a chest of drawers.

After examining it, he turned to her, "This'll be perfect. Thanks so much for your cooperation, Ms. Gates."

"You better start calling me Mandy if you want your cover to be believable," she suggested with a smile.

"You're right," his eyes twinkled. "Call me Bronson."

"I need to get to the store. You can stay here and make yourself at home. Is there anything in particular you like to eat? Besides donuts that is?" Mandy chuckled.

Bronson's eyes laughed with her teasing, "I don't expect you to buy or make me food. I'll send for takeout."

"Nonsense. It's as easy for me to cook for two as one. I rarely buy takeout. If we want to make this . . ."

"Believable" he interjected, with a wink.

"Yes, believable, then I'd cook for you."

Bronson pulled out his billfold and handed her a fifty. "Then take this to help cover your expenses."

Mandy hesitated then took the bill, "Thanks. So what do you like?"

"Anything. Surprise me."

Her brown eyes smiled, "All right, I will." With that, she spun around and left to go shopping.

Chapter 5

When Mandy returned home, she set her grocery bags on the table and went down the hall to the spare bedroom to see if Bronson had everything that he needed. At the doorway, she met him coming out.

"Need some help with those groceries?" he offered.

"Sure." She turned around and he followed her out of the house to her Mustang, the trunk of which was filled with blue plastic grocery bags. They each grabbed armfuls and carried them into the house, taking several trips to get it all.

"You bought out the store," he chuckled.

"I always buy a couple weeks' worth at a time," she said as she began putting her groceries away. He helped her as she pointed out where everything went. In short order, they had completed the task, and she followed Bronson back to the spare room where he had set up a card table full of surveillance equipment.

"You've bugged their house?" Mandy asked in shock as she stared at the computer screen that displayed split views of the various rooms in the Richards' home.

"We have all the necessary paperwork we need for complete surveillance," he answered.

"I'm just glad Cara's not home. Seems like an invasion of privacy to me," Mandy muttered.

"It's all perfectly legal, I assure you."

"A lot of things are legal that I don't agree with," she retorted. He didn't reply.

31

As they both stood there watching the screen, the camera monitoring the front door revealed Jason sauntering into the house and slamming the door behind him. "Cara! Where are you?" he bellowed.

The man in his mid-thirties tossed his keys on the kitchen table. The kitchen camera picked up as he opened the refrigerator, popped the top on a can of beer and guzzled it down. He crushed it flat, threw it in a wastebasket and opened another one. The various cameras picked up his movements throughout the house as he searched for his wife. Finally, he flopped down on the couch, flipped on the TV, and drank his beer.

"Look, he doesn't even care where she is," Mandy huffed in disgust.

"Did you expect him to?" Bronson asked as he pulled a cinnamon candy from a tin in his pocket and offered her one. She shook her head to decline.

"He's very controlling, so yes, I'm surprised." Mandy answered just as Jason picked up the phone and began dialing. A second computer registered the outgoing phone call and began recording the conversation as Jason called Cara's parents. Mr. Kestler's voice seethed with controlled anger as he informed his vile son-in-law that a temporary restraining order had been issued and that he was to stay away from his daughter. A lawyer had also been retained and he would be receiving divorce papers as soon as possible. The conversation ended with Jason's violent curses and the sound of him throwing the phone across the room, busting it into pieces in the fireplace.

"I can't stand to watch this anymore. He disgusts me," Mandy turned on her heel, and left the room. "Do you want turkey or ham on your sandwich?" she called back over her shoulder to Bronson who still stood observing the monitor.

"Turkey and if you have some cheese, that would be great," he replied.

"Swiss or Cheddar?"

"Swiss please," he sat down at the computer and watched Jason drink himself into a stupor until Mandy returned with his sandwich.

"So do you do this type of thing often?" Mandy asked as she stood looking over his shoulder and took a bite of her own sandwich.

"What? Hang out in pretty women's houses pretending to be their boyfriend so I can spy on their neighbors?"

Mandy nearly choked on her sandwich.

Bronson released a chuckle. "No, this isn't typical," he shook his head. "I do conduct a lot of surveillance, but it's never been from a beautiful woman's bedroom before." He looked over his shoulder at Mandy whose face had flushed crimson.

She spun toward the door. "Do you want Sprite or root beer?"

"Root beer, please," he chuckled as she left the room.

While Bronson continued monitoring Jason, Mandy sat at the kitchen table grading papers. Hours passed without any activity next door until finally Jason left the house. Bronson called for a surveillance team to trail him off premises.

The afternoon sun's pinks and purples streamed through the trees in the back yard as Mandy stood over her barbeque grill checking her vegetables and salmon steaks. Suddenly she felt two strong arms slip around her waist. She jumped a little.

"Play along, Mandy," Bronson's deep voice whispered as he swept her hair to the side. Goose bumps beckoned as he trailed kisses along her neck.

"What are you doing?" she breathed.

"Your neighbor's watching. We need to set the stage."

Mandy's eyes darted toward the Richards' house. Her hand caressed his arm that enveloped her.

"I don't see him," she whispered, trying not to move her lips as Bronson placed another warm, intoxicating kiss on her neck.

"It's not him. It's the little old lady on the other side."

Mandy spun around to face him, put both her hands on his chest and whispered, "Mrs. Wallington? She's the biggest gossip in the neighborhood!"

"I'm counting on it," Bronson's eyes fell to her lips, and she knew that her heart would hammer out of her chest. She couldn't breathe as his lips lowered and grazed across hers.

"Don't look so petrified, Mandy, or she'll know something's up," he muttered as his lips tempted hers once more.

"I'm not this easy and she knows it," Mandy whispered, leaning her forehead against his.

"Would you kiss a man on the fourth date?" His voice was deep and alluring.

"Possibly," she replied, and he kissed the corner of her mouth. "But this isn't our fourth. We haven't even had a first." She nuzzled her cheek against his five o'clock shadow.

"Sure it is – the park, the school, last night and now today,"

Mandy quickly lifted her head to meet his eyes with her protest, but stopped short when she saw his filled with something much more provocative than the mischievous flirtation she expected to find there.

This time his lips took hers with more determination, coaxing her to respond. The cinnamon taste of his mouth drew her in, and she began to react to his kiss, sliding her arms around his neck. Just when she thought she might abandon control and release herself to his charms, he pulled back a little and pointed to the grill.

"Your fish needs flipping."

"Huh?" she asked, completely bewildered.

"Your fish," he pointed again.

"Oh!" she turned awkwardly around, still reeling from the moment, and grabbed the spatula to rotate her nearly overcooked salmon. "Can you please hand me those plates?" She pointed to the lawn table.

Bronson held a plate in each of his outstretched hands, and she placed the vegetables and fish on each one.

Mandy was about to suggest that they eat inside beyond Mrs. Wallington's prying eyes when Bronson looked up at the sky, "It's nice out here. Why don't we sit outside and eat?"

When Mandy's eyes traveled next door, it was to observe Mrs. Wallington standing in her back yard with her mouth hanging open in astonishment.

"Oh great, I'm never going to hear the end of this," Mandy groaned through clenched teeth. She gave Mrs. Wallington a forced smile and nod.

"It can't be that bad," Bronson insisted, taking a seat.

"You don't know the woman," Mandy whispered as she waved at the lady. The neighbor returned the greeting and pretended to go back to clipping her rose bushes. Mandy sat down across from Bronson.

"Surely she's seen you with boyfriends before," he reasoned.

When Mandy didn't answer but put a piece of grilled zucchini in her mouth, Bronson studied her expression, "Are you saying she hasn't ever seen you with anyone?"

"I really don't date that much," she shrugged her shoulders as if it were perfectly normal for an attractive twenty-six-year-old brunette, with big brown eyes and thick dark eyelashes, not to have men lined up at her door.

"You're kidding me?" He stared at her in disbelief.

"No," she cut into her salmon, not meeting his gaze.

"How is that possible?" he asked, surprise evident in his voice.

Mandy released a nervous chuckle. "I just haven't found a man that I felt like I could trust."

Bronson raised one doubtful eyebrow, "Really?" He cut into his salmon. "Why?"

Mandy sighed. "There are the neighbors for starters; then my sister married someone about as bad as Jason. My father wasn't fit for much." She shrugged her shoulders. "I just figure safe is better than sorry."

"We're not all like that, I can assure you. Some of us are really quite trustworthy," he smiled and she couldn't resist returning his friendly expression. He took a bite of his salmon and complimented her on its flavor.

"Is that what you call what you were doing a few moments ago – being trustworthy?" her voice dripped sarcasm.

"Did I overstep my bounds?" his eyes flashed flirtatious innocence, and he took a sip of his soda.

"No, I suppose not . . . for a fourth date anyway," she smirked and took a bite of her fish.

After dinner, Mandy loaded the dishwasher, while Bronson went back to his post at the computers. Jason returned around eight o'clock. When Mandy heard his car drive up, she went back to the room where Bronson sat at the monitors.

"He's back," Bronson said over his shoulder.

"Yeah, I heard his car," she took a seat in a folding chair next to Bronson.

They watched Jason repeat his earlier routine, grabbing a beer and vegetating in front of the television.

"Looks like this will prove to be a boring surveillance," Mandy commented.

Bronson smiled at her, "Yeah, well, nobody said investigative work was all glory and glamour."

They sat there in silence for several minutes watching the monitors, but Jason didn't move from his couch potato position. Mandy shifted in her chair so that she faced Bronson instead of the computer screens. "I was thinking we should come up with an explanation for you suddenly being here all the time."

"What did you have in mind?" he glanced at her and then back at the monitor.

"I was thinking maybe we could say you're an old boyfriend."

"Suddenly back in your life," Bronson nodded, and she agreed.

"The thing is, you'd have to be coming back to town from somewhere because why would you be here? If you lived around here you'd have your own place to stay," she prompted.

"Good point." Bronson thought for a moment. "What if I've been away . . . somewhere like . . . Chicago. I spent a few years up there, so I could answer questions about the area if asked."

"Okay," Mandy nodded. "Now we just need a reason for why you came back."

"How about downsizing," he suggested. "I could have come back to Chattanooga to visit family and look for a job."

"And maybe your parents don't have a computer so you're using mine to search for jobs online and print resumes," Mandy suggested.

"That's good." He nodded.

"So if I'm just being a good friend and helping you out, maybe there's no need for all this . . . uh . . ." Mandy wasn't sure how to say it and she could feel the blush rising to her cheeks, so she rushed on, "these public displays of affection."

Bronson smiled, "Oh, but we've already started that. Mrs. Wallington's already seen it, so we better stick with it."

"But how do we explain it where it makes sense? I'm really not the type . . . and Mrs. Wallington knows that."

"I think we've already established that you're the type," his eyes met hers pointedly, and then he winked with a slight flirtatious grin. Again, Mandy felt herself blush and diverted her gaze to the monitors. He had her there.

After a minute of silence, Bronson suddenly put a hand on her arm, "Oh, and I was thinking . . . I'll need a key to your house so I can get in here when you're at work."

"A key to my house?" Mandy's eyebrows rose.

"Yeah . . . I've got to get in here to work, and I don't want you to have to arrange your schedule around mine," Bronson explained.

"But how am I going to explain *that* to Mrs. Wallington?" Mandy retorted.

"Just tell her it's more convenient since I'm looking for a job using your computer," Bronson suggested.

Mandy stood up, "All right, I guess you're right. You do need a key." She went into her bedroom and looked through her jewelry box for the spare. While she was in front of her dresser mirror, she noticed her hair didn't look its best. She set the key down on her dresser and reached for a brush, raking it through her hair a few times. Smiling at the thought of Bronson in the next room, she had to admit she was having fun.

As she reached down for the key her more cautious side kicked in and she muttered to herself, *"What on earth are you doing?"* But she really had no choice. Cara's only hope was for Bronson to arrest Jason. And Bronson needed this key for his surveillance. She carried it back to the spare bedroom and handed it to Bronson.

"So what brought you back into my life?" she asked as she sat down beside him once more. "How do we explain that?"

"It's always best to stay as close to the truth as possible," he suggested. "Let's say I was riding in the park, and we ran into each other while you were jogging. We went to lunch, one thing led to another, and we realized we still cared for each other."

"I guess that works," she agreed and glanced at Jason dozing on his couch. "He doesn't look energetic enough to be involved in drug running," she commented.

Bronson released a laughing sigh, "Energetic has very little to do with it."

~*~

After they'd worked out the details of their story, Mandy left Bronson to his work. He stared at the monitor, trying to think of some excuse to walk out that bedroom door and be near her. He reminded himself that he was here to work. He had to nail Avery Hallstead, one of the biggest drug dealers in the area. There was every indication Jason worked for him. It was just a matter of time before Bronson and his surveillance team had enough to convict.

Bronson thought of his meeting with the captain. He'd hesitated when the captain suggested he use Mandy as his cover. Bronson knew she would be a distraction. Ever since he met her in the park and pulled her onto his horse, he'd found her attractive. But, he couldn't tell the captain that!

Just as he suspected, thoughts of Mandy were already pulling his mind off task. She was just too much fun to tease, too irresistible not to kiss.

Jason stirred and Bronson punched a button on the keyboard to shift the camera angle. It was a false alarm though; Jason just rolled on his side and kept sleeping.

Chapter 6

Sunday morning, just as Mandy suspected, Mrs. Wallington cornered her by the garage.

"Who is that handsome man you were with last night?" The elderly woman rested a hand on her hip.

Mandy's heart raced, hoping she could relate the story in a believable way. "He's an old boyfriend who's back in town looking for a job."

"Oh?" Mrs. Wallington's eyebrows rose.

"And don't be alarmed if he's here during the day when I'm not. He's using my computer to search for jobs and print resumes."

"Do you want to give me a key so I can let him in?" Mrs. Wallington suggested.

"Uh . . . no, that won't be necessary. He has one," Mandy opened her car door and pretended to be looking for something inside her car. She didn't want to meet the woman's eyes.

"Really?" Mrs. Wallington's voice rose with surprise.

Mandy rushed on with her explanation, "I know him really well. We dated for years. So it's okay that he has a key."

"All right, if you think that's wise," Mrs. Wallington's voice carried obvious doubt.

Mandy met the elderly woman's gaze, "I'm positive."

Mrs. Wallington put a hand on Mandy's arm, "Be careful, dear. I know you've been alone for a while now, but rushing into something this fast isn't . . ."

Mandy interjected before the woman could finish, "Don't worry, Mrs. Wallington. I'm not going to do anything I'd regret." Her neighbor still looked worried. "I've got to run now, or I'll be late for church." Mandy slipped behind the wheel of her Mustang and started the ignition. She began backing out and waved through the window.

All through church Mandy kept thinking of the situation with Bronson. She didn't want her neighbors thinking she was loose. She'd worked hard to avoid even the appearance of evil, and here she had a man practically living at her house and kissing her in public! Okay, not in public, but out in the back yard for her neighbors to see! Before long the whole neighborhood would be talking – it was what Bronson wanted. But what if it got back to the people at church? How would she explain what was going on? She certainly couldn't blow Bronson's cover.

When Mandy returned home, Bronson's red truck was parked on the right side of her driveway. She pulled past it, into the garage, and shut the door. When she stepped inside, she pulled off her heels and carried them toward her bedroom. Tossing them just inside her bedroom door, she continued on to the spare bedroom where Bronson sat in front of the monitors.

"Hi!" he greeted glancing over his shoulder at her. He took a double take and whistled, "Don't you look nice."

Mandy rolled her eyes. "Nobody can hear you inside here. No need for false flattery."

"Who said it was false flattery?" he quipped, rising to his feet and motioning for her to take a seat. She stepped toward the extra chair but remained standing.

Studying the monitor for a moment, she asked, "Anything happening?"

"No, he's been sleeping in all morning so far." Bronson stretched his arms high above his head.

"I thought I'd put on a roast with potatoes and carrots, then take a little nap," she explained.

"Sounds great," he smiled. "I mean the roast and potatoes." Then added, "Don't suppose I'll be getting a Sunday nap. You'll have to manage without me there."

Mandy rolled her eyes. Was he making fun of her? Did he think her a prude and now used every occasion to try shocking her? She let his comment roll by and simply stated, "Dinner should be ready around five. Would you like a sandwich now?"

"No thanks. I brought a sandwich with me and already ate it. Don't want to be a mooch," he said, then glanced back at the computer screens.

"You're not a mooch. You gave me money for food, remember?" she stepped back and leaned her hand on the doorframe.

"I know. I just don't want to abuse you with my presence - having you wait on me and bring me food." He looked so handsome standing there in his jeans. There was absolutely no way he could ever abuse her with his presence.

"Really, it's not a problem. I'd be making food anyway," she replied and then went to the kitchen to make her own lunch. After eating, she took a nap, and a few hours later she awoke to the sound of dishes clanging.

She opened her sleepy eyes and sat up for a moment. It sounded like Bronson was in the kitchen rattling plates and silverware. She got out of bed, straightened herself in the mirror and brushed her hair. Once in the kitchen, she saw Bronson bending down digging through her cabinets.

"May I help you find something?" she offered.

"Oh, yeah," he rose to his feet. "Jason left the house. The mobile surveillance team has him now, so I thought I'd help you with dinner and heat up a can of green beans. I was just trying to find a small saucepan."

Mandy approached him and went to the cabinet beside the one in which he'd been searching. Retrieving the pan, she reached past him and set it on the stove. In doing so, she'd gotten close enough to smell his aftershave. She glanced up at him and he thanked her, giving her a look that sent her insides twirling. Nervously, she stepped around him and pulled the roast out of the oven. He helped her set the table and soon he was sitting across from her eating dinner.

It was an odd feeling sitting there with him. In a way, she felt he belonged there – like they really were a couple, and yet she knew nothing about him. She decided that if she knew more about the man, she would feel more comfortable having him around.

"How long have you been a police officer?" she asked.

"Seven years," he replied and put a piece of carrot into his mouth.

"Do you like it?" She stabbed at several green beans.

He finished chewing his bite of carrot, then replied, "Yeah, I do. There are parts of it that get a little monotonous."

"Like watching Jason Richards drink himself into a stupor in front of his TV?" she interjected and ate forkful of beans.

"Yeah," he nodded. "But other times it can be a real rush – like when you nail the bad guy or when you come to a victim's rescue in the nick of time." He put some roast in his mouth and complimented her on the dinner.

She thanked him, and they continued to eat their dinner. After a few minutes she asked, "Have you always had a dog for your partner?"

"Champ's been with me for about three years now. He's a drug dog - trained to sniff out the stuff," Bronson cut his roast into smaller pieces.

"Really? That's fascinating."

Bronson took a sip of his drink and answered, "Yeah, he's really smart."

"So is he yours?"

"Technically he belongs to the department, but when he's ready to retire, they'll probably let me take him home," Bronson explained.

"Where is he now? You could have brought him along." Mandy took a bite of potato.

"He's at the kennel. I figured Jason might suspect something if Champ were here too."

Mandy gave an understanding nod. "You must miss him. I guess you get pretty attached."

"Yeah, he's a good dog. I can see why they call them man's best friend." Bronson smiled and took a sip of his drink.

"So he's your best friend?" she grinned.

"Well," Bronson chuckled. "I let Champ believe that, but I've got another friend who might be upset if he thought he was upstaged by a dog."

Mandy smiled. "Who's that?"

Bronson wiped a napkin to his lips. "My friend, Gerard. He and I attended the Academy together and have been friends for years. He works in homicide, so we don't generally work the same beat. But we do the Civil War re-enactments together."

"I think the re-enacting is fascinating. I'm a Civil War buff myself," Mandy leaned her chin on her hand, eager to hear more.

"Oh, really?"

"I teach history – math and history."

Bronson nodded. "The re-enacting is fun – you should come out and do it sometime. It gets a little expensive buying all the period clothing and gear, but it's a lot of fun."

"Do they let women do that?" Mandy put a few more green beans on her plate.

"Sure. There's even a shop over in Chickamauga that sells dresses and uniforms," he said.

"I didn't know that." Mandy cut a piece of potato and bit into it.

"Yeah, I'll have to take you over there sometime," he took another bite. "This really is delicious roast, Mandy. We could use a good cook in our company. You should join us."

Mandy gave a little chuckle. "I don't know how well I could cook without my modern conveniences," she waved an arm toward her microwave and stove.

He jiggled his fork. "Cooking over an open fire does take some getting used to."

"So how long have you been re-enacting?" she asked just as Bronson's cell phone rang.

"Three years," he said just before answering the phone. He rose to his feet, told the person on the phone that he understood and then hung up. "Well, back to work. Jason's coming down the street on his way home." He gathered up his plate and carried it with him back to the computer room.

Mandy released a sigh. She'd been enjoying their conversation and would have loved to continue it. But, she decided to stay out of his way and let him work. She spent the remainder of the evening washing dishes, watching a movie and then went to bed after Bronson left at ten o'clock that evening.

Chapter 7

Monday afternoon when Mandy took her lunch break in the teacher's lounge, she sat down next to Jan at a small round table.

"How's your day going?" Mandy asked.

"Rough. There's a couple boys in my second period class who are driving me nuts," Jan groaned.

"Hmmm . . . sorry," Mandy commiserated and then her cell phone rang. She answered it and heard Bronson's voice.

"Hi," she smiled involuntarily. "How's it going? Anything new?" Mandy glanced up at Jan whose inquisitive eyes met hers. Mandy debated on getting up and leaving the table. Should she tell Jan about the surveillance operation? She listened to Bronson explain that Jason had left for work that morning and nothing much had happened. He apologized for bothering her at school, but he couldn't find where she kept her bandages. While splicing a wire he nicked himself.

She leaned her head on her hand and spoke quietly into the phone, "I keep them in the bathroom, in the cabinet under the sink." She really hoped Jan didn't hear what she'd said, but she probably did. She waited for Bronson to find the bandages and then told him goodbye.

"Who was that?" Jan asked.

"Nobody," Mandy shrugged.

"From the look on your face when you answered the phone, it sure looked like somebody," Jan lifted a single accusatory eyebrow.

At times like these, Mandy really wished Jan wasn't so adept at reading her every facial expression. Mandy's eyes surveyed the crowded lounge. She bit her lip and stood up, holding her tray. "Bring your food and come with me." She gestured with a nod toward the door, indicating Jan should follow her.

Her friend complied without question. Jan followed her down the corridor to Mandy's classroom. Mandy set her lunch on her desk and went back to shut the door behind Jan.

"What's going on?" Jan finally asked.

"Do you promise that you'll never breathe a word of what I'm going to tell you?" Mandy sat down behind her desk and motioned for Jan to take a seat on the other side.

"I promise," Jan said, pulling up a chair.

Mandy continued, "Do you remember the re-enactor?"

Jan nodded.

"He's really a police officer, and he's conducting surveillance from my house."

"What?" came Jan's shocked response.

Mandy explained about Cara and Jason. Then she told her about Bronson's plan to catch Jason in the act of drug trafficking. She related their cover story and asked Jan to go along with it should anyone ask. Jan agreed and sat there obviously shocked by the twist of events.

"What about your nosy neighbor? Does she know the truth?" Jan finally asked after several moments of silence.

"Oh, no. She can't know or it would ruin the whole thing. I mean, she's a sweet lady, but she's simply incapable of keeping her mouth shut about anything," Mandy insisted.

"I bet she thinks you've gone to the devil having a man in your house all the time!" Jan chuckled.

"I'm sure she does," Mandy sighed and thought about her amorous encounter with Bronson. She couldn't help smiling at the thought of it.

"You've got that look on your face again," Jan pointed.

"What look?"

"That, *I'm totally smitten* look," Jan replied and ate a potato chip.

"Is it that bad?" Mandy put her hands to her cheeks to cool her blush.

Jan chuckled with a nod.

"Mrs. Wallington probably thinks I'm the biggest floozy on earth. I bring home this guy she's never seen, and then while I'm grilling in the back yard, he comes up behind me and starts kissing my neck."

"Really?" Jan breathed, her eyes widening.

"He tells me to play along . . . that we're setting the stage. I turn around to face him and ask him to stop because Mrs. Wallington is watching. But that's what he wanted."

"Wow, so what happened?" Jan leaned in, excited to hear the rest.

"He starts kissing me, and I swear I could feel the heat from Mrs. Wallington's stare."

"Are you sure that heat wasn't coming from someone else?" Jan teased.

Mandy decided to play it nonchalant, "It's just a charade. It's not real."

"But did it feel real?" Jan prodded, leaning forward again and waiting expectantly for a reply.

"Yeah," Mandy whispered, nodding her head affirmatively. "Yeah, it was amazing."

~*~

When Mandy returned home after school, she saw Bronson's familiar red truck in her driveway. She smiled and felt a little flutter in her stomach at the thought of spending another evening in his presence.

She put her bike in the garage and went inside the house through the garage entrance. She kicked off her shoes by the door and put her book bag on the kitchen table. Just as she started back toward the spare bedroom, Bronson appeared in the doorway and motioned her back.

She followed him and he pointed to the monitor. "He's home early. He brought a suspicious-looking package with him and put it in the freezer."

"Really?" Mandy took a seat in her usual folding chair. She'd gotten hot from bicycling in the August heat and felt like resting in the air conditioning. Lifting her hair from her neck and holding it behind her head, she asked, "So are you moving in?"

Bronson sat down beside her. "Not yet. We need something more concrete than this. Besides it's his supplier we're after. A big drug dealer named Hallstead. Jason's just a pawn, I'm sure."

Mandy watched her neighbor move around the house and then step into the bathroom. He didn't bother to close the door since he thought he was alone. Mandy quickly rose to her feet. "Well on that note, I'll go change out of these sweaty clothes." She went to her bedroom, took a shower and changed. After reapplying a little makeup, she opened her door. She wasn't one to wear much makeup in general, and normally she wouldn't have bothered, but having a handsome police officer like Bronson in the house made her self-conscious of her appearance.

Mandy poked her head in what she now referred to as "Bronson's office" and asked, "Would you rather have fried chicken or taco salad?"

Bronson was under the desk adjusting some sound equipment. "Either sounds good to me. You decide," he replied, obviously engrossed in his task.

Mandy left him to his work and decided she'd make the taco salad. It would require less work, and she'd have more time to grade a stack of test papers. She prepared the meal and brought Bronson's to him in his office. He was on the phone when she came in, so she quietly left it for him and slipped out.

She ate alone in the kitchen and spent the remainder of the evening grading papers, then watched a little television. Around nine-thirty she stuck her head in Bronson's office, "Anything new?"

"No," Bronson shook his head and turned sideways in his chair so he could both see her and keep an eye on the monitors.

"Do you need anything from me before I go to bed?" she asked.

"No thanks. I'll just wrap things up here before the night shift comes on and lock up when I leave."

"All right. Good night," she gave him a slight wave and he returned the sentiment.

She changed into a t-shirt and pajama bottoms and climbed into bed. It felt weird having him in the next room – weird but safe. She'd been yawning earlier, but sleep didn't come easily for her. She lay there thinking about Bronson and the rather anticlimactic evening they'd had. There had been a part of her that hoped for something more. She glanced at her clock radio when she heard him slip out around ten-thirty. Mandy rolled over in her bed, pulled the blankets up around her neck and felt an odd letdown in knowing he was gone.

The next four days were almost identical repeats of Monday, and Mandy began to wonder if Bronson had changed his mind about playing the amorous boyfriend. Then again, she reasoned that within the confines of the house, there was no one to observe such a display of affection, so what justification could there be for it?

The next rainy Friday afternoon, Mandy came home from school to find Bronson at his usual perch. She said hello to him and then went through the house opening windows and the front door, allowing the aroma of fresh rain into the house. She looked out her screen door for a minute or two, loving the view of the lush green vegetation dampened by the summer thunderstorm, which had now passed.

She retrieved the steaks she had marinating in the refrigerator and set them on the counter. The next thing she knew, she heard Bronson's deliberate footsteps approaching. From the sound of them, he seemed in a hurry. She glanced over her shoulder and saw him looking at the screen door. When he continued straight toward her, she turned to face him, and he reached around her to move the steaks aside.

"What are you doing?" she asked.

"Play along," he whispered as in one bold motion, he lifted her up onto the counter, letting his hands linger upon her waist. Mandy could feel her heart hammering with his sudden attention and the smoldering expression in his brown eyes. Without another word, his lips took hers in a slow kiss. Mandy tensed, feeling a crimson blush rise to her cheeks, but his command to "play along" echoed in her mind. Resisting the urge to ask questions, she put her arms around his neck and fully participated in whatever delightful ruse Bronson had going this time.

As he tugged her closer to him and his kisses fell to her neck, Mandy glanced toward the screen door. There stood Jason Richards, his hand raised as if he were about to knock, but evidently unable to decide if he wanted to just yet.

Mandy tapped Bronson's shoulder. "Someone's here," she whispered.

If Bronson heard her, he ignored her words and kissed her lips one more time before looking toward the door. He offered Jason a friendly wave, lifted Mandy from the counter and set her feet to the floor. With his arm around her, he accompanied her to the door and pushed at the screen.

"Can we help you with something?" Bronson asked, his hand caressing Mandy's shoulder.

"I need to talk to Mandy for a minute," Jason said as he stepped inside the house.

Mandy waited for Jason to continue. She needed to regain her bearings. Facing Jason any time took all her wits, but now she felt as if Bronson had drained every coherent thought from her mind. All she registered were the tingles still racing through her body and the heat of his hand on her shoulder.

"I was wondering if you've talked to Cara lately? I can't get her parents to let me through to her," Jason asked.

"Oh," Mandy's face showed her irritation. It was no secret that she disliked Jason. He must be desperate if he was coming to her for information. "I talked to her a couple days ago. She's doing fine . . . Safe," Mandy added, enunciating the word.

Jason ignored Mandy's obvious jab and continued, "So she hasn't had the baby yet?" He appeared sincerely concerned, but Mandy knew what an actor he was. One could never believe a word he said.

"No, the baby hasn't come yet. Cara's doing fine and staying with her parents," she repeated.

"If you talk to her again, will you tell her I'm trying to reach her?" Jason asked.

"I think she's aware of that. But there is a restraining order, you know," Mandy retorted.

"That doesn't mean I can't speak with her on the phone," he grumbled.

Bronson pushed the screen door open, indicating it was time for Jason to leave when Mandy said, "I'll tell her, but I can't promise anything."

Jason nodded and left.

"What a loser," Mandy muttered when Jason was out of earshot. She looked up at Bronson who still had an arm around her shoulder. She stepped out of his embrace and shut the door, "So I suppose that little display was for Jason's benefit?" she asked, turning her back to Bronson so he couldn't see the smile playing on her lips. She went back to the counter where he'd so blissfully interrupted her dinner preparations.

Bronson cleared his throat, "He'd just made a call to the Keslers. Cara's dad stonewalled him again, and Jason stormed out of the house. The outside surveillance team said he was coming this way.

"You sure are quick on your feet," she bit back a grin and glanced at him over her shoulder.

"I've had some time to think through how I should react in such a circumstance," he stated as if pulling a woman onto a kitchen counter and lavishing her with kisses were countermeasures straight out of a police handbook.

"Oh really?" she chuckled, retrieving the grill lighter from a cabinet over her head.

He offered only a sheepish grin in response. "I better get back to work," he pointed his thumb toward his office and left.

Mandy pulled some frozen French fries out of the oven, spread them on a baking sheet and put them in her preheated oven. Next, she stepped out the back door to start her grill. Looking over her backyard, she released a satisfied sigh. Everything looked fresh and greener after a rain. It washed the pollen out of the air and cooled things down.

But, the weather wasn't the only thing causing her content state. Even though she knew the episode with Bronson was only a farce, she couldn't help enjoying the game while it lasted.

As she went about preparing the grill, she told herself she had the best of both worlds – a handsome man to dote on her and protect her, and yet no pressure to commit long term. Mandy had come to believe that in the long run, men were only a disappointment – especially men like Bronson who seemed too good to be true. This charade gave her the excitement of romance without the sting of reality. When this case was over, Bronson would leave, and she could look back on these weeks as a fond memory. The only problem was, just thinking about Bronson leaving produced a hollow feeling in the pit of her stomach. She'd grown accustomed to him being there. And despite her resolve to steer clear of men, she felt drawn to Bronson. Even if she could trust no other man, she trusted Bronson and felt safe with him near.

She put the steaks on the grill, closed the lid and stepped back from the heat. Lost in her thoughts, she didn't notice Bronson come out of the house until his arm slid around her waist and he rested his chin on her shoulder.

"Smells good," he said, sniffing the air.

"You're not working?" she asked, unable to keep the grin from spreading across her face.

"He's stepped out, so I get a dinner break," he explained as he brushed her hair aside and kissed her neck.

Mandy discreetly tried to glance toward Mrs. Wallington's house to see if her neighbor was around, but she didn't see the woman. "I don't think Mrs. Wallington's out here."

Bronson turned her around to face him, "I'm thinking you need a little practice."

Mandy could feel her pulse accelerating, "Practice?"

"Yeah, you looked a little stiff and embarrassed in there. We've got to appear natural or people are going to catch on," he explained as he slipped his arms around her and pulled her to him.

She didn't know if he was serious or just being a tease. A twinkle glimmered in his eyes just before he lowered his head to give her a long slow kiss.

"Now that was better. You're not as stiff," he observed, still holding her against him and looking down into her eyes.

"You caught me off guard earlier. I wasn't expecting it," she defended.

"But you've got to be ready at all times. That's why I think we need more practice." He shifted her arms, draping them over his shoulders.

She rose on her tiptoes, put her mouth to his ear and whispered, "Why, Officer Reilly, I believe you're just being a tease."

When her eyes met his once more, his face was stern, and he pressed a finger over her lips, "Uh – uh, I'm always Bronson, and I'm serious. This case could be a little more dangerous than we expected. Your safety could depend upon how well we play this part."

She smiled, thinking he was only teasing, but his face remained grim. He was serious and she wondered what kind of danger lurked ahead.

"Is there a problem?" she asked.

"No, not at the moment," he shook his head. "These are just dangerous people, and I wouldn't want anything to happen to you." He put a hand to her cheek and looked into her eyes.

~*~

Bronson was half teasing Mandy about her need for practice. If truth were told, he wanted an excuse to kiss her. He spent half the day looking for opportunities to kiss her. Yet, she did need to relax and be in the moment with him. The thought occurred to him that perhaps she didn't find him as attractive as he did her. Maybe that's what caused her tension.

"Look," he said, holding her hands in his. "I realize this is all new to you - having to kiss and act as if you're in love with a man you don't even know. I tease you about it, but I do want you to know that if this is making you uncomfortable, we can stop this charade right now. I can walk out that door and let your life return to normal this evening."

Mandy shook her head, "I don't want that. I want you to stay." She bit her lip as if she were embarrassed by what she'd said. Her words were like music to his ears.

"Good," he smiled. "I know I come on strong, but we have to make sure Jason's thoroughly convinced. One slip, one misstep, and he could catch onto us. While Jason is a nasty character in his own right, he's nothing compared to the people he works for. "

Mandy gave a somber nod. "I understand. I'll try to do better. I'm just . . . not used to this, I guess. You would've been better off if Jason had lived next door to a better kisser," Mandy released a nervous chuckle.

"Believe me," Bronson shook his head. "There's nothing wrong with your kisses. It's just apparent that it's me you're not used to. That's all I meant by practice - just getting used to me being the one to steal those kisses."

"Maybe if I stole them for a change…" Mandy whispered, took Bronson's face in her hands and pulled his lips to hers. She kissed him like she never had before, and Bronson couldn't deny how attached he was becoming to her. With that attachment came worry that somewhere along the way he might slip up and she might be hurt. He pulled her against him, and his lips made unspoken promises to her that he would protect her no matter what.

Chapter 8

A couple of weeks into the surveillance operation, Mandy returned home on a Thursday afternoon to find Bronson at his usual post sitting in front of the computer monitors.

"Well, the verdict's in," came her cheery quip as she entered his room.

"Hi!" he returned her chipper greeting. "What verdict is that?"

"It's official. Mrs. Wallington thinks you're a hunk but that you're not good enough for me because you never take a lick at a snake."

Bronson chuckled that low, rumble chortle that had become music to Mandy's ears.

"Oh, is that all? She thinks I'm lazy, does she?"

She approached his desk and leaned against the end of it facing him with a smile.

"But, does she find me trustworthy?" Bronson pointed an index finger skyward dramatizing the fact that that particular characteristic was all that truly mattered.

"I don't know, I'll have to ask her the next time we discuss your suitability," Mandy smirked and then stood upright. "What do you want for dinner? Fried chicken or grilled tuna?"

"Tuna, I love the way you grill fish," he flashed his dimples.

"Thanks," her eyes lit up as she left the room.

~*~

As Mandy worked over the grill, Bronson stepped outside, letting the screen door slam. She turned to face him and he gave her a jubilant embrace. Mandy had never cooked on her grill quite so much until Bronson came along. The man loved grilled foods and that was fine with her since it always meant she'd be the object of his affections. Pretended or not, she increasingly lived for these amorous moments.

His suggestion that they "practice" meant it didn't even matter if there were neighbors around to observe them. Sometimes he'd catch her completely off guard inside the house, coming up behind her as she graded papers or watched television.

"I think we have him!" Bronson whispered into Mandy's ear.

"Really?"

"Are those steaks almost done? Then we can go inside, and I'll tell you all about it," he looked to his left and right finding no neighbors outside.

"Almost," she turned around and gave them one more flip as Bronson slid his arms about her waist stealing kisses from her slender neck. Each time his familiar affection returned, Mandy's pulse quickened and every ounce of her felt like warm chocolate melting in a fondue pot.

As they sat down at the kitchen table, Bronson explained that he'd just picked up a conversation between Jason and one of Hallstead's men. He had scheduled a rendezvous for that night at nine-thirty.

They ate dinner and after Bronson helped her clean the kitchen, he prepared to leave. It was about an hour before the meet when Mandy stood with him at the front door. "Now, be careful," she said, reaching up to let her hand graze along his cheek. "And no matter how late it is when you wrap things up at the station, let me know how it goes."

"Are you sure? You have school tomorrow and it might be really late," he said.

"It doesn't matter. Promise me, you'll let me know," she met his eyes and felt a nervous tremor as he agreed. Would he be in danger? She couldn't stand the thought of anything happening to him.

Another officer came to take Bronson's place manning the monitors, and Mandy stood at the door watching Bronson get into his truck and drive away. She tried to kill time watching television, but her eyes simply stared at the screen as she thought about Bronson and worried for his safety. Two and three hours passed with no word from him.

Jason parked his car by the Tennessee River and sauntered to the end of the deserted dock. He flicked his flashlight off and on twice and waited. Within less than a minute, a motor boat cut its engine and coasted next to the dock. He reached out his hand to grab the rope they threw to him, and fumbled with it as he tried to tie it to a wooden post. Two men got out of the boat, and looked at him in disgust, "You Jason?" One asked.

"Yeah, you got the stuff?" he shot back. He sniffed and ran his hand across his face. "I want to get this over with."

The other man shook his head and opened the suitcase he had in his hand. "Now let's see the money."

Jason reached into the duffel bag he'd slung across his shoulder. He took it off and gave it to the man. At that moment, lights seemed to appear from everywhere just as two narcotics officers bobbed above the water's surface in scuba gear and commandeered the boat. Two others climbed onto the dock, each grabbing a criminal. Bronson ran into the fray and pointed his gun at Jason when he reached the end of the pier.

Just as he began issuing the arrest and reading them their rights, Jason, obviously pumped up on his own dose of narcotics, elbowed the officer behind him and kicked Bronson's arm. Bronson was caught off guard, and before he could recover, Jason slugged him in the face. Bronson's gun went off, and pandemonium broke out as several officers tried to assist. The criminals decided to make a run for it. They jumped for the boat, followed by several officers.

In the melee, the drug runners took a gamble by throwing the duffel bag into the water to buy time so they could start the boat. Twenty dollar bills littered the water, and clogged the engine. It sputtered and finally kicked to life, but the rope was still tied. By this time the officers had surrounded them, and there was no way out. The officers boarded the boat and cuffed all three men. Leading them by the arms, the officers took the thugs to the squad cars.

Bronson radioed his superiors with one hand and blotted his bleeding eyebrow with the back of his other, glad he'd chosen to wear his bulletproof vest that night. He fingered the indentation near his heart, realizing how close to death he'd come.

It took several hours to get everyone to booking and file his report, so it was nearly midnight by the time he arrived at Mandy's door. Uncertain as to whether she'd still be awake, he used his key to enter and quietly closed the door behind him. The officer manning the monitors had long since left, having received the news that the criminals had been apprehended.

Bronson hovered over Mandy. She'd fallen asleep on the couch in her sweats and t-shirt. Bronson noted that it was the same t-shirt she'd worn the first day he met her in the park. His mind darted back to that rainy morning. Even from that first day, there was something about this woman that drew him to her like a moth to the flame.

Unwilling to disturb her, he decided to remove his computer equipment from the spare room, under the cover of night so as not to alert the neighbors that the entire affair had only been a ruse. Quietly he unplugged the computers and loaded them into his truck.

He re-entered the house and remembered that she'd made him promise to tell her the outcome no matter how late it was. Even though he knew the officer would have told her of the arrest, he realized she'd want to hear it from him. He eased down beside her on the couch and patted her shoulder.

"Mandy"

"Huh?" she began to stir.

"Mandy," he gently brushed a stray hair from her eyes. "It's me, Bronson."

She opened her eyes and blinked several times, "How did it go?" She sat up and leaned against the corner of the couch.

"We got him."

She reached up and gently ran her finger along the edge of the bandage over his eyebrow. "What happened to you?"

"It's nothing. Just a little cut. He got in a good punch before we took him in." He leaned his hand on the couch beside her.

She flicked on the end table lamp and looked him over. "Are you hurt anywhere else?"

"No, I'm fine. Really," he chuckled, not wanting to worry her. "But thanks for caring." He gave her that mischievous grin that he often did before he found an excuse to shower her with affection. But there would be no more excuses. The case was now closed.

"So, you won't be needing my spare room anymore, then?" she stated the obvious.

"No, I cleared everything out for you." He pointed his thumb in the direction of the room he'd used.

"Already?" came her surprised response.

He chuckled, "I thought you didn't like my computers – 'an invasion of privacy' I believe were the words you used."

Mandy didn't feel like his witty banter right now. A horrid ache had tightened inside her throat and she thought tears might actually escape her eyes. She stood up and went to the kitchen for a drink.

"You want a soda?"

"Please."

She poured two glasses of root beer, handed him one and sat down on the couch sipping the other.

"So what's next?" she asked.

"Jail for Jason and his cohorts. On to the next case for me, and in about a month I'll have to testify before the grand jury."

"Testify," she whispered distastefully.

"Just part of the job, Ma'am," he offered his best *Dragnet* impression. He guzzled the last of his root beer and then set it on a coaster on the coffee table. "Well, I better get out of your hair so you can get some sleep." He rose to his feet and stretched. "I guess you'll be happy to have your house back to yourself."

No! She wanted to scream. *No, it won't be nice to be alone again. No, I won't be happy to be without your handsome face, your helpful ways or your fantastic kisses. I don't want to ever live another day without you in it.* But she just sat there in the awkward silence.

"So," she began, "I guess maybe I'll see you around?"

"As convenient as fate has been in bumping us into one another, Ms. Gates, I don't particularly want to leave it in her hands," he winked. "I was thinking I could treat you to dinner Saturday night – you know – make it up to you for all those delicious home cooked meals."

Mandy couldn't keep the smile from spreading across her lips. "That sounds great."

He leaned over and kissed her cheek, "Thanks for everything, Mandy."

She accepted the compliment, and he started for the door. Just before leaving he called back. "Six-thirty sound okay?"

"That'll be fine," she waved as he slipped out the door and locked it behind himself. She rose to her feet, stretched her arms over her head and exclaimed, "Yes! Yes! Yes!" with every step to her bedroom.

Chapter 9

Bronson gazed across the candlelit restaurant table. Mandy, self-conscious of his scrutiny, stared out the window toward the moonlit Tennessee River. She glanced up to meet his eyes.

"What?" she released a nervous chuckled.

"I just can't get over the fact that a gorgeous woman like you is sitting here with an ugly fella like me."

"Oh give me a break," she rolled her eyes.

"I'm serious!" he insisted.

"Don't you at least look in the mirror when you shave?" she teased.

"Okay, then ordinary Joe," he relented.

"Now you're just fishing for compliments," she bantered and lifted the fork from her napkin.

"There's only one compliment I'm fishing for," he cut into his steak and put a piece into his mouth.

"And what would that be?" she quizzed.

"Oh, no," he waved his fork dramatically. "If I tell you, then it's not a compliment." He plunged his fork deep into the meat.

"You're as bad as a woman!" she retorted.

"Now that was definitely NOT the compliment I was hoping for," came his adamant reply.

"Hmmm . . . " Mandy didn't particularly feel like embarrassing herself by rattling on about everything she found fantastic about him in hopes of finding the one trait he wanted to hear. Instead she simply said, "I'll think about it and get back with you."

"So, my good qualities are so hard to pinpoint that you have to think about it?" he rallied and took a bite of steak.

"I did NOT say that. Now you're putting words into my mouth!" she defended.

"All right, all right, settle down. I'll give you some time," he chuckled.

As they continued their dinner, Mandy's mind drifted into itemizing a list of Bronson's attractive qualities – like the way his eyes flirted with her when he teased, the deepening of his dimples that gave him that boyish quality, and his helpful nature like carrying out the trash without being asked. She loved the way he kept her on her toes with his quick wit. Mandy never particularly noticed feeling fear, but with Bronson around she couldn't deny a sensation of complete and utter safety. No one in the world could harm her with him near, and that sense of safety and security never seemed more dramatic than when his arms held her tight.

Lost in her thoughts, she hadn't said a word for several minutes as she stared out the window at the moon and city lights bouncing off the river.

"You're quiet. What are you thinking about?" he finally asked.

"Oh, I was just . . . just wondering whether you thought they'd keep Jason locked up until the trial."

"The bail's been set extremely high. I doubt he'll come up with anything to approach that figure," Bronson assured. "We shouldn't have anything to worry about."

"Do you think we need to worry if he does get out?" Mandy asked with sudden anxiety.

"Maybe," he tilted his head to one side. "He knows it was me who arrested him. He's seen me at your house. It wouldn't take a genius to put two and two together. That's why I fought so hard for the bail to be set high."

Mandy felt a nervous tightening in her chest, and she wished she hadn't brought up the subject. She hadn't thought about Jason being released and causing them trouble. She had only thought of

Cara and her safety. Fortunately, Cara was still with her parents and adamant that she'd never go back to Jason after what he'd done to the baby.

"Do you think he'd come after you if he got out?" she asked, then lifted her napkin to her lips.

"It's possible. But it's not like it's something I haven't dealt with before," Bronson reasoned. "It'll be fine, Mandy." He reached across the table and covered her hand with his. "He's not going to raise that kind of money. His mom can't bail him out of this one."

"I hope not . . ."

After a stroll downtown along the shops, Bronson tugged Mandy's hand and led her to a hansom cab parked in front of the aquarium.

"Care for a ride?" he asked as he pointed to the horse drawn carriage, pulled her toward it, and slipped some money into the driver's gloved hand.

Mandy couldn't help smiling at the reminder of all the daydreams she'd been embroiled in with Bronson and horses. He helped her into the carriage and slid in beside her, putting his arm around her shoulder. Her chest tightened and her mouth went completely dry as she thought about their cozy position.

They'd feigned affection so many times that snuggling against him at this moment seemed completely natural, but then again, it held a novelty it never had before because it was no longer "part of the job." She wasn't entirely sure how to react, so she turned her head away from him looking out the side of the conveyance at the beautifully restored buildings.

"Trustworthy," she muttered more to herself than to him.

"What?" Bronson asked.

"Oh nothing," she waved her hand.

"No, you said something. What was it?" he coaxed.

"I said *trustworthy* – I feel secure and safe with you. I trust you. That's what you were asking at dinner wasn't it? If I trusted you?"

Bronson nodded, and his expression turned somber as if he were preparing to reveal some dark foreboding secret. In response, her expression matched his worrisome furrowed brow.

"Mandy . . . I was wondering . . ." he paused.

"Yes," she encouraged him to continue.

"Would you care to keep seeing each other? Socially, I mean?"

With Mandy's sigh, the tension evaporated from her complexion, "Oh, is that all?"

"What do you mean is that all?" he leaned back a little.

"With that look on your face, I thought you were going to tell me something like you had six months to live, were married, or had robbed a bank," she chuckled.

"No, none of those things," He shook his head with a twinkle in his eye. "So, are you interested?"

Am I interested? Who in their right mind wouldn't be interested? She thought, but her response was simple. "Sure, that would be nice."

"Great," he smiled and pulled her closer. She nuzzled up next to him, amazed at how comfortably her body fit next to his.

Chapter 10

Bronson sauntered down the hallway of the precinct with Champ, his German shepherd, beside him. He gave his friend Gerard a cheery wave and kept walking.

"It's somethin' else about that scum Richards raising bail, don't you think?" Gerard called over his shoulder.

Bronson stopped cold.

"Who'd o' thought he could come up with that kind o' money?" Gerard marveled.

In an instant Bronson had Gerard by the shoulder turning him around, "What? He's out?"

"Released on bail a couple hours ago." Bronson lifted his watch – 5:00 p.m. Mandy would be home!

Gerard looked surprised as Bronson spun on his heel and ran down the hallway with Champ keeping pace beside him. "What's wrong?" he shouted, but Bronson didn't answer.

Blood chased through Bronson's veins like a rabbit hounded by wolves. He suddenly didn't feel like he could breathe. He yanked open the squad car door for Champ and climbed in after the dog. Champ's tongue hung out of his mouth, and his chest was heaving in and out, but his eyes looked at his owner in concern.

"We've got to hurry, boy," was all Bronson said as he patted the dog's head.

Bronson peeled out of the parking lot, and tried calling Mandy from his cell phone. There was no answer. With the first spot of traffic, he turned on his siren and used the shoulder as a lane to pass slow cars. Flying as fast as he could, he turned off the siren and lights a few blocks before Mandy's house. There was no use alerting Jason to his arrival. He parked his car several houses down and crept discreetly toward Mandy's house, Champ alongside him. With pistol drawn, he let himself in the back door with a key.

His eyes darted to the scattered school papers sprawled all over the kitchen table and spilling onto the linoleum. A broken lamp lay shattered on the kitchen floor. His chest tightened and his pulse quickened. He eased the door shut without entering the house and in low tones radioed for backup.

"Stay," he whispered to Champ, who obeyed instantly by sitting on his haunches.

Bronson slowly open the door and left it open as he crept into the kitchen. He made his way to the hallway, his weapon in a ready position. His eyes fell to the space beneath Mandy's closed bedroom door. Shadows moved beneath it.

He stepped back so that Champ could see him and tapped his thigh twice signaling the dog to join him. In an instant the dog joined him.

"Ready?" Bronson whispered and the dog halted but did not sit.

Bronson crept down the hallway with his back hugging the wall outside Mandy's room.

He could hear a faint moan. Bronson spun around, kicked in the door and pointed his weapon at Jason Richards, who immediately dragged Mandy, gagged and tied, in front of him using her as a shield. Jason aimed a gun at her temple.

"Put it down or she gets it," Jason threatened. Mandy's eyes widened in fright. Blood trickled down her cheek from a wound on her forehead and dripped onto the beige carpet. Bronson's heart ached when he thought of what Mandy had endured.

"Now, now," Bronson said loudly and raised his hands making to surrender his weapon by beginning to crouch. Champ charged into the room in full attack and knocked Jason to the ground. Jason pulled Mandy along with him, and she fell to the floor.

Bronson piled on next, knocking Jason's gun aside and elbowing Jason's wrist so that he released Mandy.

~*~

"Run, Mandy!" Bronson commanded as Champ snarled and growled. Mandy scurried away on her knees. Running was impossible with her legs bound and her wrists tied.

Bronson and Jason tussled around on the floor in a blur with Champ joining in the mix, biting Jason in strategic debilitating locations. As Mandy crept down the hall, she heard a shot and instinctively put her hands over her face.

Moments later, she heard footsteps and cried out a muffled scream.

"It's okay, honey, it's me," Bronson soothed as he knelt next to her and removed the gag from her mouth.

"I hoped you'd come!" she cried. "All I could do was pray you would come."

"It's all right. It's over. He won't be hurting anyone else," he consoled as he loosened the ropes from around her wrists. The instant her hands were free, she put them around Bronson's neck and hugged him fiercely, burying her head on his shoulder.

He held her for several minutes, letting her cry against him. Finally, he put his hands on her shoulders and eased her back a little, "Let me take a look at your head." Mandy was reluctant to give up the comfort of his shoulder, but she did so he could examine the wound.

He gritted his teeth and winced along with her when his fingertips grazed across the painful lump forming beneath the laceration.

"He hit me with the lamp," she explained as Bronson cut the ropes around her feet with his pocketknife. Then in one effortless swoop, he'd lifted her into his arms and carried her to the sofa. "I'll get something to clean that."

Bronson hurried to the bathroom to retrieve the first aid kit from under the sink. He returned, knelt beside her, and tended to her wound.

Within minutes, police officers poured into the home. An ambulance took Jason's body to the local morgue, and the officers vacated the house leaving Bronson to "question the victim."

Bronson insisted that Mandy remain lying down on the couch as he sat next to her. With a gentle stroke, he swept her hair away from her bandage. His clipboard rested on his knee and he leaned over to place a tender kiss on her lips. Her hand went to his chest and slid around his neck. Her eyes met his sympathetic ones, and she noted the compassion and adoration there. A smile turned up his lips as he pulled the pen from his clipboard and prepared to take down the report.

"Is this how you interrogate everyone?" she teased as she laced her fingers through his hair.

"No, just the ones that can't keep their hands off me," he winked.

Mandy feigned insult, lifted her hand from the back of his head and gave his shoulder a little slap.

"I see you're feeling a bit better – enough energy for meanness," he quipped. His voice softened sympathetically, "Do you want to talk about what happened?"

"Do I have a choice?"

"Sure, we don't have to do this now if you'd rather rest awhile first," he set the clipboard on the coffee table to emphasize the point that red tape could wait.

"No, I want to get it over with and then I can rest," Mandy sat up a little and leaned against the arm of the couch.

With a deep breath, she related the encounter. When she came home from work, she came in the front door and went to the kitchen. She started to set some papers that needed grading on the kitchen table. Jason must have been hiding inside the house because he came up behind her and slammed the lamp over her head. She passed out for a little while and then woke up in her bedroom gagged and tied.

All she could think to do was pray – pray that Bronson somehow would rescue her before Jason did something even worse to her. She had no idea what his plan was, but from the glint in his eye, she knew they wouldn't be going for a picnic in the park.

It wasn't long before Jason heard the floor creak in the hall and thought someone could be in the house. Bronson burst through the door. Jason pulled her in front of him, held the gun to her head, and of course, Bronson knew the rest.

Bronson filled out the form with her account and then encouraged her to lie down. Mandy fell asleep with exhaustion - the broken lamp and scattered papers still blanketed the floor.

When she awakened a couple of hours later, Bronson had stacked the papers, cleaned up the broken glass and was pulling dinner out of the oven. He set the pan on top of the stove and tossed the oven mitt on the counter.

"You shouldn't have done all this," she yawned and stretched her hands high above her head as she entered the kitchen, brandishing her white gauze bandage just above her left eye.

"It's the least I could do. I feel horrible that I put you in danger. I should never have asked you to participate in this. At the very least I should have sent someone else to arrest him so that it would never tie back to you."

She stepped closer to him. "Bronson, there's no way you could have known he'd do something like this or even that he'd raise bail. Don't beat yourself up. You and Champ saved me, and that's all that matters."

At the sound of his name, Champ, who lay by the back door, lifted his head and pointed his ears.

"Still, I feel bad." He took her hand in his.

"Don't. It's all over now," she gave his hand a squeeze.

"Except I still have to testify in a few weeks," he shrugged, and leaned back against the counter, pulling her toward him.

"Testify? Why? Jason's gone." She looked up into his eyes.

"Hallstead - his supplier. He's a much bigger fish than Jason ever was. He's the one we really need to pin." Bronson explained

"Then it's not over?" Mandy could feel the nerves in her stomach tighten

"No," he answered and slipped his arms around her waist.

"Do you think he'll come after you?" Her concerned eyes met his.

"Possibly." His expression grew serious. "From now on I want you to have around the clock protection." He put a hand to the uninjured side of her face and caressed her cheek. "I doubt he'll come after you, but he might use you to get to me, and we can't afford to take any chances."

"Are you my protection?" She gave him a hopeful smile.

"We'll rotate our watch. I'm on duty until midnight and then another set of officers will pick up the watch from outside your house."

Mandy nodded with understanding.

~*~

The following week, Cara came back to the house during the days to make some repairs and pack to move. She wanted to make a clean break and start over fresh. She hired a realtor and soon a "for sale" sign was stuck in the front lawn. Mandy helped Cara after school. Together they patched holes in the walls, repaired furniture, and packed up Cara's belongings. Bronson pitched in and helped Mandy paint in the afternoons. He always scheduled himself to be her bodyguard during her off-work hours.

One afternoon as Bronson painted the bedroom and Cara and Mandy packed the kitchen, Cara confided, "I have such mixed emotions about everything. Sometimes I miss Jason so much, I cry myself to sleep. Other times I feel like a prisoner must feel when he's set free from a life sentence in a penitentiary."

Mandy listened without comment and Cara continued. "I keep feeling like he's going to come through that door, and it'll all start again."

Mandy patted Cara's shoulder, assuring her that she was safe now and that Jason would never hurt her or her baby again.

Cara offered a weak smile and explained, "You have no idea what it's like to live your life in a constant vigil. I was always looking out for the next little thing that would send Jason into a tirade. I can't even imagine what it will be like without living on egg shells."

"Peaceful, I'd imagine," Mandy smiled as she wrapped a glass in newspaper.

"Yeah . . . but," Cara lowered her voice to a whisper. "I know it sounds really sick to admit this, but in a way I'm afraid life will be boring without him."

Mandy raised a single eyebrow, a bit surprised by the comment, but she tried to cover her astonishment. She brushed Cara's comment aside with, "Oh, the baby will be here in less than a month. Life will be anything but boring for you!"

Cara smiled and rubbed her stomach, "You're right. And just think, my baby will never have to face life with Jason."

Mandy offered a melancholy smile. It was a shame that a baby's well-being would be better served without his father in his life.

~*~

By the end of the week, the repairs were completed, and Cara had moved into the basement apartment of her parents' home. Mandy was glad for her friend, but feeling at loose ends because Bronson had scheduled some time off work to attend the Battle of Chickamauga re-enactment for a few days. Various officers would be assigned to protect Mandy during his absence, but it wouldn't be the same without Bronson. He made her feel safe. Friday morning on his way to get his horse for the re-enactment, Bronson stopped by Mandy's house before she left for school.

When she opened the door to see him standing there in full Confederate uniform, she couldn't hide the glowing admiration that spread across her countenance.

"I just love you in Confederate gray," she greeted as he stepped into the house, and she closed the door behind him.

"Thought I'd stop by since I'll be gone for a few days."

"I'm glad you did," she smiled as she touched a button on his wool uniform.

"Had to bid my lady farewell before I ventured off to war." He pulled the cap from his head and put an arm around her waist, pulling her toward him.

"Your lady?" Mandy leaned her head back and gazed into his eyes.

"Yes, *my* lady," Bronson winked as he now extended his other arm around her, his palm against the center of her back, pulling her even closer.

"Return to me, my dear Captain," she threw herself into the act with the exaggerated Southern drawl of a Georgia peach.

"No matter where the hazards of war shall take me, my heart shall ever be yours," he answered with an accent richer than his own.

"But my dearest, promise me that you shall return to me from this wretched war?" She brushed at imaginary tears.

"I promise," he vowed with his cap to his heart.

"And I shall be waiting expectantly for your return." She put her palm to his cheek.

He held her face in his hands and looked deeply into her eyes, "I love you."

Mandy smiled and continued in her Georgia peach role, "And I you, my dearest."

"No, I'm serious, Mandy. I love you," Bronson's voice lowered to a more serious tone.

Mandy's eyes widened. He wasn't acting anymore.

"I love you too, Bronson," her voice lost its thick accent.

"When I get back, we need to do something about that, now, don't we?" he curled his finger under her chin and winked.

In his farewell kiss Mandy could feel the promise of dreams transforming into blissful realities. Then he was gone – leaving her standing awestruck at the screen door.

74

Chapter 11

Men in blue marched toward the hill defended by Confederate gray. Gunshots blasted and cannons boomed. Bronson sat atop his bay commanding his regiment who valiantly defended their post. Rallying them onward to victory, he instructed the color guard to raise their banner to the wind. Rows of men rushed forward to meet the enemy.

Artillery fire rent the air and men fell like flies on either side. Bronson charged forward, his sword drawn. Amidst the gunfire, he lunged forward and slumped over his horse. Shocked by the searing pain in his chest, he dropped his sword to the earth. Bronson's hand went to his uniform, and he pulled it back covered in bright blood. His vision darkened and his body slid from the animal. His boot caught in the stirrup and his horse continued a few steps, dragging him alongside, then stopped. Bronson's foot slipped from the stirrup and fell limp to the ground. The bay turned, whinnied, and nudged his master's body with his nose.

The day's battle continued in full glory throughout the morning and into the afternoon. Finally, the rebels, holding their ground, drove back the Union troops. With the final victory shout, one-by-one the men rose from the earth like the dead rising on resurrection morning. Dusting off their trousers, they gathered their guns and swords and meandered back to camp.

Gerard, resurrected from his mortal wounds, bent over to gather his sword and return it to its sheath. He replaced his cap and surveyed the area, noting Bronson's bay standing in the field beside its master.

Gerard sauntered toward the pair. "I saw that fall, Bronson! That's what I call some acting. Did you mean to get your foot caught and drag for a while?" Gerard chuckled as he neared Bronson's position.

"For Pete's sake, stop milkin' it," Gerard rolled his eyes as he approached Bronson who still lay slumped on his side. "Or have you decided to take a nap out here in the field?" Gerard nudged Bronson's shoulder with his boot, and Bronson fell over onto his back.

"What?" Now you're bringing ketchup along to . . ." Gerard stopped mid-sentence and knelt beside his friend. "Oh, my! What in the world?" he exclaimed.

Gerard slipped his hand to Bronson's neck and felt for a pulse. Bronson had been shot in the back and the bullet had come through the other side. The crimson saturating his chest was not a hot dog condiment but blood – lots of it!

Gerard immediately called for help from the few stragglers who remained in the field. Two men ran forward, and Gerard ordered one man to go for Jim Akers, a paramedic. He instructed the other to stay with Bronson while he rode Bronson's horse to find a telephone. In a flash, Gerard was off to the nearest ranger's station.

Due to the rural position and the critical condition of the victim, Life Force was dispatched and within a short period, a helicopter landed in the middle of the Civil War re-enactment and took Bronson to Erlanger hospital in Chattanooga. Gerard flashed his police identification and hopped aboard.

During the short flight Gerard watched the paramedics frantically working on his friend whose skin color was now as gray as the uniform he wore. When they finally landed at the hospital, the gurney burst through the double emergency room doors and an orderly wheeled Bronson away. The on-duty physician put his hand to Gerard's shoulder, "You'll need to stay here, sir. We're taking him immediately to surgery."

Gerard peered through the windows as Bronson's gurney disappeared around the corner.

"If you need to make some calls, there's a phone right over there," the physician pointed to a payphone hanging on the wall. Instead, Gerard reached to his belt for his cell phone, but remembered he didn't have it on him. He had nothing of modern convenience on his person since that was customary when re-enacting.

He reached inside his pocket. At least he had some change. He went to the phone, called the precinct, and informed them of what had occurred. He asked one of his coworkers to bring him a change of clothes, a cell phone and a list of Bronson's nearest relatives' phone numbers.

Gerard slumped in a chair holding his head in his hands as he prayed for his friend. They'd worked together on the force for the last seven years. They'd attended the police academy together and had started re-enacting three years ago. Bronson was too young to die. He was only twenty-nine. He hadn't even had a chance to live yet. He hadn't gotten married or raised a family. Just when he had finally met someone he was crazy about, he had to get shot – and not even in the line of duty - but out in a field playing Civil War soldiers! Who in the world was using real bullets out there anyway? "Surely, he'll live," Gerard muttered to himself. But Bronson had lost so much blood, and he'd been laying there for hours!

This was the train of Gerard's thoughts when two officers entered the waiting room and headed straight toward him. Gerard leapt to his feet. A short, stocky female officer with her dark blonde hair pulled back in a ponytail handed him a bag.

"Thanks!" Gerard took it. "And did you bring me a phone and the list?"

She pulled a cell phone from her pocket and handed it to him along with a folded piece of computer paper from her back pocket. Gerard unfolded the paper and scanned the brief list.

"Mandy's not on here," Gerard lifted his eyes which bounced from the female officer to her lanky male companion and back to her again.

"Who's Mandy?" the female officer shrugged her shoulders.

"Mandy Gates, Bronson's girlfriend. Her name's not on here."

"I just printed out the emergency numbers. It probably hasn't been updated in about six months."

Gerard went to the pay phone again, but the phone book was missing. He dialed 411 on his cell phone and requested the number for Mandy Gates in Ringgold, Georgia. No listing.

"Why don't you call his parents? They should probably be notified first anyway, and maybe they have her number," the female officer suggested.

Gerard doubted it. Bronson was pretty private about his love life. His parents would be the last people on earth he'd give Mandy's number to. But they did need to be told. He started to dial Bronson's parents when the male officer suggested, "You may want to step outside. I don't think they want you using a cell phone in here."

Gerard nodded and went outside the building to make his call. The Reilly's lived in Knoxville, so it would take them a couple of hours to arrive. Rather than reveal something Bronson might not want his parents to know, he didn't bother asking for Mandy's number.

Instead, he returned to the two officers with his keys held out, "Here, take my keys and go get my car and bring it back here. It's got Bronson's and my stuff in it. You'll find his cell phone in his bag in the trunk, and we can get Mandy's number from it." Gerard handed them the keys and gave them instructions on where they would find his car.

~*~

Mandy unlocked her front door and tossed her book bag inside the door as she flipped through her mail. A card size pink envelope caught her eye, and she went to it first, tossing the rest of her mail on the kitchen table. She recognized Bronson's handwriting. Smiling, her heart pattered a little faster. She carefully tore open the envelope and read the card. It had a scenic photograph on the front and no printing inside. The interior simply read,

You make my life beautiful.

I love you,

Bronson

Mandy smiled wistfully, thinking of Bronson, and held the card to her heart just as the phone rang.

"Hello," she put the card to her face and inhaled deeply of Bronson's cologne.

"Mandy, this is Gerard – Bronson's friend."

"Hi Gerard! I thought you were with Bronson?"

"I am. Mandy – uh – " Gerard hesitated. "There's been an accident and I think you better come down to Erlanger."

"What? What's happened to Bronson?" Mandy grew pale.

"He's been shot."

"What?! How? He wasn't even on duty! He's re-enacting this weekend!" her mind tried to reason away the panic that seized her. She slumped onto the couch, holding her head in her hand.

"He was re-enacting and somehow he got shot," Gerard answered.

"You use *real bullets* when you're re-enacting?!" Mandy's voice rose to a frightened pitch. She never would have let him go if she'd know they used real bullets!

"No, no we don't, but somehow – I don't know how – Bronson got shot this morning. Just come on down here, and I'll tell you everything I know."

Mandy looked at the card, which she now clutched tightly in her hand, threatening to mutilate it into nothing but a wad. She loosened her grip on the it and noticed the trembling of her hands.

"Is he going to be okay? How bad is it?" Her head pounded from the sudden panic that had gripped her. A painful lump formed in her throat as tears welled in her eyes.

"I don't know. He's lost a lot of blood."

"Oh my goodness!" even Mandy's voice quaked.

"Look Mandy, you still have an officer protecting you – right?" Gerard asked.

"He's just outside," she answered.

"Get him to drive you over here. You don't need to be driving right now. Come around to ICU. That's where I'll be – in the ICU waiting room."

Mandy nodded her head as if Gerard could see her, "Okay, all right, yes that's a good idea. I'll be right there."

Mandy shoved the card in her purse and went for the door. She asked the attending officer for a ride to the hospital and he kindly put on the siren so they could travel at full speed to the hospital.

Chapter 12

Mandy hurried into the ICU waiting room. It bulged with people sprawled in recliners with pillows and blankets as if they were camping out for the night. Others sat along the walls in couches and chairs. Gerard greeted Mandy at the door with a hug, letting her cry on his shoulder. He nodded at her accompanying officer, giving him leave to go, "I'll take care of her now."

"Have you heard anything? How is he?" she wiped the tears from her eyes with a tissue.

"He's still in surgery," Gerard put a consoling arm around her shoulder and led her to a chair where he sat down beside her.

"Tell me what happened. I don't understand how he could have gotten shot," she sniffed.

Gerard related what he'd seen that morning – Bronson slumped over and falling from his horse. Gerard simply thought Bronson was throwing himself into the role as he always did. There had been gun blasts and cannon thunder all day. There was no way anyone could have realized Bronson had actually been shot at that point, but from the appearance of the wound and the blood loss, it must have happened then.

"Do you think one of the re-enactors used real bullets?" Mandy gasped.

"I don't think so. I think it was a hit," came Gerard's somber reply.

"A hit?" her eyes widened.

"I think someone used the re-enactment as a way to get to Bronson without anyone realizing who'd done it or even that he'd been shot. They were probably hoping that by the time anyone found him, it would be too late and he'd be dead."

"But why?" she cried.

Gerard lowered his voice and spoke slowly, "Bronson's been receiving a lot of threats, Mandy. He didn't want you to know because he didn't want you to worry."

"What kind of threats?" she patted her tissue to her eyes.

He lowered his voice to a whisper and leaned toward her, "Death threats. They don't want him to testify in the Hallstead case."

Mandy let the words "death threats" hang in the air for a moment and then shook her head in confusion, "Why didn't he tell me? Is Hallstead out on bail?"

"No, he wasn't allowed bail, but he can run a hit from within prison. The man's racket is tri-state," Gerard shifted his arms, leaning his elbows on his knees.

Mandy put her hands to her face and then slowly ran her fingers through her hair, releasing a deep breath. This was a lot bigger than she had wanted to believe. Sure, Bronson had alluded to the fact that there was a bigger case than just Jason's abuse and drug running, but she had no idea that they were dealing with people who could orchestrate a hit from within prison!

"They've sent officers to investigate onsite, but I doubt they'll find anything among the re-enactors. The perpetrator was probably hiding in the woods and picked Bronson off from a distance," Gerard explained.

"How long has he been in surgery?" She dabbed a tissue to her eyes.

Gerard glanced at his watch, "A little over an hour."

Mandy rose to her feet, crossed to the doorway and looked through the windows. She hated hospital waiting rooms. How many worried hours had she spent in one of these cold rooms pacing the floor like a caged animal – helplessly waiting and worrying? How many prayers had she sent heavenward the night her sister was nearly killed? Or the day of her mother's heart attack?

In these rooms time stopped and all the menial day-to-day cares of life melted away, leaving only a small crucible holding the few things that truly mattered to you. At times like these, everything condensed down to the essentials – the person you loved and whether he would live or die. Mandy had always been a praying person, but somehow in situations like this prayer became the unwavering tether connecting her to her Source of strength.

The hour of surgery turned into three. Bronson's parents were just entering the door when the physician came out to speak with Gerard and Mandy. Gerard motioned them over and the doctor introduced himself and explained Bronson's condition to the group.

"The bullet went clean through – which is a good thing. As you know, he lost a lot of blood, and we've given him some. There's some damage to muscle and nerve tissue, and we'll just have to see how it heals before we can say whether there's any kind of permanent damage there. He's extremely weak, and he's still unconscious. If he makes it through the night, then we can rest easier."

"What do you mean, *if* he makes it through tonight?" Bronson's mother interjected with barely-restrained hysteria.

"I thought you said you fixed him up," Howard Reilly tightened his arm around his wife's shoulder.

"We did. We did all we could do, but he laid there for at least three or four hours without help. That's a long time to be losing blood and not receiving medical attention after a serious injury."

"I just don't see how this kind of thing could happen to a re-enactor!" Howard's face grew red with the injustice of it all. His gaze could have bored holes through the doctor's forehead.

"I can't answer that. Perhaps Officer McNally can shed some light on that," the doctor queued Gerard into the spotlight.

As Bronson's parents quizzed Gerard, Mandy stepped toward the doctor and touched his sleeve.

"When can I see him?" Mandy's big brown eyes pled with the doctor.

"He'll be out of recovery in about twenty minutes, and we'll move him to ICU. I'll make a note on his chart allowing you to visit him for just a few minutes. I'm sure it will do him good to hear your voice."

"Thank you," she gave the doctor a weak smiled and dabbed at a tear with her tissue.

"Just pick up the red phone in about twenty minutes and tell them Dr. Madison said you could see Officer Reilly."

"Thank you."

Noting that Bronson's parents and Gerard were now seated and embroiled in conversation, the doctor nodded sympathetically at Mandy and slipped behind the ICU doors.

Oblivious to Mandy's presence, Bronson's parents continued to carry on their conversation with Gerard. This gave Mandy an opportunity to observe them at a safe distance. She sat down on a chair catty-cornered to the couch upon which the three sat. Gerard was sandwiched in the middle with Mr. Reilly reiterating how he couldn't understand how such a thing could happen when one was simply "play acting." On Gerard's left, Mrs. Reilly kept insisting that if Bronson had listened to her and gone into dentistry, none of this would have ever even happened. She'd never approved of him being a cop! And what business did he have pretending to be a Civil War soldier?

Mandy couldn't keep from finding comedic relief in their reactions. Mrs. Reilly's hands waved around dramatically and her curly strawberry blonde hair bounced with her animation. "You boys never listen to me. I told you both to forget the police academy and go to dentistry school. But, no! Neither of you could be dissuaded from your destructive course!"

"That's why we moved, you know." Mr. Reilly interjected. Bronson's eyes were like his father's – his hair too, except Mr. Reilly's had turned salt and pepper gray.

Gerard rolled his eyes.

"Hillary just couldn't stand the thought of Bronson in danger all the time. That's why I suggested we move to Knoxville. Out of sight – out of mind, you know." Mr. Reilly looked at Gerard who ran his hand through his curly blonde hair.

"Dentists don't have to deal with death. They get all the perks of being a doctor without the death. Nobody dies in a dental chair," Mrs. Reilly reasoned. "They may think they're going to, but they never do."

"We could have kept our nice house that we got for a steal in the 60's. It was totally paid for. But nooooo, Bronson's got to go join the police force and push his mother to the brink of hysteria on a daily basis." Howard Reilly moved his hands about in a flittering motion to demonstrate his wife's frazzled state.

"Now dentists do have to deal with blood. But it's not very much at once. Pack some gauze in it, and it goes away," she shook her head comfortingly. Mandy smiled to herself, visualizing strapping Bronson in a white lab coat, a mirror in one hand and a drill in the other.

"You realize we only paid $14,000 for that house in the 60's. Sure we got $90,000 for it, but we had to turn around and pay $200,000 for the house in Knoxville." Howard pounded two fingertips into the palm of his other hand to illustrate the $200,000 dollars.

"And Bronson was always so good with his hands. He could work on those tedious model cars for hours – those itty bitty wheels and hubcaps!" Mrs. Reilly illustrated the tiny size of the model pieces with her thumb and forefinger. "Oh my! He had just the skills a good dentist needs, I tell you!"

A broad smile crept across Mandy's face as she continued to listen to the pair alternatively carry on two entirely separate conversations while Gerard's head bobbed back and forth between them like a ping pong ball. Finally, she glanced up at the clock on the wall and realized it had been twenty minutes. She stood and crossed the room to the red phone, leaving Gerard to play conversation tennis with the Reillys. Normally, she might have felt neglected having not been properly introduced, but when would poor Gerard have had a chance to insert a word into the conversation? If he had, then she'd be stuck in the middle of their verbal tennis, unable to weasel away to see Bronson.

Mandy picked up the red phone and told the attendant exactly what Dr. Madison had told her to say. The door buzzed and Mandy entered. She stepped down a hallway that opened up into a large room divided into curtained quarters for each patient. She walked toward the large desk in the center of the room.

"Officer Reilly is right over there," the nurse pointed to Mandy's right. Anxious about his condition, she slowly approached the partition. A friendly nurse in a pair of blue slacks and a white coat with little blue flowers on it greeted Mandy.

"Good evening, Mrs. Reilly, come right this way."

"Oh, I – uh," Mandy started to correct the woman and tell her that she wasn't married to Bronson when her eyes caught hold of his pitiful form in the hospital bed. Tubes ran out of his nose. He looked so pale. He wore no shirt, but had a large bandage on his shoulder and chest.

The nurse pointed to the tubes in his nose, "The tubes are still there from surgery. We'll be taking those out shortly." She pointed to a tube coming out of his chest, "This one over here will have to stay for a little while. It's for drainage."

Mandy winced.

"We need him to lie very still, so we're in no hurry for him to wake up. But you're welcome to talk with him. It'll be good for him to hear your voice. Do you have any questions?" the nurse asked.

"Is he doing any better?" Mandy gripped the cold metal rail that ran along Bronson's bed.

"His heart rate is getting a bit stronger, but his blood pressure is still a little low. He also has a bit of a temp so we've given him a round of antibiotics to prevent infection. This is his heart rate, his temp, and his blood pressure," she pointed to various electronic devices measuring Bronson's vitals.

"Your husband's a strong man, as you know, Mrs. Reilly. He's holding his own. Dr. Madison will be going off duty in a little while.

He'll come around and answer any other questions you have before he leaves. Dr. Jenkins comes on duty next. He's an excellent doctor – they're both the very best in their fields."

Mandy nodded and thanked the nurse. The woman gave her a sympathetic pat on the arm and left her alone with Bronson.

Mandy stepped closer to Bronson's bed and put a gentle hand to his cheek. "Oh, Bronson," she whispered. A helpless weight descended upon her chest as she watched him lying there completely incapacitated. How strange that this virile man she'd come to depend upon as her rescuer and protector now lay helpless before her! A horrible tightening cramped inside the hollow of her throat, and she turned her head away, a prayer filling her heart as she took a moment to gather her strength.

She patted the tears that spilled from her eyes and faced him, leaning over to place a soft kiss on his forehead. A tear spilled upon his brow, and she dried it tenderly with her thumb.

The nurse said to talk to him. What was she going to say? An awkward tension spread over her and she forced herself to speak.

"Bronson, it's me — Mandy. Can you hear me?" She smoothed the troubled wrinkles from his brow and caressed his cheek lovingly.

"Bronson, you're going to be all right. Remember, you promised to come home to me. And I promised I'd wait for you. Remember?"

"Oh, and," she reached into her purse and pulled out the card, "I got your card. I love it. It's beautiful." She held it up as if he could see it and that she could prove to him that she cherished it so much she'd probably carry it in her purse every day of her life.

She put it away and let the bag slip to the floor next to the bed. She leaned over and caressed his hand, curling her fingers around his.

"Bronson, you know I love you, don't you?" She whispered into his ear.

He didn't say anything, but Mandy could have sworn she felt his fingers tighten around hers.

~*~

Mrs. Reilly suddenly stood up and posed a question into the air, "When can we see him? I think we should be able to see him! Where did that doctor go?"

A man lying in a recliner, who'd evidently slept there the night before and planned to again, answered, "You pick up the red phone over there and tell them the name of the person you want to see. If they're not in the middle of a shift change or aren't dealing with an emergency on the floor, they'll probably let you come back." The man looked down at his watch. "But I think they're coming up on a shift change."

Mrs. Reilly disregarded the man's last sentence. She had already reached the red phone and lifted it to her ear, "I need to see Bronson Reilly. This is his mother."

"What do you mean 'call back in thirty minutes?' I need to see him now."

She listened for a moment and then huffed, slamming down the receiver.

It was then that Gerard realized Mandy had disappeared, and he was the one assigned to guard her. He stood up and looked around the room. Just as he headed for the door, Mandy entered the waiting room.

"Oh, Mandy, you had me worried. I thought I'd lost you," he smiled.

"I just took a moment to go back and see Bronson," she explained.

Mrs. Reilly's ears perked up, "See Bronson? You've been to see my Bronson?" She put her hand dramatically to her abundant bosom emphasizing the word "my."

Mandy gritted her teeth for a second; unnerved that she had now been discovered. Her pleading eyes met Gerard's.

"Mr. and Mrs. Reilly, this is Bronson's friend, Mandy Gates."

Mr. Reilly cocked an eyebrow, evidently reading more into the word "friend" than its traditional use. Mrs. Reilly, oblivious to the fact that anyone other than herself could hold center stage in her son's heart, moved closer to Mandy. "And you've seen him? How did you get back to see him when they won't even let his own mother see him?"

"I – I went in a while ago before the shift change. They made me leave just now." Mandy answered, suddenly feeling about the size of an ant in comparison to this formidable woman. It wasn't that Mrs. Reilly was taller than Mandy. She was actually a few inches shorter. She was a little heavy set, but her demanding presence was what set Mandy ill at ease.

The thought occurred to Mandy that if she were really Bronson's wife, she'd have to deal with this woman frequently - at the very least on holidays and birthdays. It was the only flaw she'd found in Bronson so far – other than his propensity to leave important things unsaid – like the fact that someone wanted him dead!

"I just don't see why they let *you* in before his own parents!" Mrs. Reilly bellowed. Mandy remembered that she was a schoolteacher and that perhaps she could use the same psychology on this woman as she did with her students – start out tough and if things go well, soften over time.

"You three were talking when the doctor said we could call on the red phone. You continued to carry on a conversation amongst yourselves. Since I was not part of that conversation, I decided to call on the red phone when the opportunity arose." Mandy explained the facts with that schoolteacher look and tone that said, "You weren't paying attention in class so you missed out on important information that would later be useful on the exam."

"Well!" Mrs. Reilly huffed and widened her eyes.

Mr. Reilly, evidently impressed that a young woman like Mandy could put his wife in her place, smiled and warmly extended his hand to her, "I'm Howard Reilly, Bronson's father and this is my wife Hillary. I take it you already know Gerard."

Mandy took the man's hand and smiled, "Nice to meet you. Yes, Gerard and I know each other."

"And how long have you and Bronson been," he hesitated and his eyes darted to Gerard and back to Mandy, "*friends?*"

"A little over a month," she answered.

"A month? You've only known him for a month and you're getting to see him first!" Hillary Reilly bellowed again.

"Settle down Hillary. She already explained that we weren't paying attention. You snooze you loose – right, Gerard!" Mr. Reilly chuckled lightly.

Gerard laughed and used the moment to return to their seats before someone else came in and grabbed them. The four sat back down. This time Gerard managed a seat by himself and left Mandy trapped between the Reilly's.

Fortunately for Mandy, she wasn't there long before Dr. Madison entered the room to give them a report. Bronson was looking better. How he faired that evening was still critical, but if all went well, he should be in his own room by the morning. The doctor suggested that they take this opportunity to get some dinner during the shift change.

Bronson's parents didn't want to leave. They had already picked something up and eaten in the car ride down to Chattanooga. Mandy asked Gerard if he'd give her a lift home so she could get some clothes and her car and come back to camp out in the waiting room. Happy for the break from Bronson's parents, Gerard agreed.

Chapter 13

When Mandy arrived back at the hospital with her pillow and small bag of belongings, Bronson's parents were coming out of the ICU. Tears flooded down Mrs. Reilly's cheeks, her mascara smearing. Her husband's arm cradled her consolingly. They were so distraught that they didn't notice Mandy and Gerard until Gerard approached them. Mrs. Reilly threw her arms around Gerard's neck and sobbed on his shoulder, leaving a big black stain on his white t-shirt.

"What's happened?" Gerard asked darting a worried gaze back to Mr. Reilly. Fear gripped Mandy. Had Bronson taken a turn for the worse?

"Nothing, nothing, she's just extremely distraught about seeing him that way."

Mandy and Gerard released a relieved sigh.

"I'm going to take her down the road to a hotel. Give us a call on my cell if there's any change," Mr. Reilly explained.

"Okay, sure," Gerard nodded as Mrs. Reilly released his neck and her husband helped her out of the building.

"She had me terrified there for a minute," Mandy wiped her brow.

"She can be a bit – well – intense." Gerard offered Mandy a weary smile.

"I gathered." Mandy settled into a chair.

"Are you sure you want to stay here all night?" Gerard asked.

"I'll see. I'd like to stay a while and see how he does tonight. I may just crash here." She set the tote bag of books she'd brought with her on the floor at her feet.

"I'll stay a while with you," Gerard sat down in the chair next to her. "I'll call for someone to stay with you when I leave."

"Is that really necessary? Do you think after what they've done to Bronson they'll still try to get to him through me?"

"I doubt it," Gerard reached into a paper bag he had and pulled out two candy bars. "But I'm not changing anything about the orders Bronson put into effect. We're not going to take any chances." He offered a candy bar to Mandy and opened his.

~*~

Mandy was glad she stayed the night because they let her spend more time in the ICU with him. About three in the morning, she had propped her pillow up on the guardrail of his bed and her head lay on it with her hand clutching his. She'd dozed off to sleep until she felt the weight of a hand on her head.

"Mandy," Bronson's voice sounded parched and cracked.

She lifted her head and his free hand slipped weakly to rest on her shoulder.

"Bronson! You're awake!" she cried.

"Where am I?" he groaned.

"You're at Erlanger. You were shot from your horse at the re-enactment. Gerard and Life Force brought you here," Mandy caressed his cheek, but still held his hand.

Bronson touched his wounded shoulder. "I remember a searing pain and then falling, but that's all." He moved his hand to a knot on his head. "I must've hit my head when I fell."

"Yes, I think you did. You've got a nasty bruise there. You laid there for several hours before anyone noticed you. They thought you were acting." Mandy was reluctant to release his hand, but knew he needed water. She rose to her feet and reached for his cup on the night table. She held up a straw to Bronson's lips so he could take a sip of ice water.

"Who shot me?" he asked.

"We don't know. Gerard thinks it was one of Hallstead's thugs." She set the cup on the counter beside his bed.

"Oh, yeah, I guess that makes sense," Bronson closed his eyes.

"Bronson, why didn't you tell me you'd been threatened?" she let her fingers stroke his shortly cropped hair.

"I get threats all the time, Mandy. It's part of the job. I didn't see any point in worrying you," he answered wearily.

Before she could scold him for keeping it from her, a nurse pushed back the privacy curtain and came in. "Mrs. Reilly, would you like a cup of – " the nurse stopped and put her hand on her hip when she saw Bronson awake. "Mr. Reilly, you're awake! How fortunate that you were here when he woke up, Mrs. Reilly!"

Bronson's brow furrowed and a curious puzzled smirk settled on his face. Mandy could feel herself blushing.

"How are you feeling Mr. Reilly?" the nurse began tending to Bronson, asking him questions and helping him achieve a more comfortable position.

After the nurse left, Bronson turned to Mandy with a raised eyebrow, "Mrs. Reilly?"

Mandy rolled her eyes self-consciously, "Oh I'm sorry about that. They just assumed and rather than explain and have them possibly not let me back here, I just kept my mouth shut."

"Why Mandy Gates, I didn't know you had a dishonest bone in your body." Bronson teased.

"I see you're almost back to your old self," she quipped, feeling a bit uncomfortable being caught in a fib – especially one on this subject.

Mandy and Bronson talked for a few more minutes before Bronson's eyelids grew heavy.

"Mandy, go home and get some sleep. You look exhausted," he admonished.

"I don't want to leave you," she laced her fingers through his.

"I'm all right. Go home and rest and come back to see me in the morning. I'll need your beautiful face to cheer me tomorrow," he lifted her hand to his lips and kissed it.

"So you're saying I look like an exhausted hag right now?" Mandy teased, faking a hurt expression.

"I didn't say that and you know it. But it makes me feel sad to see you so tired. Go get some rest, and I'll feel better that you did."

"All right, I guess," she reluctantly stood up, leaned over and kissed him. Sleep found Bronson before she even left the ICU.

Chapter 14

Bronson survived the night. His temperature reduced and his blood pressure rose into a normal range. The next day he had his own hospital room.

Hillary sat attentively in the chair beside her son's bed ladling food into his mouth while Howard perused the morning newspaper beside her.

"Really, Mom, I couldn't eat another bite," Bronson raised his hand to emphasize the point.

"There's just a couple more bites of fruit. Surely, you can finish it off. It'll make you feel better," she insisted.

Howard noted that Bronson finally acquiesced and forced down another spoonful of the bland fruit cocktail. Each of them looked up at the door when they heard light tapping.

"Yes, come in," Bronson answered. His face lit up as Mandy entered the room carrying a gift basket, and Howard believed there was a bit more color to his son's cheeks.

"Hi! How are you feeling this morning?" Mandy greeted Bronson with an expression that conveyed her adoration of him.

"Wonderful, now that you're here," he winked. She bent over to kiss him and handed him the basket. Howard set down the business section and watched the blissful couple and his stewing wife. Hillary's face had grown a shade redder. After thirty-two years of marriage, he knew what that thin pursing of her lips into a straight line meant.

Howard reached over and put his hand around Hillary's arm. "Honey, why don't you and I walk down to the gift shop for a little while," he coaxed.

Hillary wriggled from her husband's grasp, an irritated expression growing more prevalent in her eyes. Her attention never left the couple even to acknowledge Howard's suggestion.

Mandy helped Bronson rummage through the basket. "Just a few things to make your hospital stay more tolerable," Mandy pulled out two CD's by Bronson's favorite musical groups, a portable CD player with headphones, and a sports magazine.

Bronson lifted a box of chocolate pecan caramel candy, "Oh, and my favorite- Turtles! This is great, Mandy. Just what I needed," he smiled, slipping his good arm around her neck and tugged her closer for a thank you kiss.

Mrs. Reilly's ample rump fidgeted side-to-side in the hospital chair. Howard lifted a single eyebrow. This was something new for their son. He never even mentioned the girls he'd dated in the past, much less kissed one right in front of them. Howard therefore deduced without much effort that Bronson must have serious intentions toward Mandy. Hillary, on the other hand, had had quite enough when, upon Bronson's request, Mandy pulled a chocolate from the box and put it into his mouth.

"Give me that, Bronson Abernathy Reilly!" Hillary ripped the box of candy from Mandy's hand and slammed it down on the night table.

Mandy's mouth dropped, obviously shocked at the sudden outburst. Bronson's eyes also trained on his mother as if he were demanding explanation for such a display.

"Now Hillary," Howard soothed in a calm monotone.

"You just told me you couldn't eat another bite of food. If you have room in your stomach, you should be eating this nutritious breakfast instead of that rot!"

"Oh, Mom," Bronson muttered and rolled his eyes.

Hillary's finger shook as if she were scolding a three-year-old with his hand caught in the cookie jar. "Don't take that tone of voice nor roll your eyes at me, young man!"

Bronson simply closed his eyes and relented, "Yes, Ma'am." He could have been Champ commanded to sit and roll over. Mandy stood there for several moments, flabbergasted.

"Hillary, I feel like a walk down to the gift shop," Howard rose to his feet, tugged on his wife's arm and then laid the newspaper over the arm of his chair.

"Then go," she breathed in irritation.

"Why don't you come along with me? We could both use the walk," he persisted.

She simply twisted her arm from his grasp, took the basket from the couple and set it on the night table beside the chocolate.

"Bronson, you look tired. You need a nap," Hillary ordered.

"I'm not tired," Bronson assured his mother.

"Oh, yes you are," she insisted as she fluffed his pillow.

"Hillary," Howard calmly interjected.

"Mom, I've been sleeping for hours, I'm not tired," Bronson reasoned.

"You look exhausted," she countered.

"Hillary," Howard tugged at her arm again, this time more insistently as he pulled her toward the door.

"I'll be back in fifteen minutes, and I'm expecting to find you resting when I return," she shook her finger as Howard literally dragged her from the room.

Mandy shut the door to the room and turned back toward Bronson.

"Abernathy?" she teased.

Bronson rolled his eyes, "It's my mother's maiden name."

"You poor thing," Mandy chuckled.

"In more ways than one," his mouth twisted into a grimace.

Mandy sat next to him on the bed, "Are you feeling any better?" She smoothed away the fretful creases on his forehead.

"It's not bad unless I have to get up and walk around - which, unfortunately, I need to do right now."

"Too much chocolate – eh?" Mandy chuckled as Bronson eased himself into an upright position.

"Too much hospital food," he shifted his feet to the floor and grimaced with the pain in his shoulder.

"Do you need some help?" she offered. He swayed a little, dizzy as he rose to his feet. He nodded affirmatively as he waited for the wave to pass.

He put his arm around her shoulder and she supported him as he shuffled to the bathroom. Satisfied that he could stand on his own, Mandy shut the door behind him.

When the Reilly's reentered the room, Mandy was helping Bronson back to his bed. Hillary immediately maneuvered herself between the pair and scolded, "I told you to be resting when I returned and here you are walking around!"

"Nature calls sometimes you know, Mom," Bronson chuckled.

"You should have called for a nurse or waited until your father and I returned."

Bronson sat down on the bed, and Hillary's voice lowered to a loud raspy whisper as she put her mouth to Bronson's ear, "She has no business helping you do such things."

"I just helped him walk there and back. It wasn't like I went in there with him," Mandy defended.

"Still!" Hillary huffed.

~*~

Mandy arrived at the hospital on Bronson's fourth day there. She opened the door to his room and smiled a little wider when she noted his parents were not there.

"Hi!" she greeted and he looked pleased to see her.

"You ready to go home today?" she asked.

"Definitely. Mom is driving me nuts," Bronson rolled his eyes as Mandy drew closer. She bent over and kissed his forehead.

"You think she'll stop driving you nuts just because you're not in the hospital?" Mandy retorted.

"I'm hoping she'll go back to Knoxville."

"I hate to tell you this," Mandy grimaced, "But I overheard your parents talking about staying at your house and taking care of you for several more weeks."

Bronson swore and ran his hands through his hair. "I don't think I can take much more of this."

"Look on the bright side, your mother loves you," Mandy noted as she sat down on the edge of his bed.

"Mmmm," Bronson groaned.

"Unfortunately, she hates me," Mandy added, a frown creasing her brow.

"She doesn't hate you," he soothed, putting his hand to her arm.

"Oh," Mandy sighed, "She hates me all right. She begrudges anything I do for you. I think if it was up to her, she'd carry you back to Knoxville just to get you away from me."

"Speak of the she-devil," Bronson muttered under his breath just as Hillary and Howard came through the door.

"I've loaded all your stuff in the car," Howard said. Hillary walked straight to her son, ignoring Mandy's presence.

"I just have to wait for them to sign me out," Bronson replied.

"That could take awhile." Hillary turned to Mandy, "You may as well run along Ms. Gates. We'll get Bronson settled in at home. I've decided to stay on and help Bronson get to and from physical therapy for the next few weeks. He's going to need lots of care so that he's ready to testify at that trial."

Bronson's pleading eyes met Mandy's as if he were begging her not to leave him to his mother's bossy care.

"I'll stick around," Mandy said. "I've got a light work load tonight," she added, giving Bronson's hand a reassuring squeeze.

~*~

Little did Mandy know that Bronson's mother meant every word she said. She did stay with Bronson and dote on his every need. The Hallstead trial came and went without further event. No one was ever able to pin the shooting on them, but at least Hallstead and his thugs were behind bars with no parole in the near future.

Hillary's constant presence made seeing Bronson awkward. It didn't stop Mandy from visiting him, but Mrs. Reilly made it clear that Mandy's presence was not required nor particularly wanted.

A month after the shooting, Mandy arrived at Bronson's house while Mrs. Reilly had gone to the grocery store.

"Darn, you just missed her." Bronson snapped his fingers. "I know how you hate it when you don't get a chance to spend time with mother," Bronson quipped sarcastically from his recliner. Mandy rolled her eyes and bent over to kiss his forehead.

"Cara had her baby," Mandy said.

"Really?"

"Yeah, a little boy. Eight pounds, thirteen ounces," she removed her sweater and draped it over her arm.

"Did everything go okay?" Bronson asked.

"Yes, the baby's healthy and so is Cara," Mandy started to go to the couch and sit when Bronson grabbed her arm and held her in position.

"Oh, no you don't. I'm not settling for a forehead kiss when we've got the place to ourselves," he winked.

Mandy leaned over again and gave him a peck on the lips.

"We can do better than that, can't we?" Bronson protested and started to insist upon further affection, but the look on Mandy's face halted his plans.

"What's wrong?" he asked.

"It's your mother," Mandy stated flatly.

"What has she done now?" he sighed.

Mandy pulled a note from her purse and handed it to Bronson. He scanned it, then wadded it into a ball, and angrily threw it in the unlit fireplace.

"I'll talk with her," he exhaled in frustration.

"Talking won't do any good, Bronson. Where does she get off telling me that I'm smothering you and that I need to give you space to breathe? She's the one who's suffocating you. She's taken a powerful, strong-willed man and turned him into a marshmallow!" Mandy waved her hand at him indicating his relaxed position in the recliner. "I do good to spend ten minutes alone with you a few days a week, but I'm smothering you?"

"I'm sorry, Mandy. She'll be gone soon."

"Bronson, she'll never be gone. She's your MOTHER. I mean, I love you, but good grief! I just don't think I can deal with someone like this for –" She started to say for the rest of her life, but that was being a bit presumptuous. So instead she said, "any length of time."

"Are you saying that if we ever decided to consider marriage, my mother would be a factor in your decision?" There, he'd said it — the "m" word they'd been skirting ever since the shooting.

"Yes," Mandy answered solemnly.

"So you're saying that you won't marry me because of my mother?" his eyes widened.

"Bronson, that's not the point," Mandy shook her head.

"I believe it *is* the point," he insisted.

"But we've never even discussed marriage," she waved away his comment.

"We are now," he retorted, staring up at her.

"But it's just a hypothetical conversation," Mandy reasoned, trying to avoid his line of questioning. She went in the kitchen to get a soda.

Bronson followed her. Mandy glanced back at him. Even with his arm in a sling, he still looked irresistible in his jeans and t-shirt. But this wasn't a time to be trapped by Bronson's handsome good looks or boyish charms. Mandy steeled herself for his persuasive advances.

"It wouldn't be hypothetical if I asked you," he ventured.

"Huh?" Mandy played dumb as she popped the top of the can of root beer and handed it to him and got herself another one.

"I'm asking, Mandy. Will you marry me?" He set the can down on the table dramatically.

"What?" Mandy giggled nervously and then her tone grew more irritated. "You're asking me to marry you in the middle of a conversation about your *mother*?"

Bronson exited the room abruptly, leaving Mandy standing there dumbfounded. She took a sip of her drink and sat down at the kitchen table. "Where in the world did he go?" she muttered.

Within a few moments, Bronson reappeared and knelt on one knee beside her chair. He reached into his sling, pulled out a velvet box and lifted it to her.

"Look, Mandy, I know it's not the most romantic moment in the world. I've been planning an elaborate evening for this since before the shooting. I intended to give it to you before now, but . . . What I'm trying to say is, I love you. Will you marry me?"

Mandy slowly opened the lid to find a beautiful diamond ring inside.

"Bronson, I don't know what to say," she lifted the ring from the box and shook her head.

"What about yes?"

"I don't know if I can say yes," she whispered tentatively.

"Why not? You love me and I love you. That's all that matters – right?" he looked up into her eyes and she almost said yes. The word was actually forming on her lips when Mrs. Reilly walked through the kitchen door carrying armloads of grocery bags and found Bronson kneeling in front of Mandy.

Bronson didn't move. He just knelt there frozen, his eyes pleading with Mandy to forget that his mother was present and to agree in spite of it.

Mandy replaced the ring, gently closed the lid on the box, and set it on the table. She leaned over and whispered in Bronson's ear, "I'm sorry, Bronson. I love you, but I just can't." With that she was gone.

"I told you that girl was no good for you," Mrs. Reilly shook her insistent finger.

Bronson slowly rose to his feet and fingered the velvet box on the table. Taking a deep breath, he turned to his mother, "Mom, I need you to leave."

"I understand. You need a little time after a jolt like this. I've got another errand to run. I'll go do that and when I get back we can talk all about what happened."

"No Mom. I need you to leave. Go back home to Dad. I can take care of myself now. You've done enough here."

"You're not blaming me for this are you?" she defended, placing her hand melodramatically to her heart.

Bronson marched over to the fireplacem, snatched up the wad of paper, unfolded it, and shook it in the air.

"Why did you do this to Mandy? No, why did you do this to ME? I can understand that you don't want someone taking your place in my heart, but can't you understand I have room in my heart for a wife and a mother? Can't you see that I'm crazy about Mandy? Do you enjoy tormenting me? Do you enjoy driving the woman I love out of my life?"

"I – uh – you don't need her, Bronson. You're just blinded to her wiles right now and you're hurt. But one day you'll thank me. You'll see."

"Mom, Mandy has no wiles. She has no guile, deceit or agenda. She is who she is. That's what I love about her. You - on the other hand – " He wanted to say she was a manipulative witch, but decided against it. "Just leave Mom. And don't come back until you can accept that I'm marrying Mandy - until you can treat her with respect." With that, he grabbed his keys and the ring and stormed out of the house.

Mrs. Reilly yelled from the porch as he opened the car door, "But you can't drive with one arm!"

Bronson pulled the sling off his arm and flung it into the front seat. "I can do a lot of things you think I can't!"

Chapter 15

Mandy couldn't breath. Tears had been flowing since the moment she started the ignition and backed out of Bronson's driveway. What had she done? An immediate sense of loss swept over her. But how could she put up with that woman for the rest of her life? Marriage was a hard enough prospect without bringing a jealous mother-in-law into the picture!

She told herself that Bronson simply must not be the one for her. If he was, then everything would be ideal – not like this. Everything would be rosy and perfect like a dream – like one of her daydreams where her hero sweeps her off her feet and carries her away to safety and exhilarating, undying love. There wouldn't be an irritating mother-in-law in that picture. It was simple in Mandy's line of reasoning - Bronson must not be the one for her. She'd get over him. Someday, somehow she'd forget about him. This is what she told herself as she parked her car and stepped out, trying to avoid Mrs. Wallington who sat on her front porch. It was no use. Mrs. Wallington was on her way over.

"Mandy, honey, how is Bronson? Is he doing any better?" Mrs. Wallington asked with concern.

"He's fine," Mandy kept walking toward the house.

"You don't look fine. You look like you've been crying," the elderly woman put a hand on Mandy's shoulder.

Mandy turned slowly to face her neighbor. "I really don't feel like talking about it right now," she snubbed back a remnant of her tears.

"Okay, that's fine. You don't have to talk about it." Mrs. Wallington patted Mandy's shoulder. "Can I help you with anything? Lighten your burden in any way?"

"Yeah, lighten my burden of one old woman," Mandy gritted her teeth and muttered under her breath.

"What?" hurt filled Mrs. Wallington's eyes.

"Oh, Mrs. Wallington, I wasn't talking about you!" Mandy put her arm lovingly on her neighbor's arm. "I was talking about Bronson's mother."

"Jealous is she?"

"Yes, and now she's won," Mandy grumbled.

"Won what?"

"Bronson," Mandy stated flatly.

"What do you mean she's won Bronson? You're not giving up are you?" Mrs. Wallington's voice rose in surprise.

"Yes, I give up." Mandy snipped angrily. "Is that so horrible? I give up! She wins. I lose." She opened the door and went inside. "He's probably not the man for me anyway. If he was, it wouldn't be this difficult." She tossed her purse dramatically on the chair.

"What we obtain too cheap we esteem to lightly," Mrs. Wallington stated calmly.

"What?" Mandy shook her head, confused. She flopped down on her couch.

Mrs. Wallington sat down next to her. "You're a history teacher, dear, don't you recognize it? It's Thomas Paine: 'These are the times that try men's souls. The summer soldier and the sunshine patriot will in this crisis shrink . . . but she that stands it now, deserves the love and thanks of [her man].'"

Mrs. Wallington winked and then continued, "'Tyranny, like hell, is not easily conquered; yet we have this consolation with us, that the harder the conflict, the more glorious the triumph. What we obtain too cheap, we esteem too lightly; 'tis dearness only that gives everything its value. Heaven knows how to put a proper price upon its goods; and it would be strange indeed, if so celestial an article as [a man's love] should not be highly rated.'"[1]

Mandy chuckled, "I believe you took some liberties with Mr. Paine's words."

"A little," she shrugged. "But the point's the same. If it's worth having, it's worth fighting for." The elderly neighbor made a fist in the air to emphasize her point.

"But do I want to keep fighting for the rest of that woman's life?" Mandy leaned her head back on the couch in exasperation.

"You wouldn't be the first woman to put up with a domineering mother-in-law," Mrs. Wallington reasoned.

"I guess not, but still . . ." Mandy was feeling worn down and it resonated in her voice.

"Maybe your love for him just isn't strong enough," Mrs. Wallington shrugged her shoulders and stood to leave.

"I love Bronson," Mandy defended. "More than anything."

"Ah, but do you trust your love for each other? Do you trust that it can withstand anything? No marriage is perfect, Mandy. Bronson's mother is probably just the tip of the iceberg. You'll find all kinds of little things that annoy you about each other. But if you put your trust in the love you've committed to one another, then you can make it through anything."

"So you're saying love is enough?"

"No. Love coupled with commitment is enough. Annoyances arise. People make mistakes. In-laws interfere and even good looks and romance fade, but if you're committed to love him forever, then that commitment to love will carry you through." Mrs. Wallington patted Mandy's shoulder. "Think about it, sweetie." She left Mandy pondering her words.

1 Thomas Paine, The American Crisis, no. 1, 1776

~*~

It wasn't long before Bronson appeared on Mandy's doorstep.

"She's not home, Bronson," Mrs. Wallington called.

"Her car's here," he pointed to her vehicle as proof.

"She went for a run in the park."

~*~

Running cleared Mandy's head. It gave her time to think about things. Her feet pounded the pavement on the cool autumn afternoon. The trees had turned the most beautiful shades of bright yellow, vibrant orange and deep red. It was difficult to stay mad with this kind of beauty surrounding her.

As she rounded the corner, she stopped abruptly and looked up at Bronson in his Confederate coat and hat atop a black horse. He still had on his jeans, and she could make out his t-shirt beneath his coat.

He extended the palm of his good arm to her, "My lady."

She hesitated and then took his hand. He pulled her into the saddle in front of him. Bronson held her securely with his wounded arm and nudged the horse. It darted into the forest. The leaves crunched and fluttered under the galloping hooves. They rode for some time and then finally reached a beautiful green open meadow. The sun lit up the cloudless azure sky and a gentle fall breeze caused a few scattered leaves to tumble across the green field. Bronson stopped the horse at the edge of the woods. His injured arm encompassed Mandy's waist while the other held the reins.

"Whose horse is this?" Mandy asked.

"Let's just say I commandeered it."

Bronson moved his lips to her ear, "Mandy I'm sorry we fought. I told my mother to leave, and that she wasn't welcome back until she could treat you with respect and realize that I love you and want to marry you."

"You really told her that?" she turned her head a little to look at him.

"Yes, and I meant it. You're the world to me - the air I breathe. As much as I love riding through the beauty of God's creations, I love your beauty even more. You're my life, Mandy." He reached into his pocket and put his arm around her to hold the ring in front of her. "Please marry me."

Bronson slipped it on her finger.

"It's a perfect fit," she whispered.

"And so are we," he kissed her cheek and she turned to fall into the ardent embrace of her irresistible protector, her rescuer and the only man who embodied her dreams.

Epilogue

It was an inordinately cold Thanksgiving morning as Mandy awakened to the cry of "Mama, Daddy, I 'ant to get up."

Mandy nudged Bronson with her elbow and he rolled over on his side.

"Your turn," she muttered groggily.

"Uhhhhrgg," Bronson moaned as he sat up and put his feet to the carpet. He shuffled out of the room with his eyes still closed and soon returned with a three-year-old boy. He flopped the child onto the center of the bed and climbed in beside him. Mandy and Bronson each put an arm around the little one and kissed a chubby cheek simultaneously.

"Are Gamma an' Gampa comin' today?" Lucas looked up to his parents sharing a morning kiss over his head.

"Yes they are," Bronson mussed the boy's hair. "Bet you're hoping they bring you a dollar, aren't you?"

"Yep, Gampa always bings me a dahwa," the child's eyes lit up.

"What time is it?" Mandy yawned.

"Nine-thirty," Bronson answered.

"Nine-thirty, already?" Mandy hopped out of bed and threw on her robe. "I've got to get the turkey in the oven."

"We'll help, won't we, Lucas?" Bronson stood up and put the child on his shoulders, following Mandy to the kitchen.

They spent the morning cooking turkey and dressing and pumpkin pies. Spices filled the autumn air as the doorbell rang.

"It's Gamma and Gampa!" the excited three-year-old toddled to the front door and pulled it open with both hands.

Mandy removed the last pie from the oven as Bronson's parents bubbled into the house.

"Oh, my! Your house is just so pretty! I love the decorations and it smells simply divine!" Mrs. Reilly gushed. Mandy caught a wink from Bronson's eye and then he hugged his mother and father. Howard Reilly scooped his grandson into his arms.

"I brought you something," he reached into his pocket.

"A dahwa?" the child suggested in anticipation.

"Nope," Howard shook his head and the child's expression fell. "Two dollars!" he exclaimed and held two crisp dollar bills in the air. The little boy squealed, wiggled from his grandfather's arms and ran to his father.

"Gampa gave me TWO hoe dahwas!"

"Wow! Did you thank him?" Bronson patted the child's shoulder.

"Thankoo Gampa!" Lucas cried.

"You're welcome, Lucas." Howard flopped down in the recliner on the North end of the room. "You should have seen that traffic between here and Knoxville! We got stuck in a jam for nearly an hour, and all we went was about two miles!"

Hillary sat in a wingback chair opposite her husband while Bronson sat on the couch between them. Mandy took a moment to relax next to her husband on the couch while Lucas climbed up into her lap.

"Oh, and my arthritis was just acting up the whole way. I kept asking Howard to stop so I could stretch out my knees." Everyone looked at Hillary.

"There had to be at least ten thousand cars in that line of traffic." Howard held his arms apart illustrating the immense length of the line of vehicles.

"It gets that burning, twinge, aching thing going in my knees, and I swear I'm just going to pass out from the pain of it all." Everyone watched Hillary cradled her knee in her hands dramatically.

"Who knows what caused it. I never even saw a wreck," Howard continued.

"I've been to the doctor several times, but he just hasn't done a thing for me," she whined.

"I think it was just construction. Why in the world were they working on the road on Thanksgiving?" Howard complained.

Bronson squeezed his wife's hand and winked. That's the way every holiday went at the Reilly's - a lot of good food, love and conversation tennis.

Second Sight

A Sequel to *"In Love We Trust"*

by Marnie L. Pehrson

For Cathy, thanks for prodding me to write this sequel! But most especially for your encouragement, support & vision for the future!

Dan Vanderhoff straightened his tie and then rose from his chair at the boardroom table. He shook hands with his associates, retrieved his briefcase and exited the legal offices of Madison and Montague. It had been a long day, but a smile spread over his handsome face. He'd done some fancy footwork, but he believed he'd found a loophole for his client. Of course, the other lawyers on staff had been of service, but the fledgling partner was quite proud of himself for masterminding the project. He knew a win on this case would earn one more feather in his cap in the eyes of his senior partners.

Whistling a happy tune as he exited the building, he found his way to his Lexus in the parking garage and headed out of D.C. toward the Maryland suburbs, home to his beautiful wife and two-year-old son, Jamie. The gloomy drizzle on the January afternoon did little to dampen his spirits as he left the expressway.

The traffic light at the end of the off ramp turned green and Dan turned right. Just as he did so, a Ford truck came barreling across the overpass, slammed on its brakes and skidded across the slick oily pavement, hurling into Dan's Lexus, crushing it like an accordion into the car in front of him.

The metallic twirling and clank of a stray hubcap falling to the pavement was the last sound the young lawyer heard before his eyes closed for the very last time.

~*~

Gerard McNally raked his fingers through his wavy blonde hair and placed his cap on his head. Staring in the mirror, he straightened his tie and clipped on his badge. He gathered the contents of his pockets that he'd tossed on his dresser the night before and shoved them into his pocket. Another day on the force. With every day that had passed since his friend Bronson Reilly retired to start his own detective agency, Gerard grew less and less satisfied in his work.

Bronson urged him weekly to turn in his badge and come to work with him, but Gerard wasn't one to quit a good job. Plus, Bronson's agency was young yet, still in its infancy. Who was to say it would work out? Bronson had a wife and child to think about, but Gerard was on his own. Why toss aside a promising career on the force when there was no one to worry over his safety? Of course, that meant no one to come home to, no one to snuggle up by a fire with or fill a home with the wonderful smells of a home cooked meal. Then again, Gerard reminded himself that his apartment had no fireplace, and he could always inhale tantalizing aromas from Logan's Roadhouse down the street.

Gerard shoved an arm into his navy down jacket and started for the door. He locked his apartment, zipped up his jacket and started for the stairwell.

~*~

The blonde police officer nodded and his pale blue eyes smiled as Sable Graham passed him in the stairwell. She shoved her fists deeper into her pockets, quirked a half smile at the officer and kept on ascending to the second floor. She pulled a crumpled paper from her pocket and unfolded it.

"Apartment 254," she mumbled under her breath as her eyes lifted to read the number on the door she passed and continued onward. When she stopped in front of the apartment designated on the paper, she lifted her sleeve, noting the time as seven twenty-three. She knocked soundly and waited.

The terraces between apartments were outdoors, and she could see her breath in the winter morning air. The petite brunette in her late twenties fidgeted, bouncing slightly to stay warm as she shoved her gloved fists deep into her pockets once more. After waiting a minute or two, she knocked again, a little louder.

"Just a minute…" she could hear a groggy female voice answer from inside the apartment.

When the door flung wide, it was to see her old college roommate, Ellerie Tash standing before her, her robe wrapped haphazardly about her waist, her auburn hair mussed and one eye closed with morning sleep.

Ellerie's mouth dropped open, "Sable! Sable Graham! What on earth are you doing in Georgia?" Ellerie's arms went wide and hesitantly Sable stepped forward as Ellerie pulled her into a gigantic bear hug. Sable's arms went rigid at her sides for Ellerie had grabbed her so suddenly that she hadn't had a chance to pull her hands from her pockets.

Sable's long hair caught under Ellerie's immense embrace and the only thing Sable could do was hope that Ellerie released her grip before her locks yanked from her head. Finally, Ellerie freed her friend, grabbed her by the arm, and pulled her into the apartment. Once inside, Ellerie shut the door.

"What have you been up to all these years?" Ellerie led her friend over to the couch and fairly shoved her into the seat. Flopping down beside her, Ellerie tucked one long leg under the other.

"Working mostly," Sable smiled at her jubilant friend.

"Aren't we all!" Ellerie rolled her eyes, "Except for when I can escape to Daytona, that is!"

"You always did love the beach," Sable chuckled. Never mind that Ellerie didn't have the complexion for it, she'd have her freckled body donned in a bikini frolicking in the surf every chance she could.

5

"Gosh, sometimes it seems like yesterday that we were vying for the fraternity brothers at William and Mary!" Ellerie exclaimed in the thick Southern accent of a Georgia native.

"Seems like ages ago to me," Sable sighed.

"What's wrong, Sable?" Ellerie's voice lowered and she took Sable's gloved hands.

"Oh, nothing," Sable shook her head negatively. "I'm just tired. It's a long drive from D.C. to Chattanooga!"

"Why didn't you fly?" Ellerie asked.

"I felt like driving," Sable shrugged. "Plus, I plan to stay a while and this way I won't have to rent a car."

"Really? Then you simply must stay with me! I have a spare bedroom, and I've been looking for a roommate." Ellerie leaned her arm across the back of the couch.

Sable looked around the disorderly apartment. Ellerie hadn't changed much since college. Talk about a clutter bug! But she was a likeable personality. She was the first person Sable thought of when she decided to escape Washington.

"I was kind of hoping you might say that," Sable smiled.

"So what brings you to Fort Oglethorpe, Georgia, of all places?" Ellerie patted her hand on the back of the couch.

"I just had to get out of D.C. I needed a sanity break and when I thought back to the last time I felt sane, it was at William and Mary, and then I thought of you," Sable shrugged.

"Funny that the word *sanity* would evoke my name in your memory!" Ellerie chuckled, stood and crossed toward the kitchen. "Have you had breakfast? I was just fixin' to make an omelet. You remember my omelets?"

"I certainly do," Sable smiled and followed her friend. She removed her gloves and shoved them into her pockets, then took a seat at the bar that separated the kitchen from the living room.

"You were working at a law office there in D.C. last I spoke with you – right?" Ellerie asked as she cracked an egg into a ceramic bowl.

"Madison and Montague," Sable replied.

"There was talk of you being made a partner, too," Ellerie remembered as she cracked another egg.

"Yeah, but it didn't work out," Sable shrugged.

"Why not?" Ellerie pried as she tossed the egg shells toward the garbage disposal.

"Let's just say, I never took Schmooze 101 in college."

Ellerie nodded with understanding. "You never were one for doing what it took to brown-nose your way to success, were you?" She smiled and continued, "That's what I've always liked about you, Sable. You get what you get with you. You give your best and if that's not good enough, there's no toady bootlicking to turn 'em around." Ellerie chuckled, whisking the eggs feverishly. "So who's the lucky sycophant who got the position?"

"Oh, just some guy you wouldn't know," Sable waved away the question and leaned her elbows on the counter.

"So you're off on vacation?"

"Something like that," Sable looked around the apartment. Piles of dirty dishes filled the sink, the dishwasher hung open and an assortment of dishtowels lay wadded on the counter, hanging on the oven door. One cowered in a corner by the refrigerator.

"How long are you here for?" Ellerie asked as she drizzled chopped onions, tomatoes, mushrooms and peppers into the frying pan.

"As long as it takes," Sable muttered.

"Takes to do what?" Ellerie's eyebrows furrowed.

"Get the rest I need. I'm on a leave of absence until I feel up to returning." Sable tapped her fingers on the bar.

"Are you all right, Sable?" Ellerie's head cocked to the side, studying her friend closely.

"I'm not sick or dying if that's what you're worried about. Just burned out and need a break," Sable closed her eyes wearily and she shook her head side-to-side.

"Then, you've come to the right place!" Ellerie smiled and she slid a colorful, mouth-watering omelet in front of her friend.

~*~

Officer Allan Reager covered his nose and mouth with a handkerchief as he stepped out the front door of the small two-bedroom home. He turned his eyes toward the brown scraggly hickory tree, its limbs clutching and clawing skyward as if grasping heavenward with its last dying breath - much like the young woman whose body he and his partner had just found inside. It was freezing, but Reager dabbed his handkerchief to his brow to absorb the perspiration, then reached for his radio to call for an investigative team.

"Reager, come back in here for a minute," his partner, Gerard McNally, called from inside. Reager finished his call and took a deep breath, closed his eyes momentarily and stepped back into the house.

Blood pooled on the kitchen linoleum around the young woman's torso. The license Gerard found in her purse said that twenty-four-year-old Jessica Honeycutt weighed 120 pounds, stood five-foot-seven and evidently lived at this residence. You couldn't tell it from the bloodied gray corpse, but from the driver's license photo, she had been an attractive brown-eyed brunette.

Gerard handed Reager the license, "I think she knew the killer. In fact, I think she could have been out on a date with him."

"Really?" Reager asked as he looked at the license and handed it back to Gerard. "What makes you say that?"

"For one thing, there's no forcible entry marks on the door. Whoever it was, she let him in. Then, look how she's dressed." Gerard squatted down before the body and motioned for Reager to do the same. The young woman lay on her side, her blouse opened down the front. Several buttons were popped off. With an unopened pen Gerard pointed to a brown stain on the woman's blouse. "See that?"

"Yeah."

"I bet if we analyze that, it'll be soy sauce." Gerard stood up and went to the table where he'd placed the contents of the woman's purse. "See here," he held up a strip of white paper in his gloved

8

hand. "Fortune from a fortune cookie – *It's easier to ask forgiveness than to obtain permission.*"

"That's true, you know," Reager shook his head positively.

"And look here," Gerard pointed his pen to two tickets on the kitchen table. "Two tickets to the Chattanooga Symphony at eight o'clock last night."

"Which she evidently didn't use," Reager noted.

"I think she went out to a Chinese restaurant with her killer – spilled some of her dinner on her blouse, came back here possibly to wash it off, but before she could do it ..."

"Looks like a combination rape, manslaughter," Reager finished.

'The third one of these in the last month," Gerard's eyebrows furrowed.

"You think it's the same guy? A serial killer here in No-where-ville, Georgia?" Reager asked.

"Sure looks like it," came Gerard's somber reply.

~*~

"The laundry room is in the basement," Ellerie motioned for Sable to follow her down the stairwell. The two women had spent the better half of the morning catching up with each other and getting Sable settled into Ellerie's spare bedroom. Ellerie called into work and took a personal day. They'd taken a trip to the grocery store and now Ellerie was showing Sable around the apartment complex.

"There's a quarter machine here. Four washers, four dryers," Ellerie thumped her hand on a dryer.

Sable nodded and turned toward the door where an elderly woman entered the washroom.

"Mrs. Higby! How are you today?" Ellerie greeted jovially. "Sable, this is Mrs. Higby in 312. Mrs. Higby, this is my old roommate from college, Sable Graham. Sable's going to be staying with me for a while. She's visiting from D.C."

The elderly woman set her basket on a nearby dryer and extended her hand toward Sable.

"What a pretty name! Nice to meet you, Sable," Mrs. Higby extended her withered hand in Sable's direction. Sable hesitated momentarily, staring at the woman's appendage and then took it. A chill started at Sable's palm, crept to her wrist, up her arm and sent an icy shiver throughout her body as a dark foreboding settled at the center of her being.

Sable leaned forward and whispered into the elderly woman's ear, "Repair things with your daughter today. Do not delay." As Sable stood erect once more, her somber green eyes met the woman's astonished expression. Bewildered, the white-haired woman released Sable's hand. She glanced at Ellerie then at Sable and back, then grabbed her laundry basket and waddled out of the room without another word.

"What on earth did you say to poor Mrs. Higby? She looked as if she'd seen a ghost!"

Sable stood there silent for a moment, almost trance-like. Ellerie took her by the shoulder and shook her. "Sable, what did you say to poor Mrs. Higby?"

"Huh?" Sable turned to Ellerie.

"What did you say to her?"

"I just told her it was nice to meet her," Sable lied.

Ellerie's expression narrowed suspiciously. "Looked like you said something besides that! Whatever you said sent her on her way fast enough!"

"Maybe she remembered she had something else to do," Sable shrugged and started out of the laundry room and up the stairwell. With a suspicious expression on her face, Ellerie flipped off the light and followed her.

"I need to lie down for a while," Sable said as she entered the apartment. "You don't mind if I take a nap do you, El?"

"No, I don't mind," a worried frown creased Ellerie's face as she watched her friend disappear into the bedroom and shut the door.

Something wasn't right with Sable. Sure, she hadn't seen her in five years, so the conversation would naturally be sluggish, but Sable was withdrawn, private - more so than Ellerie ever remembered her being. Then there was that whole incident with Mrs. Higby! Ellerie decided that the next time she got the chance she'd ask Mrs. Higby what Sable had said.

Sable sat down on the bed, massaging her temples with her fingers. She felt so drained – sapped of all energy. The same way she felt every time it happened. Why couldn't she just be normal like everybody else? Normal like she used to be before the accident. She'd come here to get away from it all, but there was no escaping the curse. It followed her no matter where she went. The only thing she could do was hope that in this quieter location, there would be fewer encounters.

Sable kicked off her shoes, pulled down the bedspread and slipped under it. Curling into a ball, she let sleep envelop her.

Chapter 2

Gerard lay in his bed, his hands propped behind his head. Mahler's *Resurrection* played on his stereo. It had been a long day. He and Reager had visited every Chinese restaurant in the Chattanooga and Northwest Georgia area, showing Jessica Honeycutt's photograph to each waiter, manager and busboy they could find. No luck. No one seemed to remember the young woman. Yet, the lab had definitely turned up soy sauce on her blouse. Maybe she and her date bought takeout and ate somewhere else? In that case, she may never have even set foot in a restaurant.

Gerard's mind refused to stop whirling, plodding along on the case like a dog with a bone. He sat up in bed and looked at his clock. It was only a quarter past ten. He stood, slipped on his jeans and a sweatshirt and picked up a pair of dirty gym socks from his bedroom floor. He tossed them in a basket and decided now might be a good time to do a bit of laundry. He gathered up the towels, shirts, pants and other assorted apparel from a nearby chair. He picked up similar items from the floor of his bedroom and bathroom, then dropped them in the basket. Next, he rummaged through his change jar for some quarters, shoved them in his pocket, and slipped on his shoes. He tucked the basket under his arm and left his apartment.

Before Gerard arrived in the laundry room, he could hear the whirl of washers and dryers and caught the fresh scent of fabric softener in the air. After the effort expended to gather his laundry, he really hoped there would be a free machine. When he stepped in the laundry room, he spotted the ebony haired beauty perched atop a dryer, her legs crossed at the ankles and her nose in a book. She wore a pair of jeans and an attractive v-neck burgundy sweater, her long black hair cascading around her shoulders.

Gerard set his basket on a dryer beside her. "Any free machines left?" he asked peering around the cinderblock room which was lit only by a single bulb hanging directly over Sable's head.

"Hmmm?" she asked, lifting her attention from her book and briefly meeting his gaze. "Oh, I think there's one over there," she pointed across the room. Her eyes returned to the page.

"Thanks," Gerard replied and started across the room with his basket.

As he passed her, Sable discreetly lifted her gaze from the book and watched him cross to the washer. There was something manly about his gray sweatshirt and the fit of his Levis that stirred an attraction within her. She forced her eyes back to the page, but her mind was on other things. When was the last time she'd been out on a date? Much less had a handsome man show her any affection? Too long, much too long - before the accident. What she wouldn't give for one day of normalcy! She watched him load his clothes in the washer. What would it be like to spend an hour in the arms of a man like that?

Before she could shove the thoughts from her mind, Gerard hopped up on the dryer next to hers and extended his hand. "You must be new here. I'm Gerard McNally. I live in 315."

Sable kept both hands securely on her book, staring at his outstretched hand. She recognized him now. This was the cop she'd passed in the stairwell on her way up to Ellerie's this morning. Not a cop. She couldn't possibly shake a cop's hand. No telling what vile kinetic residue he encountered on any given day. She wouldn't, couldn't expose herself to it.

"I'm Sable. I'm visiting Ellerie Tash in 254," she replied never taking her hands off her book.

Gerard quirked a quizzical eyebrow and dropped his outstretched appendage. He probably thought she was a snob or one

14

of those obsessive compulsive sorts who won't shake hands for fear of germs.

"Where are you visiting from?" he asked, letting his leg swing and his cross trainer pound rhythmically on the dryer. He must have chosen obsessive compulsive. Either that or he didn't let a snob deter him.

" D.C. Ellerie's an old friend from college," Sable replied.

"So what are you reading?" Gerard peeked over to look at the title at the top of the page, "*The Heavenly Surrender*" he muttered. "Sounds like a . . ."

"Chick lit," Sable finished for him. She turned the book over to display the cover, "McClure... she's my favorite."

"Ah, so you're one of those romance readers – eh?"

"Can't live it, may as well read it," Sable muttered under her breath.

Gerard chuckled, "I find that hard to believe."

"What?"

"That you don't have men pounding down your door," he replied.

"What's that? Some sort of pick up line?" she reopened the book and pretended to start reading.

"No, just an observation. Unless, of course, you'd like it to be a pick up line," he smiled.

Just then the dryer Sable sat on buzzed and she hopped down. She set the book on the dryer and grabbed her empty clothes basket. His eyes never left her as she filled her basket and plopped the book on top.

"Guess, I'll see you around, McNally," she smiled.

"See ya," he waved as she turned and left.

~*~

Unusual woman, Gerard thought as he watched her leave. If nothing else, she'd taken his mind off the case for a few minutes. So, she was Ellerie Tash's friend. She didn't look like she'd be a friend of

15

Ellerie's. Ellerie was like a super friendly greyhound that barrels up to your car, plops his paws on your open window and pants in your face, welcoming you to the neighborhood. He wouldn't have matched Sable up as Ellerie's friend in a million years. *Friends* Gerard mused. Jessica Honeycutt would have had friends, wouldn't she? And perhaps they would know who she had a date with that night!

~*~

Gerard hovered over Officer Davis who sat at his computer. "How long do you think this is going to take?"

"You never know. Depends upon how ingenious she was with her password," the brown-headed officer tinkered with the Palm Pilot on the desk in front of him and then punched some keys on his own computer. Pages of scrambled numbers and letters ran across his computer screen as his program worked to obtain the password to Jessica Honeycutt's Palm Pilot.

"Let me know as soon as you've got it," Gerard put his hand on the officer's shoulder and then turned to go back to his office.

"Got it!" Davis exclaimed before Gerard could take two steps.

"Really? Already?" Gerard turned around.

"Yep. It was a combination of her sister's name and her own birthdate – molly0312," the officer unplugged the Palm Pilot and handed it to Gerard.

"Thanks!" Gerard slapped the officer's back and took it.

Back in his office, Gerard worked his way through the Palm Pilot searching for her schedule, addresses and phone numbers. Nothing turned up on her schedule for Tuesday evening, but there were several addresses. Soon he was back at the tech genius' desk. "Hey, Davis, can you print out a list of all the names, addresses and phone numbers she's got in here?"

"Sure," he nodded and took the Palm Pilot once more.

"Oh, and print out any appointments she's had in the last few months or had scheduled in the future."

"Will do."

~*~

Gerard and Reager stepped through the glass doors of the large insurance building in downtown Chattanooga, walked toward the elevator and Reager pushed the up button. They took the elevator to the tenth floor and stepped off, approached the main desk and asked to see Joy Stablemeyer. The secretary directed them to the fourth office on the right. Gerard tapped on the open door and a young woman in her mid-twenties glanced up from her desk.

"Officers, please come in," she motioned to two vacant chairs opposite her. Gerard could tell by the plethora of crumpled tissues that the young woman self-consciously raked into her waste basket that she either had a horrendous cold or was quite close to the deceased. From the tears in her eyes, he deduced the latter.

"I'm sorry officers. I don't even know why I came to work today. I'm just not fit for anything," she sniffed and patted a wadded tissue to her eyes.

"We're terribly sorry to intrude upon you like this, Ms. Stablemeyer. I'm Officer McNally and this is my partner Office Reager. Thank you for agreeing to meet with us."

"Certainly," she motioned again for them to be seated. Reager shut the door and they both sat down.

"So you were Miss Honeycutt's best friend?" Reager began.

"Since high school," she sniffed.

"Where did you go to high school?" Reager inquired.

"Hixson. We graduated in '99."

Reager jotted the school and year down on a pad of paper.

"Do you have any idea who would have done something like this to your friend?" Gerard asked as sympathetically as that question could be delivered.

"No," she shook her head negatively. "I have no idea! She was such a nice person. Jessica didn't have any enemies."

"We have reason to believe that it could have been a date that did this to her. Do you happen to know if she had a date Tuesday night?" Gerard asked.

Joy shrugged, "She didn't mention anything. I even met her that day for lunch, and she didn't say a thing about a date."

"Was she seeing anyone?" Reager asked, still jotting notes on his notepad.

"No, the last guy she seriously dated was Todd Ellison, and she broke it off with him six months ago." Joy twiddled a pen between her thumb and forefinger.

"Todd Ellison," Gerard repeated. "I saw his name in her Palm Pilot." Gerard glanced at Reager.

"I'm sure it was just left in there. She didn't keep in touch with him. He's on to greener pastures, I'm sure." Joy set down the pen and laced her fingers together on her desk.

"So did she date anyone recently – even one time – that you know of?" Gerard asked.

"I set her up on a blind date with a friend of mine once, but she didn't care for him. You see Jessica just couldn't get over Todd."

"I thought you said she broke it off with him?" Gerard asked.

"That's because he cheated on her. She had to get rid of him, but that didn't mean her heart let go. I was always badgering her to get out and see other people. Now I wish I hadn't pushed so hard!" Joy's eyes suddenly filled with tears. She pulled a tissue from a box on her desk and blew her nose ferociously.

The officers waited for her to regain composure.

"Do you think she would have used a dating service perhaps?" Reager suggested and Gerard's eyes lit up with the possibility.

"Yes, maybe one of those online dating services? I saw a computer in her bedroom," Gerard added.

"It's possible." Joy shrugged and wadded the tissue in her fist. "But if she did, she wouldn't have told me about it. She knows how I feel about that kind of thing. It's just asking for trouble," Joy's voice grew agitated and she set down the tissue. This was evidently a soapbox issue for her. Then as if she were coming to some intense realization she exclaimed, "Oh no! Do you think? Do you think she used one of those dating services and the guy they matched her up with murdered her?" Joy's face now possessed an expression of terror.

"So you think she could have been dating someone she met online?" Reager threw the question back at her.

"It's possible. She was way too trusting, and she did love to play on her computer at night." Joy threw her tissue on the desk and grabbed another one.

Gerard suddenly stood and extended his card to Ms. Stablemeyer, "Thank you so much for your time, Miss. If you think of anything else, please call us."

She took his card, placed it prominently on her desk and shook his outstretched hand. "I will. I'll call you if I think of anything that might help."

Just as they were about to step out the door, Gerard turned toward her once more, "One more thing, did Jessica enjoy the symphony?"

Joyce swiveled in her chair to face them. "Oh yes, she always bought a pair of season tickets. Sometimes I went with her and sometimes Roger did."

"Roger?" Gerard asked, still standing in the doorway.

"Roger Wesley – just one of our friends from college," Joyce explained.

"Could she have been with this Roger the night of the murder?" Reager asked.

Joy's expression grew somewhat irritated. "Roger would never do anything to hurt Jessica. He was crazy about her."

"Crazy about her?" Gerard repeated.

"Oh, he had a crush on her. Of course Jessica was oblivious to the fact. She just saw him as a friend. We were all friends. Sometimes I hang out with Roger, sometimes we all three go places together. He's just Roger! He wouldn't hurt a flea!" Joyce waved her hand as if the notion were preposterous.

Gerard pulled out the list of names and addresses from Jessica's Palm Pilot. Roger's name was there along with his address, work and home numbers.

"Maybe she mentioned something to him, then? Any other friends you'd recommend we speak with?" Gerard asked.

Joy leaned back in her computer chair. "No, you could talk with her sisters. But as for friends, it was mainly just me and Roger."

Gerard stepped back into the office, "Would you mind taking a look at this list and telling us who you know here and how they were related to Jessica?"

"Sure," she took the list and examined it.

Joy identified the various people on the list and marked notes out to the right of each of their names. She gave them the paper and the officers left.

Gerard spoke into his cell phone as Reager drove past the Chattanooga Aquarium, "Hey Davis, this is McNally. How about meeting us over at Jessica Honeycutt's house and bring any of your computer gizmos you'll need to analyze her machine."

Chapter 3

Sable finished her book and booted Ellerie's computer in the corner of her living room. She sat down and went to the Web to check her email. She wasn't really expecting anything, but she'd finished her book and had nothing else to do. It always made her feel a little let down at the end of a good book, sad for it to be over. Checking her email would give her something to do, plus she figured enough spam had probably collected in her box to fill it. She cleared out her inbox, and just as she was about to turn off the machine, an instant message screen popped up with a bell noise.

"El, you off work today?" It was a message from someone named ChattCowboy.

"Ellerie's at work. This is her friend. She'll be home after 5:30," Sable typed.

"I didn't know she had a roommate."

"I'm just visiting," Sable replied. "Gotta run." She disconnected from the internet and shut down the computer. She really didn't have anything else to do, but she didn't feel like chatting with some cyber cowboy friend of Ellerie's.

~*~

Officer Davis clicked away on Jessica Honeycutt's computer, checking files and folders.

"Whatcha got?" Gerard asked as he entered the bedroom and sat down on the burgundy comforter.

"Nothin'. Not a dad blamed thing," Davis shook his head and turned to look at Gerard. "If I didn't know better I'd say it was a brand new computer straight out of the box."

"Why do you say that?" Gerard leaned forward, looking at the monitor.

"Everything's back to factory settings. No data. There's not even an internet connection set up." Davis pointed at the screen.

"Why would someone keep email addresses in her Palm Pilot if she didn't have an internet connection?" Gerard asked.

"Don't know," Davis shrugged. "She didn't have an internet connection on that Palm Pilot, did she?"

"I don't think so," Gerard pulled it from his pocket and handed it to Davis.

"No, it's an older model. Doesn't have email functionality. Maybe she had a computer at work." Davis suggested.

"Her friend Joy said she liked to spend time on her computer at night. Why wouldn't it be set up with email and have some files on it?"

Davis turned back around toward the computer and began typing on the keyboard. "Let me snoop around here a bit more on this machine. Why don't you and Reager see if she used a computer at work?"

~*~

Gerard sat at Jessica's office desk while Reager sat across from him looking through manila folders. Gerard's cell phone rang and he answered it.

"Davis here," the voice answered his greeting.

"Yeah, watcha got?" Gerard leaned back in the office chair.

"The computer's been wiped – reset to factory settings. Basically a complete format of the drive and the factory settings reinstalled," Davis explained

"Can you tell when?" Gerard asked, tapping a pencil on Jessica's desk.

"Tuesday night around 7:45 p.m.," Davis answered.

"So the killer wiped her computer," Gerard deduced.

"Looks like it. The thing is though... the average Joe wouldn't know how to do that."

Gerard looked at Reager who had risen to his feet and was now digging through Jessica's file cabinet. "So we're talking about someone with technical expertise." Reager met Gerard's gaze.

"Right, and he'd probably need to know what kind of computer she had going in," Davis explained.

"Hmmm..." Gerard grunted. "Any chance of restoring the data?"

"Unfortunately not," Davis paused.

Gerard groaned.

"So what did you two find out at her work?" Davis asked.

"We could probably use you over here. She does have a computer with Internet. But her boss said they were really picky about what they let employees access. There's a firewall and no programs like instant messenger."

"K, what's that address and I'll be right over."

Gerard gave Davis the address and disconnected the call.

~*~

Ellerie returned home from work, parked her car in front of the apartment complex and approached the mail boxes. She'd hated to leave Sable at home all day by herself, but she couldn't very well miss work every day just because Sable had turned up on her doorstep. Sable sent her off assuring her that she'd probably just nap the day away.

As Ellerie unlocked her postal box, she heard a female voice call from behind her, "It's such a shame about poor old Mrs. Higby, don't you think?"

Ellerie turned her head in the direction of the voice to find Melissa Carlisle coming down the stairwell. "Hmmm? What?"

"Mrs. Higby, she passed away in her sleep last night."

"You're kidding me?" Ellerie gasped, flinging her hand to her chest. A swell of tears threatened behind her eyelids.

"I'm afraid not, and the poor old soul must have known her number was up because she called her estranged daughter yesterday. She hadn't spoken to her in years and years! Anyway, she called this Liza and told her she was sorry and wanted to make things right between them!"

"Really? Where did you hear that?" Ellerie's mouth dropped.

"Her daughters are in her apartment right now. They told me." Melissa pointed over her shoulder toward Mrs. Higby's apartment.

"How odd," Ellerie noted, "I wasn't aware that Mrs. Higby had any children she didn't get along with."

"Well, the others say this particular daughter was always a handful," Melissa explained. "The funeral's tomorrow at Lane's."

"What time?" Ellerie stuffed her mail under her arm and closed the box.

"Ten in the morning. There's a viewing tonight from seven to nine." Melissa stepped closer to her.

"Thanks, Melissa," Ellerie placed her hand on Melissa's shoulder and numbly carried her mail up the stairs. It just wouldn't be the same without Mrs. Higby. The sweet old woman was always so cheery – like a surrogate grandmother to all the younger people who lived in the building. It was news to Ellerie that Mrs. Higby even had an estranged daughter. She couldn't imagine anyone not getting along with her.

Sable sat on the couch watching a Columbo rerun when Ellerie stepped into the apartment. Ellerie set her purse on the counter and placed her keys on the hook. "What did you say to Mrs. Higby in the laundry room yesterday?"

"Huh?" Sable muttered, turning her head toward Ellerie.

"What did you say to Mrs. Higby yesterday?" Ellerie repeated with a serious expression on her face.

"I told you already," Sable rolled her eyes, but Ellerie came to stand stubbornly in front of her.

"No, you tell me the truth. Mrs. Higby's dead, and I want to know what you said to her!"

Sable had never seen Ellerie so demanding. Usually, she let everything roll past like an eighteen wheeler whizzing down I75 to Atlanta. "Nothing," Sable shook her head and shrugged.

"You're lying." Ellerie put her hands on her hips. "You never could lie, Sable. We always got caught in school because you were the worst liar on the planet! I don't even understand how you can be such a good lawyer, you're so bad. Now tell me the truth."

Sable waited for nearly a minute, hoping to hold out longer than Ellerie, but Ellerie didn't budge. She just stood over her, a sour expression puckering her face.

"Okay, all right," Sable sighed and rose to her feet. She flung her arms, and stepped toward the kitchen. "I told her that she needed to make amends with her daughter."

Ellerie's mouth dropped wide. "How? How did you know to say that? Do you know Mrs. Higby?"

"Never met her before in my life," Sable muttered as she slammed a cup on the counter and turned toward the refrigerator.

"Until today, I didn't even know she had a daughter that she hadn't spoken to in years! How could you know it?" Ellerie stared at Sable as if she were from another planet.

"I just did," Sable shrugged.

"How?" Ellerie demanded.

"It's sort of a curse," Sable sighed.

Ellerie stepped toward the bar and leaned her hands on it. "Sable, tell me what's going on!"

Sable stood there, weighing her options. Finally, she decided that she couldn't intrude on Ellerie's life like this and expect her to remain clueless. "Have a seat," Sable motioned to the bar stool and Ellerie sat down, leaning her elbows expectantly on the counter.

Sable poured herself a drink and put the soda back in the refrigerator. "It all started three years ago when I was driving home in a thunderstorm," she took a sip of her drink. "Lightning struck my car, and I veered off the road. I hit a telephone pole and woke up in a hospital several hours later."

"Were you hurt?" Ellerie acted as concerned as if it had just happened yesterday.

Sable shook her head. "Amazingly enough, all I had was a busted lip and a concussion, but after a few days passed, I noticed something had changed." Ellerie's eyes remained riveted on her friend. Sable continued, "I first noticed it when my father came to visit me at my apartment. He took my hands in his and everything went ice cold. It was as if someone dropped the temperature in the room by about fifty degrees. Then I was overpowered with this intense need to confess everything I'd done as a teenager that he didn't know about. I apologized profusely for being a smart mouth and for staying out after curfew. I even told him about the time Paul Bowan and I made out behind the bleachers."

"Oh my! You certainly were cleansing your soul." Ellerie chuckled. "What possessed you to do such a thing?"

"I don't know. It just all came flooding back, and I had this overpowering urge to make everything right with my father. Two days later, he was dead – a heart attack."

"Gosh, Sable! I'm so sorry. I didn't know your father had passed away!" Ellerie exclaimed.

"It's all right." Sable shrugged and leaned her hands on the counter opposite Ellerie. "Like I say, we made our peace with each other. But Dad was just the first encounter. As a criminal lawyer, you can imagine the types of people who come into our office." Ellerie nodded affirmatively and Sable continued. "I began to notice that sometimes when I'd shake someone's hand, I'd get that icy cold feeling and then within days the person would either be harmed or die. The creepier the reaction, the more horrifying the death. Sometimes a word or phrase would come to my mind when shaking the person's hand – like it did with Mrs. Higby yesterday. Not always, but sometimes. As you'd imagine, I tried to shake as few hands as possible, but that's quite difficult in my line of work."

"Yes, I'd imagine so," Ellerie remained riveted to Sable's story.

Sable raked a hand through her hair with a sigh. "Anyway, it just got to be too much and I had to get away. I need to seriously consider a new line of work or something. I just can't deal with it anymore. I think I might become a professional hermit."

"So you're telling me that you knew Mrs. Higby would die, and you knew to tell her to make peace with her daughter?"

Sable nodded.

"Wow!" Ellerie sat up straight on the stool and stared at Sable with awestruck wonder.

"Yeah," Sable exhaled.

Chapter 4

Ellerie hated funerals, but she had to pay her respects to poor Mrs. Higby. She decided to stop by the viewing that evening for a few minutes. Of course, she couldn't talk Sable into going with her.

"Why on earth would you ask me to go to a funeral home?" Sable cocked one eyebrow and stared at Ellerie as if she had horns sprouting through her auburn tresses.

"Well, there's nothing to predict there, Sable. They're already dead!" Ellerie flung her hands in the air. Since Sable only continued to glare at her, Ellerie grabbed her purse and headed out the door. "I'll be back in about an hour."

After signing the guest book and taking a quick glimpse at the body, Ellerie approached the daughters, offering her sympathy. Just as she prepared to leave she turned to find Gerard in his police uniform approaching the women. She smiled and stepped aside, letting him offer his condolences. After he had spoken to them, he turned toward Ellerie.

"So, El, how're you doin'?" Gerard smiled.

"Doing good… doing good." Ellerie pursed her lips into a tight smile. "Horrible about poor Mrs. Higby, isn't it?"

"She will be missed," Gerard shook his head. "Sweet woman."

"Made good cookies," Ellerie added.

"Yes, she did. I've been the beneficiary of Mrs. Higby's baking talents on more than one occasion," he nodded. "She's almost been like a surrogate mother to me since I moved down here from Nashville."

Ellerie gave him a wan smile. "Speaking of cookies, Ger, I've got a brand new bag of double stuff Oreos at home. Why don't you drop by and dunk some?"

Gerard smiled broadly and patted his stomach, "Don't tempt me."

"Seriously, stop by." Ellerie put a hand on his arm. "I'd like you to meet my friend Sable. She's visiting from D.C. for a while. I think you'd like her."

"Met her already," Gerard replied dryly.

"Really? When?" Ellerie's voice rose with the question.

"Last night in the laundry room." Gerard rubbed his chin. "She's a bit stand-offish, isn't she?"

"Oh, that's just because you're a stranger," Ellerie flicked his arm with the back of her hand. "She doesn't know we're buds!"

"I see," he nodded.

"Sable's going through a hard time right now," Ellerie lowered her voice. "She could use some friends and a little ... distraction." Ellerie's lips lifted into a knowing smile.

"Distraction – eh?" Gerard laughed. "Is that what I'm good for these days?"

"Oh, come on, Ger. I think you'd really like her if you got to know her," Ellerie grabbed his hand and dragged him toward the door. Suddenly she turned toward him again, "Oh, you were done here – right?"

"Yeah, I guess so," he shook his head, chuckling at Ellerie's typical antics.

Ellerie knew Gerard well enough to know he couldn't resist a good mystery. And she could tell by the look in his eyes the moment she mentioned Sable's name that he was intrigued. Sable needed some distraction, and Gerard need something a little more playful than homicide investigations. They were exactly what each other needed.

Ellerie rummaged through her stack of keys, searching for the one to her apartment.

"Got enough keys there?" Gerard teased. "Why don't you just knock?" He reached over and rapped on the door with his knuckles.

"Oh!" she pounded the heel of her hand to her forehead. "That's right! Sable's inside."

A few seconds later, Sable opened the door. She stood for a moment, shocked to see Gerard with Ellerie. Ellerie stepped inside and he followed her.

"Gerard says you two have already met, but I got the idea that you got off on the wrong foot because you didn't know Gerard and I are friends," Ellerie jabbered as she hung up her coat and keys and tossed her purse on the counter.

Sable stared awkwardly at Gerard whose eyes meandered over the apartment. "Somebody's gone and performed a neatness in here, El," he observed.

"That's Sable. We'll be able to eat off the toilet seats before you know it," Ellerie quipped matter-of-factly as she removed a jug of milk from the refrigerator and let it thud on the counter.

"Come clean my place next, will ya?" he smiled. Sable returned an obligatory grin and slid onto the bar stool farthest away from where Gerard stood.

"Sable has a law degree. You won't find her cleaning your apartment anytime soon, bud," Ellerie teased as she set the bag of Oreos next to the milk.

Gerard slid onto the barstool next to Sable's while Ellerie set three mugs on the bar. "So you're a lawyer. What kind of law do you practice?" he asked.

"Criminal," she replied as she poured Gerard a cup of milk. "What department do you work in?" she asked while pouring milk for Ellerie and herself.

"Homicide" he said and leaned his elbow on the counter.

Sable nodded and when he looked down to dunk his Oreo in his milk, her eyes widened at Ellerie. *"Hom-i-cide"* she mouthed in Ellerie's direction with fire shooting from her eyes. *"Are you nuts?"*

"What are you working on now?" Ellerie directed the question at Gerard, ignoring Sable's aggravation.

31

"You may have seen it in the paper," he looked to Sable and then to Ellerie. "The young woman who was killed in her home off Gattis Circle."

"Oh, the one they're calling a date rape/murder!" Ellerie's big brown eyes grew even wider.

"Yeah, tricky one," he said.

"Do you have any leads?" Ellerie asked.

"Not yet," he gave his head a dejected shake.

"Ellerie, I think I have something in my eye. How about coming in here and helping me get it out?" Sable rubbed her right eye and walked toward her bedroom. When Ellerie didn't come immediately, Sable waved her hand at her, motioning for her friend to hurry up and follow her.

Sable flipped on the light and shut the door after Ellerie stepped into the room. "Are you out of your mind? I told you about this premonition thing I have with death and you bring a *homicide detective* here to meet me!" she whispered.

"I thought you'd have a lot in common. You predict murders, and he solves them. You're on the same team, so to speak," Ellerie reasoned.

"Ellerie, I swear sometimes I wonder how in the world you graduated top of your business class!" Sable ran a frustrated hand through her hair.

"Now don't go cutting down my networking abilities." Ellerie waved her arms as she spoke. "I'm known for them, you know. I make just the right connections. And I'm telling you that you and Gerard are like two peas separated from the same pod."

"Yeah, some sick pod from a horror flick!" Sable whispered in exasperation.

Ellerie put her hands on Sable's shoulders, "Calm down." She breathed deeply and exhaled several times, trying to get Sable to do the same. Once Sable had relaxed a little she removed her hands from Sable's shoulders. "He's a great guy. We even dated a couple times, but we just didn't click romantically – you know what I mean – how sometimes two people just can't get on that level? But we're great friends, and I just know you'll love him when you get to know him. He's just your type."

"Maybe I'm not making myself clear here, Ellerie," Sable whispered. "I get the creeps when people touch me, and you're trying to set me up for romantic involvement with a HOMICIDE DETECTIVE!! I haven't dated in three years because I can't take the chance on even holding hands with a guy. Do you really expect that the first one I would get romantically involved with would be a *homicide detective*?"

Ellerie's expression grew irritated. "Will you stop calling him that? He's just a guy. That's just his job. There's more to him than that."

"Ellerie ..."

"Listen to me. Just touch his hand and if you get a creepy feeling, I'll shut up and never say another word about it," Ellerie reasoned.

"Touch his hand? How am I supposed to do that?" Sable put her hands to her hips.

"I don't know – you're a big girl. Figure it out. Heck, just shake his hand when he leaves." Ellerie suggested.

"You beat everything, El," she muttered just before opening the door.

When they stepped into the living room, Gerard was kicked back on the couch, his long legs stretched and crossed over the coffee table as he dunked an Oreo in his mug of milk. "Did ya get it out?" he asked, looking up at them and taking a bite of his cookie.

"Huh? Oh yeah, it was an eyelash," Ellerie replied and plopped down on a recliner leaving only one place for Sable to sit - on the couch beside Gerard. It wasn't a very big couch, more like a loveseat, so even though Sable tried to sit as far away from Gerard as she could there was only a hand span between them.

Just then, a knocking sound came from the other side of the room. Sable looked to the door.

33

"Nobody's there," Ellerie said, "It's my computer. When one of my friends on my buddy list logs on to the internet, it makes that knocking sound on my instant messenger."

"Oh, that reminds me," Sable began. "You got an instant message today from somebody named ChattCowboy."

"Really?" Ellerie asked.

"Yeah, he thought you were home from work and was surprised to find out you had a roommate. I told him you'd be back after 5:30," Sable related.

Ellerie's chair was within arm's reach of the computer. She leaned over and jiggled the mouse on her computer to make the screen saver shut off. "Yep, that's him there now."

"So who's ChattCowboy?" Gerard asked.

"Oh, just some guy I met through a singles' site a couple of weeks ago," Ellerie waved her hand.

"Have you met him in person?" Sable asked.

"No, not yet," Ellerie shook her head and leaned back in her chair.

"You're looking for dates on a singles' site?" Gerard asked with surprise.

"No, not really. I guess my name got bought from one of those list places – you know – how you fill out your name and address and sometimes your birth date on online surveys or when you buy something. They must have sold my name to this singles' site. They started sending me matches in the Chattanooga area, so one day I filled in my profile as a lark and this guy contacted me." Ellerie tucked one leg under the other.

"How do they send you matches?" Gerard asked.

"By email. They send me the guys' pictures and a blurb about them and where they live. Then, I can email them through the site."

"So the site sends you emails!" Gerard's eyes lit up and he leaned forward.

"Yeah," Ellerie nodded, looking a bit perplexed as to why Gerard found this so fascinating.

"You care if I make a quick phone call?" Gerard asked as he pulled his cell phone from his pocket.

"Go ahead," Ellerie said.

Gerard set his mug on a coaster and shoved the rest of his cookie in his mouth. He stood up and walked to the kitchen as he dialed his cell phone. "Hey, Davis, do me a favor and call a few of Jessica Honeycutt's friends and find out her email address. Then see if you can figure out her password and log into her email and look for anything from a dating site or anything that looks like it's come from a guy. Save anything you find and print it for me..... Yeah, great, thanks!"

"What's up?" Ellerie asked as Gerard disconnected from his call.

"We think Jessica Honeycutt may have been dating someone she met online," Gerard stepped back toward the living room.

"Really? How creepy!" Sable looked to Ellerie, "You better stay off that site and get rid of that guy who's instant messaging you!"

"Ah, he seems like a really nice guy," Ellerie shook her head as if Sable were worrying for nothing.

"You don't know that, El. People can say anything online. Sable's right. You need to be careful," Gerard warned. Ellerie just waved her hand and rolled her eyes. "At least get his real name and address and let me run a background check on him," Gerard suggested as he sat back down next to Sable.

"Now that's an excellent idea," Sable agreed shaking her index finger at Ellerie.

"See... I knew you two were like two peas out of the same pod," Ellerie quipped. Sable shot her friend an irritated glare just as the phone rang. Ellerie rose to get it in the bedroom.

They watched Ellerie leave and then Gerard cleared his throat. "So, you went to college with Ellerie?" Gerard shifted so he could look at Sable.

"We were roommates," Sable nodded.

"And you're still friends – huh?" he queried in mock surprise.

"Not for long," Sable quipped sarcastically.

"She can be kind of pushy, can't she? But she is fun." Gerard grinned.

"Gotta love her," Sable gave him a defeated smile.

"So you came all this way just to visit Ellerie? You two must be really close," Gerard deduced.

Sable shifted on the couch so that she faced Gerard. "Actually, we've hardly spoken since we left college, only Christmas cards and the occasional phone call. I just had to get out of D.C. and when I tried to think of somewhere relaxing that would get my mind off things, I thought of Ellerie. Luckily, she's been kind enough to take me in."

"That's Ellerie, always taking in lost dogs, stray cats and . . ."

"Old roommates," Sable finished for him.

"Have you had a chance to see the sights?" he crossed his leg over his knee.

"No, just been hanging around the apartment resting."

"Would you like to? We've got some great things here in the Chattanooga area – the aquarium and downtown's fun. Then there's the battlefield, Lookout Mountain, Rock City and Ruby Falls." Gerard's voice grew more animated, "Oh, and you have to go to the Choo Choo and listen to the singing waiters at the Station House."

"Sounds like I'd keep Ellerie running ragged on her days off seeing all of that. I may have to grab a map and see some places on my own."

"Ah, you can't go alone. It's not the same." He thought for a moment and then offered, "Why don't I show you around?"

"That's very kind of you. But I know you're a busy man with your job and all. I wouldn't possibly expect you to …"

He interrupted her protest, "Really, it'd be fun. I have a couple days off coming up. I'm off tomorrow and Saturday. I have to go to the funeral in the morning, but I could take you to lunch, and we could see some things tomorrow afternoon."

Sable swallowed the nervous lump in her throat. She didn't know what to say. Ellerie was right about one thing. If Sable still had a 'type' after all these years, then Gerard McNally would definitely be it – tall, blonde, muscular, smart and don't even get her started on those hypnotic baby blue eyes. But, he was a homicide detective! How could she agree to spend two days with him? Maybe Ellerie had the right idea. Maybe if she could just get him to shake hands with her she could see if he set off any alarms. She should have shaken his hand the other night in the laundry room. She'd probably missed her window of opportunity.

"So, what do you say?" he asked when she still hadn't replied.

"Uh, give me a call in the morning, and I'll let you know if I feel up to it," came her noncommittal reply.

"I'll do that," he smiled and stood. "Tell Ellerie bye for me. I have a few things to check into for work."

Sable walked him to the door. This was her moment to find out, so she extended her hand toward him, "Nice meeting you … officially."

"You too," he smiled and took her hand. It seemed as if for a moment she wasn't even standing in Ellerie's apartment anymore. She was wrapped up snug and warm like a mug of hot chocolate on a cold winter's evening. A roaring fire blazed in a rock hearth. She noted the strong masculine arms around her and followed them up to the handsome face that belonged with them. The firelight danced in Gerard's pale blue eyes and Sable could hardly breathe as his lips descended toward her own.

"You okay?" he asked.

Sable blinked and shook her head. "Yeah, yeah, I'm fine," she stammered and stared at her hand which still clutched his. She released it.

"I'll call you in the morning then," he said. He looked at her as if he were still trying to understand what had happened to her.

"I'd like that." She shut the door behind him and leaned back against it, closed her eyes and breathed deeply. Never had she experienced anything like it. She still tingled from the warm liquid which flowed through her body at his simple touch. Heaven only knew what anything more intimate would do to her!

Chapter 5

Gerard pulled into a parking space outside Roger Wesley's condominium and turned off the headlights. He and Reager stepped out of their squad car into the chilly night air, went to the front door, and knocked. A man in his late twenties answered. The man's bold Roman nose dominated his face, making his brown eyes seem crossed, even though they weren't.

"How can I help you officers?" the man's gaze darted from Gerard to Reager and back.

"We have an appointment to speak with Roger Wesley," Reager answered.

"Oh, come on in," the man opened the door wider, turned his head, and yelled, "Roger, there are some police officers here to see you!"

Reager and Gerard stepped into the spacious residence. Gerard noted how much nicer it was than his own. His eyes scanned the Mexican tile floors in the kitchen toward the fireplace in the living area.

"Tell 'em to come in my office," Roger called, and the man who'd answered the door motioned them toward the back of the condo. He ascended the stairs to a loft. Gerard and Reager followed him to where Roger sat behind a large oak desk. A computer monitor faced them from a hutch along the wall.

"Would you like me to stay?" the man asked.

"No thanks, Derrick, I've got it," Roger replied. "Please have a seat, officers," Roger motioned to two empty chairs located on opposite ends of the loft. Reager sat in one, and Gerard moved the other chair next to his partner's so they both faced Roger.

"Thank you for taking the time to meet with us this evening, Mr. Wesley," Gerard began as he extended his hand to Roger. "I'm Officer McNally and this is my partner, Officer Reager. As I mentioned on the phone earlier, we just need to ask you a few questions about Jessica Honeycutt. We're contacting all of her friends and associates."

"Certainly, I'd be happy to help in any way I can," Roger smiled sadly. The man who'd let them into the house was obviously related to Roger. They both shared the same Roman nose, dark features, black hair and eyes, but Roger had a softer look about his expression which made his face appear less pinched than Derrick's.

"Are you and Derrick twins?" Reager asked.

"No, Derrick's eighteen months older than me, but we do get asked that a lot," Roger smiled, flashing a set of white teeth.

"We have just a few routine questions, if you don't mind," Gerard pulled out his pad and pen.

"Go right ahead," Roger motioned.

"Where were you on Tuesday night from six to nine p.m.?" Gerard asked.

"I had a board meeting at my office that night. It started at 6:30 and lasted until about 9:30. I got home around ten," Roger tapped a pencil on his desk.

"Could you please give us the names and phone numbers of a few people who were at that meeting, just to verify your whereabouts at that time?" Reager asked.

"Sure," Roger nodded and pulled a piece of paper from his printer and began scribbling three names and phone numbers on it.

"Also, if you happen to know where you were on the nights of Saturday, January 8th and Friday, January 21st, that would be helpful." Reager added.

"Hmmm…" Roger scratched his head. "Let me see," he pulled out his planner and began thumbing through the pages. "On the eighth, I went to the movies with my friend Chuck. What was the other date?"

"Friday the twenty-first," Gerard replied.

"That night I went with a few guys to the Comedy Catch," he answered. "I'll write their names and numbers down here for you as well." Roger started writing again.

"Good," Gerard nodded. "Now, we just have a few questions about Jessica. We're trying to piece together a picture of her life so we can find out who would have done something like this to her. Do you know if she was dating anyone?"

"No," he shook his head negatively with a sigh, "Not that I know of."

"Do you know who she might have been with on Tuesday night?" Gerard asked.

"No, I don't." Roger shook his head.

"Did she have any enemies?" Reager tapped the point of his pen on his pad.

"No, everybody loved Jessica," Roger's eyes held a heartbroken expression. He folded his hands together and rested them on his desk.

Gerard leaned forward, resting his elbows on his knees. "Do you think she would have used an online dating service or gone out with someone she met online?"

"Hmmm... I don't know. Maybe. She did spend a lot of time online at night, chatting with friends." Roger answered.

"Did she ever chat with you online?" Gerard pointed toward Roger's monitor.

"We'd instant message each other occasionally at night when we got bored or lonesome," Roger nodded.

"Do you happen to remember what service she used and her ID?" Reager asked, his pen hovering over his notepad.

"She used Yahoo! Messenger, like I do and her handle was JessHoney," Roger replied.

"Just out of curiosity, what's your ID?" Reager asked.

"It's ChattCowboy," Roger answered. Gerard felt the hair on the back of his neck rise. He'd just heard that handle recently. Where was it? That's right, less than an hour ago at Ellerie's! Roger was the guy instant messaging Ellerie! Was it only a coincidence?"

41

Gerard rose from his seat and motioned toward Roger's monitor, "Would you mind showing me how that instant messenger thing works?"

Roger spun around in his swivel chair so that he faced the monitor and jiggled his mouse to turn off his screen saver. He opened his instant messenger program. As fast as Gerard could do so he began scribbling down the list of buddies in Roger's buddy list. He couldn't see them all, but he wrote down the ones he could.

Roger pointed at the different names and explained how he could tell which ones were online and which ones weren't and how to send a message. He even demonstrated by sending a message to his brother downstairs.

"I don't know much about this stuff. Are you pretty handy with computers?" Gerard asked in a nonchalant tone.

"I know a little, but just enough to get by," Roger answered.

"Do you happen to know if Jessica was having problems with her computer?" Reager asked.

Roger swiveled so he faced Reager. "Not that I know of. I talked with her on Monday, and she didn't mention it."

"When you say you talked with her, was it by phone or in person or instant message?" Reager asked.

"She IM'd me Monday night. That's the last I heard from her," Roger answered, and Reager continued to make notes.

"Do you ever date women you meet online?" Gerard leaned his arm on the computer hutch.

Roger's eyebrows furrowed a little, "No, I just chat with people - haven't ever got up the nerve to ask any of them out."

"Is that because you were in love with Jessica?" Gerard countered.

An expression of surprise flickered across Roger's face. He obviously hadn't expected that question. "Who told you I was in love with Jessica?"

"Joy said you had a thing for Jessica but Jessica didn't know it." Gerard watched closely for Roger's reaction.

Mist filled the man's brown eyes, "Yeah, I was in love with her."

"Why didn't you tell her?" Gerard countered.

"I would have eventually. I was waiting for her to get over Todd Ellison," Roger turned back toward his computer and shut it down.

After a few moments of silence, Gerard extended his hand to Roger, "I'm sorry for your loss, Mr. Wesley. Thank you for your time."

Roger shook Gerard's hand and then Reager's, "I hope you catch whoever did this to her."

"We will, rest assured of that," Gerard nodded.

~*~

Derrick stepped into Roger's office after the policemen left. "So how did it go?"

"Fine," Roger wiped the corners of his eyes with a handkerchief and blew his nose.

"Are you all right?" his brother inquired.

"I just can't believe she's gone, Derrick. If I'd told her how I felt about her, she'd be alive right now," Roger lamented.

"You're putting too much on yourself, Roger. You don't know that," Derrick insisted.

"If I'd told her how I felt, we would have been together, and he couldn't have gotten to her." Roger blew his nose again.

"You couldn't protect her all the time. It was probably just a burglar. You've got to stop blaming yourself," Derrick reasoned.

"You just don't get it do you, Derrick!" Roger barked, went to his bedroom, and slammed the door.

~*~

Ellerie stood with her elbow leaning on the bathroom doorway watching Sable scrub the sink. "I don't care how shiny you get that porcelain, Sable, I'm not eating off the toilet seat!"

43

Sable turned and chuckled, "Well I hope not! I did get that ring off your bathtub though."

"What are you tonight, the energizer bunny?" Ellerie looked toward the living room, "So did Gerard leave?"

"Yeah, he said to tell you goodbye. You sure were on the phone a long time," Sable remarked.

"I was talking with Gretta from the office. She's got this crush on a guy we work with and the whole thing is progressing so slowly that it's making her nuts." Ellerie sighed.

Sable smiled, "You're giving advice to the lovelorn these days then?"

"Yeah, you know what an expert I am in that department," Ellerie quipped with a snort. "So… did you shake his hand?"

"Yes, I did," Sable dried her hands with a towel.

"And?"

"He didn't creep me out," Sable shrugged.

"That's it? Did anything else happen?" Ellerie pressed.

"He offered to show me around Chattanooga tomorrow," Sable passed Ellerie and went toward her bedroom.

"All right! I knew you two would hit it off!" Ellerie clapped her hands together.

"Don't get your hopes up, El," Sable cautioned.

"Come on, admit it. He's exactly your type, isn't he?" Ellerie insisted.

"All right, yes. If I still have a type, he'd be it. But I'm damaged goods, Ellerie. He's not going to want me after he finds out I'm a freak." Sable stood in the middle of the bedroom with folded arms and stared at Ellerie.

"You are not a freak, Sable! Give him a chance. Gerard's a big boy. He can take anything you dish at him." Ellerie leaned on the doorframe.

"We'll see won't we," Sable gave Ellerie a wink and shooed her out, then shut the bedroom door. As she changed clothes for the night, Sable admitted to herself that she felt wonderful. She was so pumped that she could have cleaned the entire apartment. It had been years since she'd felt this good. What's more, the vision of Gerard's handsome face descending toward hers wouldn't leave her mind. Was it a fantasy or a premonition?

~*~

Gerard slept in a little later than usual on Friday morning, put on a suit and drove to the precinct. When he sidled up to Davis and placed a piece of paper on the officer's desk, Davis looked up at him. "McNally, what are you doing here? The Captain's going to have your hide if he sees you in here. He's been going on and on about how you and Reager haven't had a day off in three weeks and that if you don't rest you won't be fit for solving these cases.

"I'm not here to work, just to give you some things to do while I'm off," Gerard winked.

"Gee, thanks!" Davis picked up the paper.

"I need you to perform a thorough diagnostic on all three victims' computers. Look for any kind of online dating sites in their histories, any logs of instant message conversations, and lists of their instant message buddies. If their computers are wiped, like Jessica's was, then call their friends and find out their email addresses and instant message ID's and break into their accounts. I need to know who they've been talking to online. Also take a look at this list of Yahoo usernames and see if any of them correspond to the victims or anyone the victims talked to."

Davis just nodded as Gerard continued down his to-do list, "Look specifically for any conversations any of the women had with a ChattCowboy. Also, call the people on this list." He handed Davis a copy of Roger's alibis. "See if Roger Wesley's alibis check out."

"You think Roger Wesley did it?" Davis cocked an eyebrow.

"At this point, I'm just checking out anything and everything," Gerard shrugged.

"Will do. Now get out of here before the Captain comes back with his doughnuts," Davis pointed toward the door.

"All right, thanks, Davis," Gerard slapped the officer on the back and left the precinct for Mrs. Higby's funeral. On the way, he called Sable.

~*~

When the phone rang, Sable stared at it a moment, nervous about picking it up. She'd just about decided not to go anywhere with Gerard today. She wasn't ready for the vision that kept replaying in her mind, even though she felt drawn to him.

Finally on the fourth ring she picked up, "Hello."

"Sable?" Gerard asked.

"Yes," she pressed the phone to her ear and sat down on the couch.

"How are you doin'?" She loved his voice. It was one of those baritone ones that made her weak in the knees.

"Good," she smiled involuntarily and leaned back on the cushions.

"Are we still on for today?" he asked.

"Uh, I – " she groped for an excuse, but her hesitance gave him an opening.

"I know a great restaurant overlooking the river for lunch," he tempted.

"What time?"

"I'll pick you up around noon after I change out of this suit," he said.

"Sounds good," she agreed in spite of herself.

"See ya."

"Bye," she hung up the phone and rested it on her lap.

This wasn't a good thing. She couldn't say no to him. Her old fears about getting close to someone kept telling her to stay away from him, but she wasn't thinking with her head anymore. It was as if her heart were on an auto-piloted course leading her deep into uncharted territory.

46

Chapter 6

Sable climbed into the front seat of Gerard's green Bronco, and he shut the door behind her. He tossed his denim jacket in the back seat and climbed behind the wheel. As he backed out of the parking lot, her eyes lingered on the flexing muscle of his arm where his short sleeve hit the center of his bicep. He shifted the automobile into drive and his cowboy boot hit the accelerator.

"Great day for sight seeing. It's gotta be sixty-five degrees out there," he remarked.

"It is beautiful," She looked up at the cloudless sunny sky. She had no idea where they were going or what they were doing, but somehow she felt oddly secure and nervous at the same time. Normally, she wasn't the superficial type, but as good as he looked in those jeans and tight fitting black t-shirt, she decided even if he took her somewhere boring, she could still enjoy the view.

"Do you like fish?" he asked.

"I like trout and salmon if they're cooked right," she replied.

He chuckled, "No, I mean, do you feel like going to the aquarium?"

"Oh," she smiled, "Sure."

"We have the largest freshwater aquarium in the world," he bragged as if he may have been in on the design of it.

"Cool," she smiled.

"But we'll get something to eat first," he said.

"Okay."

~*~

She looked tense. Striking, but tense, he thought. Her dark green v-neck sweater brought out the green in her eyes. He smiled as he noted her jeans and white tennis shoes, pleased that she had a practical side. He hated it when women wore uncomfortable heels when he took them somewhere they'd be walking a lot.

"So, were you born with that dark black hair?" he asked.

Her eyes narrowed, evidently surprised by his question, "Why?"

"Your name – Sable – it means jet black, ebony, or raven. Did you have that dark hair when you were born? Is that why your parents named you Sable?" he asked.

"It's an old family name, but I suppose if I'd been blonde at birth they would have named me something else," she smiled. "Then again, there wasn't much hope of me being blonde. Both my parents have black hair." She leaned her hand on the arm rest by the door.

"It's beautiful," he smiled.

"Thanks," she nodded. "The hair or the name?"

"Both," he smiled, and her eyes locked with his for a moment. He finally looked back at the road. "Have you always lived in D.C.?" he asked.

"I grew up in Virginia, went to William and Mary for college and then got the job in Washington."

"Do you like living there?" he asked.

"It has its perks, but there's a lot of crime. You don't feel safe there like you do here," she observed.

"I guess a lot of crime is a good thing for a criminal lawyer?" he smiled. "Keeps you busy."

"Yeah, well, I'm getting sick of it all," she sighed and looked away from him, out the passenger side window.

"So, are you a defense or prosecuting attorney?"

"Defense." She continued to look out the window, watching the lush vegetation so indicative of the South.

"The whole thing can wear you down, can't it?" he remarked.

"Yes," she sighed.

"I can relate to that. Are you thinking about quitting?" he asked.

She cocked her head to one side, "Actually, I am."

"What will you do instead?" he asked and turned onto a different street.

"Don't have a clue," she shrugged.

Gerard let it go, concentrating instead on explaining the older sections of Chattanooga. He gave her a little history lesson on the community and the old houses. When they passed a conveyance climbing up the steep side of Lookout Mountain, he pointed and asked, "Do you like heights? We could go up the incline."

"I'll pass," she shook her head and scrunched her nose.

"Not a fan of heights?"

"No, not my favorite thing." She leaned her head so she could watch the incline ascend the mountain.

"Good, me neither. But a good tour guide has to offer," he grinned.

"So did you grow up around here?" she began interrogating him for a change.

"Yeah, raised in the Chattanooga area," he answered.

"How long have you been with the police department?" She leaned her back against the door and faced him.

"Seven years, went to the police academy straight out of college with my friend Bronson, and we both got a job here. He's out on his own now, though. He started a private investigation business and has been after me to join him."

"Do you think you will?" She leaned her hand on the dash.

"Some days I feel like I'd like to and then others I think I'd miss my job." As soon as the words left his mouth, Gerard realized she was the first person he'd ever admitted that to.

"When I think of private investigators I envision someone slinking around and taking pictures of sordid situations. Doesn't seem comparable to being a homicide detective," Sable observed.

"You're right," he nodded. "I just don't think I'd like the surveillance and the whole messy world of a PI. Bronson always liked that part of things. Heck, that's how he met his wife!"

"Really?" He'd obviously piqued her curiosity. "So tell me. How did he meet his wife?" she asked.

Gerard grinned, "Bronson was working on a drug case and used Mandy's house for surveillance to watch her neighbor. He was there under the guise of being her boyfriend, and I guess he acted the part so well, he convinced her to marry him when the farce was over."

"You're kidding?" Sable laughed.

"Nope. They make quite a pair and have a really cute little boy. I'll introduce you to them sometime," he said.

They continued to chat about their families and interests until they reached the river and Gerard parked his car by a riverboat. He opened her door and she stepped out. He reached past her and grabbed his denim jacket and her windbreaker. "It'll be chilly on the deck. You'll need this," he said as he handed her the jacket.

"We're going on the riverboat?" Her eyes widened.

"Can't come to Chattanooga without dining on the river," he winked.

He helped her put on her jacket and then slipped on his own. They ambled toward the large riverboat and soon they were seated. After waiting about ten minutes, the Southern Belle launched from the shore.

"When you said we were eating lunch at a restaurant overlooking the river, I never dreamed you meant we'd be eating *on the river.*"

"Is it okay? You don't get motion sickness do you?" He grew concerned, hoping she didn't get sea sick now that they'd left the dock and it was too late to turn back.

"No, it's fun," she smiled. "Thanks for thinking of it." She opened her menu and looked at her choices. She ordered the trout and Gerard selected the steak.

~*~

When he suggested that they take a walk on the deck while they waited for their lunch, Sable agreed. A gentle breeze wafted off the water and the clear sky made for perfect viewing of the city as the steamboat floated down the river.

"Right over there," he pointed, "is where we'll go for dinner tonight." She looked in the direction he indicated, but there were several buildings to choose from.

"That one there?" she pointed.

"No, that's the Hunter Art Museum," he stood directly behind her, and she could feel the warmth of his left hand on her waist and the heat of his body against hers. He pointed ahead so she could line her sight up with his finger and know to which building he referred.

"You see it now?" his breath caressed her cheek, and she could feel the heat of his eyes lingering on her face. Again, the vision from the evening before flashed into her mind, and all she could do was nod in agreement, unable to speak.

"All that over there is the art district. We'll eat at the Back End Café. Excellent food and view."

Again, she could only nod and fight the incredible urge to spin around and nestle into his arms. What in the world had come over her? She scolded herself and reminded her heart that she'd never been the kind of girl to swoon over men, harbor secret crushes, or even believe in love at first sight. Then again this wasn't love at first sight, more like intense infatuation at first touch. He'd been on her mind constantly since the prior evening's handshake. Now the sensation of his palm at her waist, his face so close to hers, and his chest against her back nearly reduced her to nothing but a puddle of mush at his feet.

Over lunch and the remainder of the cruise, she got to know Gerard better, and with every new insight into his character and personality she could feel herself falling even deeper. By the time they reached the aquarium, she had finally let go of her tension and allowed herself to relax and be herself with him. It was the first time she'd fully felt like herself since before the accident. All thoughts of her accursed abilities fled.

51

As they stood in front of a large window viewing the sharks, a menacing one darted toward the glass, hovering and eyeing them for several moments.

"Hey, don't look at me," Gerard spoke defensively to the shark and pointed to Sable. "She's the one who ate fish for lunch, not me!" He put his hand on her shoulder and smiled, "You know what it is, don't you? He can smell that trout on your breath and he's saying, 'So, Miss Graham, where were you at 1:00 p.m. on the afternoon of February 4th when Mr. Trout was caught, filleted and served aboard the Southern Belle?'"

Sable laughed at him and pushed him away from the accusing shark and on to the next exhibit.

"It won't help to leave, we can all smell that trout on your lips, Miss Graham," Gerard continued to tease in a deep shark voice.

"Give me one of those mints," Sable reached for the tin of candy in Gerard's jacket pocket, but Gerard put his hand over hers.

"It won't do any good to try to cover it up, Miss Graham, we all know you're the one," Gerard continued his shark imitation. With the direct contact of his touch – his strong hand over hers – an intense warmth started at her heart and drizzled out through her extremities, filling her with a tingling indescribable sweetness. Again the vision burst upon the stage of her mind, and she was wrapped up secure and engaged in his embrace.

Without realizing it, her eyes misted with emotion, and Gerard put his hand to her cheek, "Sable, are you all right?"

She leaned into his touch and blinked her eyes, attempting to force away the vision. It continued to play somewhere in the recesses of her mind as his face came into view before her.

"Are you okay?" he repeated.

She nodded, "I'm sorry. I'm fine. I just get these little spells sometimes. It's just stress – part of the reason I'm on a leave of absence from work." She couldn't possibly tell him the full truth. He'd think she was a freak for sure, and the last thing she wanted was to drive him away.

"Do you need to sit down?" his eyes were filled with concern as he gently stroked her hair and his hand slipped to her shoulder.

"No," she smiled. "Really, I'm fine." She felt wonderful actually. Every time he touched her, it was as if he could somehow recharge her batteries and take away some of the pain and the hurt. It was as if his touch erased the scars left by others upon her soul. Their horrors and frightening scenes had damaged her, and Gerard's touch healed her.

"All right," he said, taking her hand and continuing on with the tour. "But you tell me if you need to sit down or rest."

"I don't need to rest," she shook her head with a smile. "I feel great."

~*~

Gerard didn't understand it. She looked like she felt great, but a moment before she'd appeared so distant, as if she were in another time or place. Then there was that misty lovelorn look in her eye. He wondered if she were on the rebound? Maybe heartbreak sent her escaping South to her old friend? There was definitely more to Sable Graham than met the eye. He could feel it, sense it. He felt more than mere curiosity or an attraction for a beautiful woman. He had the incredible urge to gather her up in his arms and protect her, hold her, heal her, for he sensed that somehow this raven-haired beauty was broken, wounded in some profoundly deep way. When he touched her in even the simplest of ways, he felt his heart connecting with hers as she opened up and revealed another piece of the puzzle that was Sable's mysterious heart.

He let his fingers lace with hers. Her hand felt as if it were designed to fit his. She laughed and made a joke about the male sea horses being the ones to give birth, suggesting humans take up the practice. He chuckled, but he found himself staring at her lips and wondering what it would feel like, taste like, to kiss them. The more the thought lingered, the tighter his chest became, and he could feel his pulse hammering in his throat. He wondered if she would let him kiss her? He normally didn't push himself on a woman like that – especially not on a first date. Yet, the question obsessed his thoughts throughout the afternoon and into the evening as they shopped downtown, strolled through Coolidge Park, rode the carousel, ate a candlelit dinner overlooking the moonlit river and walked toward the Walnut Street Bridge.

~*~

Halfway across the bridge Sable stopped, leaned against the rail and watched the moon and city lights shimmer on the water.

"It's a lovely city," she sighed, and he stepped closer, standing directly behind her. The warmth of his presence blocked the cool night breeze. Mustering her nerve, she turned around to face him. "Thank you for a perfect day," she smiled up into his face.

"It was fun, wasn't it?" his gaze fell to her lips, and she knew that look in his eyes because she'd seen it dozens of times as the vision replayed in her mind. He planned to kiss her, and the thought didn't even occur to her that she'd only known him for a day for it seemed like a lifetime. Her heart thumped wildly, as every part of her screamed to consummate a kiss she'd never quite been able to complete in her imagination.

His lips teased hers, hovering, grazing hers as if he were hesitant to be so bold. She sighed and it was as if the sound of it gave him courage to take her lips with his. His hands which held her face lowered to her neck, his thumb caressing her throat and his fingers disappeared into her thick ebony tresses. Her hands slid around his waist, under his jacket and rested at the center of his back as she returned his kiss, deepening their exchange until they were both completely lost in a tender, emblazoned fervor.

Finally, he held her tightly in his arms and whispered into her hair, "I've wanted to do that all day long."

"I've wanted you to do that all day long," she breathed. She placed both hands to his cheeks and let her fingers play with the stubble on his handsome face. "What took you so long?"

Again his kiss was hers, warm, lingering and exhilarating. Heaven had answered her prayer and given her not only one day of normalcy, but one day of complete and utter paradise. If she never got another, this day would live in her memory and replay in the corridors of her imagination for a lifetime.

Chapter 7

Ellerie had already fallen asleep when Sable slipped into the apartment that night. She could still taste Gerard's kiss on her lips and feel the tingling throughout her body from his touch. How could one person make such a profound impact on her existence in a single day? Yet he had. She felt reborn, as if old scars had healed and new life pumped through her veins. She lay awake for nearly an hour reliving the day and excited for another with him the next. Eventually, she drifted off to sleep.

The next morning, Sable rose early and set to work on her special pancake batter. She'd promised Gerard a breakfast of chocolate chip pancakes and expected him any minute. Her heart beat rapidly in anticipation of his arrival as she dropped the chocolate chips into the batter and folded them in. She pulled a pan from the cabinet as quietly as she could since Ellerie still slept in her bedroom.

Just as she removed a couple pancakes from the skillet, she heard a soft tap at the door and went to open it. Gerard stood there in a blue flannel shirt and jeans. With his denim jacket, cowboy boots and a black Stetson he looked like a cowboy straight off the range. Sable opened the door wider and forced a mock western accent, "Well, mosey on in cowboy, the vittles is ready."

"Don't mind if I do, Ma'am," he answered with a Southern drawl and a tip of his hat. "Smells mighty fine." Sable motioned for him to sit at the bar. She stood across from him and set two plates between them.

Gerard looked down at the pancakes topped with melting whipped butter and drizzled with syrup. "Hell bent on cloggin' my arteries are ya this mornin', Missy?" he drawled, pulled his hat from his head and set it on the counter.

He cut a small piece of pancake with his fork, but she put her hand on his to stop him, "No, no, no. That's not how you eat it. Let me show you." She cut a big piece of pancake with her fork, swirled it around in the melting butter, then in the syrup and held the fork straight up, letting the sides of the pancake flop around the fork.

"You've got to get a big bite, drenched with all the good stuff," she winked and took a bite on the end that dangled nearest her.

Gerard grinned playfully, leaned forward and ate the pancake from the opposite side of Sable's fork. When they both had consumed their sides of the piece of pancake and met in the middle, Sable lowered the fork to the counter. It was at this point, as the pair engaged in a chocolate syrup, pancake kiss, that Ellerie stepped out of her bedroom, rubbed the sleep from her eyes, and entered the kitchen. Her mouth dropped wide and her eyes grew as round as Sable's pancakes. She stood at the end of the bar watching what could only be described as a very intimate way to eat breakfast.

After a few moments unobserved, Ellerie reached for Gerard's plate and slid it toward her. "Doesn't look like anyone's going to eat this," she muttered, but the pair did not acknowledge her presence. When Gerard kissed away a blob of gooey chocolate from Sable's cheek, Ellerie grabbed a napkin and lifted it in the air. She whispered, "I'll just use one of these with my meal, if you two don't mind." With wide eyes and two raised eyebrows, Ellerie shook her head, turned, and retreated with the plate and utensils back to her bedroom.

~*~

"Dress warm," Gerard called down the hallway. "We'll be outside a lot today." Sable slipped into her bedroom to get her shoes and find a warm sweater and coat.

Ellerie stepped out of her bedroom, "Well, well, well, you two sure hit it off."

"I owe you one, El," Gerard leaned his back against the wall and faced his friend, a completely love struck grin on his face.

"You do," Ellerie pointed at him, "And I intend to collect on it!"

"Name it and it's yours," Gerard smiled.

"Hmmm... let me think on it, and I'll let you know," she winked and then looked toward Sable as she opened her bedroom door and approached them.

Gerard reached out an arm to put it around Sable's shoulder, and she slipped her arm around his waist.

"So when should I expect you two kids home?" Ellerie queried in a mock motherly voice.

"We'll see you sometime before midnight, Mom," Gerard winked. "Actually, we'll be gettin' kinda dirty today, so I'll bring her back to clean up before dinner."

"No grass stains on those jeans, girly" Ellerie scolded as Gerard grabbed his hat and opened the door. Just when he tugged her outside, Sable turned around and mouthed "Thank You!" to Ellerie.

"Two peas in a pod. When I'm right, I'm right," Ellerie muttered, proud that once again her matchmaking abilities had struck gold. But even Ellerie had to shake her head in amazement. This one would be hard to top, for even she hadn't expected them to fall so hard so fast.

~*~

Gerard's Bronco turned down a long, dusty clay road.

"Where are we going?" Sable asked as she jostled beside him when the Bronco's tires sunk into a deep pothole and climbed out of it.

"You like to ride horses?" he asked.

"I don't know. Never done it," she shrugged.

"You're kidding? You've never ridden a horse before?" he lifted a single eyebrow.

"Never had the opportunity," Sable shook her head.

"Guess there has to be a first for everything," he winked and continued down the road. They pulled up to a farmhouse with a large stable and fenced in field.

"Bronson and I board our horses here. I thought since it's such a pretty day, we'd ride through the battlefield," he explained.

Sable felt her nerves tighten. "I don't know, Gerard, I don't think I can pick it up that fast."

"That's all right," he squeezed her hand. "General Lee's a big horse; I'll just let you ride with me."

"Oh good," she breathed a sigh of relief and he smiled at her nervousness.

General Lee was a huge horse – a big black animal that stood several hands taller than the other horses in the corral. Gerard helped her climb into the saddle and then hopped up behind her. It wasn't until his arm slipped around her waist and tugged her tight against his chest that she felt safe.

"Don't worry, he's a gentle giant," Gerard spoke into her ear. "We've been together for years, back to my re-enactment days."

"Re-enactment days?" she asked as the horse started forward and down the dusty road.

"Bronson and I used to take part in the re-enactments at the Battlefield, but we quit that a few years back."

"Confederate or Union?" she asked.

"Confederate of course, what'd ya expect?" he affected a deeper Southern accent than his own and pulled his hat lower on his brow.

"Pardon me. I most certainly should have known from General Lee!" she giggled at his pretended offense. "Do you still have the uniform? I'd love to see you in it."

"I do, but I've put on a little weight since then, you know, muscle and all," he chuckled and flexed his bicep. "The old uniform might not fit."

"A picture then?" she suggested.

"I have several pictures. Remind me to show 'em to you later."
He adjusted his hand at her waist.

The horse stepped out onto the main road and trotted along
toward the Battlefield. "I won't bore you by explaining all the markers.
I'll just give you the general overview and visit a few of the high points
of the battle, if you want."

"Sounds good," she put her hand on his where it rested at her
waist. She wasn't much of a war buff, but she didn't care how many
battle stories she had to listen to. All she cared about was getting to
spend a morning next to him, feeling the rhythm of his breathing
behind her, the security of his arm around her, and listening to the
resonance of his deep voice as he explained the points of history.
Surprisingly enough, she found his retelling of the battle interesting
and enjoyed visiting the little cabin on Snodgrass Hill and climbing
Wilder Tower

Finally, General Lee trotted into an open field across the way
from the tower and Gerard stopped the horse just as it passed through
a wooded area facing a vast green meadow.

"Here's the true test, Miss Graham," Gerard lowered his voice
to that deep Southern drawl, "Tell me the answer to this question,
and I'll know whether you're the girl for me."

"Oh my, nothing like a little pressure!" she giggled.

"When you see a big green field like this, what's the very first
thing you want to do?" he asked.

Sable hesitated. What kind of question was that? And how
would her answer reveal whether she was the one for him? "I don't
know," she giggled self-consciously.

"Oh, come on now, what's the first thing you want to do when
you see something as beautiful as this?"

She hesitated momentarily and then said the first thing that
crossed her mind, "Walk out in the middle of it, lie down in the grass
and stare up at the clouds."

"Exactly!" he nudged the horse and it galloped out into the
middle of the field, pranced around for a few moments and then
stopped. Gerard hopped down and lifted Sable from the horse. He

unfastened the saddle bag, pulled out a blanket and spread it on the ground. Gerard plopped down on the blanket and stretched out on his back with his hands behind his head. He motioned for Sable to do the same and then tipped his hat over his eyes.

"I'm so glad you thought to bring a blanket. Mother would have given me fits if I'd come home with grass stains," she chuckled as she lay down beside him and looked up at the few clouds drifting in the sunny sky.

After a few minutes of comfortable silence, Sable turned on her side, leaning her head on her hand facing him. "So tell me. Are you always this romantic, or are you just trying to impress me?"

He shifted to his side facing her, a teasing grin on his face, "Oh it's all an act. I'm just buttering you up until I've caught you, and then I'll be one of those couch potato husbands who lie around evenings and weekends flipping channels and calling for you to bring me my grub."

She giggled at his description, but then a nervous twirling started in the pit of her stomach over his reference to making her his wife. She couldn't help but wonder if it were all in jest or whether there might be some underlying truth there. Did she even want to be the wife of a homicide detective? For heaven's sake, she'd only known him for a day! Would he even want anything to do with her after he learned the truth?

"What's wrong?" his eyebrows furrowed.

"Nothing," she smiled and shook her head, leaning back on the blanket.

He scooted closer, resting his palm on her stomach, "Something's wrong. Are you feeling all right?"

She pressed her hand to his, drawing strength from his touch. It never ceased to fill her with a profound sense of well-being. But this time, she felt an overwhelming urge to share her secret with him, the same way she felt compelled to bare her soul to her father before his passing. But fear gripped every cell of Sable's body. What would he think of her? Sure, Ellerie had handled it in stride, but even Ellerie didn't know the full ugly truth. She feared that if she let go and told

Gerard even part of the truth, she couldn't stop. She'd spill it all, and Gerard would be lost to her. Then again, what good would a relationship built on lies be to her? Either way, in the end she'd lose him. The question was, should she lose him today or postpone the inevitable and make it that much harder?

When her eyes filled with tears and the compelling urge to spill her secrets engulfed her, he kissed her cheek and gently let his fingers stroke her hair. Her hands went to his cheeks and she pulled his lips to hers, hoping that if she kissed him long enough and completely enough that she could endure the moment, keeping the truth buried deep inside her heart where he could not find it. But her logic failed for the tighter she pulled him toward her and the more she tried to lose herself in his kiss, the more she knew the truth must be told and the sooner the better.

When the salt from her tears mingled with her kiss, Gerard pulled her to him, letting her bury her head against his chest. Her quiet tears turned to a heartbroken sob, and he held her for several minutes, staring up at the clouds as her head rested against his chest and his arms encircled her.

"Sable, what's wrong?" he whispered with his hand to her cheek. "You can tell me. Whatever it is, we can tackle it together," He kissed the top of her head hoping to assure her that she could trust him.

She sat up on the blanket and buried her head in her hands. He retrieved a tissue from his jacket pocket and handed it to her so she could wipe her tears.

"I'm sorry that I'm such a basket case. I'm just – I'm just not what you think I am, and I'm afraid when you hear the truth you'll go away." She sniffed back her tears.

He sat up facing her. "Sable, there's nothing that you could say that would make me go away."

She inhaled deeply and exhaled, searching his eyes to see if he really meant what he'd said. Finally, she mustered the courage to begin. "I need to go back three years to explain."

Gerard folded his legs in front of him and waited for her to continue.

"I was really messed up at the time. I'd just been passed over for a partnership position in our firm by a guy named Dan Vanderhoff. It basically came down to the fact that he was better socially than I was. He could schmooze the clients, and I just never have been good at that kind of thing. I really wanted that position, and when I didn't get it, I went to my favorite restaurant and drank an entire bottle of wine with my dinner. I normally wouldn't do that kind of thing, but I just had to escape from it all if even for an evening. Of course I was in no position to drive myself home, but I did. It was a terribly stormy night. I could hardly see a thing and the last thing I remember was lightning striking my car. I woke up hours later in the hospital, and they told me that I'd hit a telephone pole. Luckily, all I had was a busted lip and a concussion. They watched me overnight and sent me home."

"Anyway, my dad came to visit me a day or so later and that's when I first noticed that something had changed. Dad held my hand and an icy chill came over me. It felt as if the temperature in the room dropped below freezing, and I felt this horrible dread. I saw myself standing over my father's grave, and I felt what it would be like to lose him. In that instant it really felt as if he were gone and all the issues we hadn't addressed over the years felt incredibly important that we resolve right then. Immediately, I began confessing the things I'd done in my life that I shouldn't have – the times I'd talked back to him, disobeyed him. I even confided the grudges I'd harbored against him, and we talked things out that we'd never discussed before. Two days later, he had a heart attack and died before he even got to the hospital."

Gerard took her hand and continued to listen attentively.

"Dad was the first experience I had like that. There were so many people I encountered in my work. If I shook hands or touched someone who was about to be harmed or die, I felt that same icy chill and often saw foreboding visions. Sometimes I'd try to warn them or let them know they needed to make peace with a family member.

Eventually I got where I couldn't stand to touch people. That's why I wouldn't shake your hand that night I first met you. You're the first guy I've even dated in three years!"

"I feel honored," he smiled and she realized he was hoping to lighten her mood a little.

"You may not feel so honored when I tell you the rest." She hesitated and he waited patiently for her to continue. "Anyway, it got even creepier. As you'd imagine in a criminal law practice, you encounter people who are guilty of heinous crimes and the foul kinetic residue of those crimes remained on them. I had such a difficult time forcing myself to defend clients that I knew beyond any doubt were guilty. I tried to get other lawyers in the office to take those cases, but I couldn't always, and it wore me down. I had horrible nightmares and it wracked me with guilt."

"Wow, that would be incredibly hard to deal with," Gerard sympathized.

"Yes, well, last week it was the straw that broke the camel's back. The guy I told you about who passed me over for partner – Dan Vanderhoff – I shook his hand when he was leaving the boardroom that day, and I got that same icy chill." Sable's eyes began to well with fresh tears, "Two hours later, he was killed in a car accident. He left a wife and a little boy."

"I'm sorry, Sable," he gently caressed her cheek with one hand and squeezed her hand with the other. "That must have been hard to lose a co-worker like that."

"No, you don't understand," Sable shook her head in frustration and her eyes met his. "That's just it... the first thing I thought... the very first thing that came to my mind was that now I'd have a shot at partner." Sable sniffed back a tear, "I'm evil, Gerard. I'm a horrible person! How could I be so cruel? How could that be my first thought?"

Gerard pulled her to him, letting her head rest on his chest. "You're not evil, Sable. You're human."

"But he had a wife and a kid and all I was thinking about was myself! I mean, I felt that icy shudder, and I didn't warn him to be careful. I didn't suggest he take a taxi. That car wreck flashed into my

63

mind, and all I could think of was me making partner so that I'd have more control over the cases I took! How sick is that? And by the time I recovered fully from the episode and tried to warn him, it was too late."

"You made a mistake. You're human."

"I'm a drunk driver! I'm one of those people that you could be arresting for vehicular manslaughter!" she cried.

"Do you drink and drive still, Sable?" Gerard asked seriously, searching her eyes.

"No, I haven't taken a drink since the accident, and heaven knows I've wanted one! I've wanted to drown out the pain so many times, but I knew if I weakened, if I let myself take a single drink I'd be lost," she swiped at the tear running down her cheek.

"You're a strong person, Sable. Not many people could put up with what you've been through and stay sane."

"But I'm a freak, Gerard! Some kind of evil sadistic freak!" Sable sobbed.

"No you are not!" Gerard looked her square in the eyes. "You wouldn't feel this bad if you were evil. You care. You couldn't control the first thought that came to your mind!"

"If I were a better person, it would have been a better thought!" she insisted.

"Listen to me." He held her face in his hands. "You're being way too hard on yourself. You were just trying to find a way to ease the pain you've been living with day in and day out. It wasn't vindictive; it was self preservation."

She sniffed, "I never thought of it that way." She considered his words for several moments. "I guess you're right. I didn't hate Dan. I just wanted to be free of the pain. You have no idea how I've wanted just a single day of a normal life!"

He held her for several minutes, until she finally calmed down and breathed a sigh of relief that he now knew the whole truth. He was still there in spite of it, and she loved him for it. Yes, it was only her second day with the man, but she knew she loved him. She had to admit that without the very power she despised, he wouldn't be in her life. Besides the fact that she wouldn't have left D.C. and found him, she wouldn't know the intense goodness and strength of the man without her unusual ability to see inside his soul. It was the first time she'd ever considered her abilities as a blessing instead of a curse.

"Can I ask you a question?" Gerard broke the silence.

"Yes."

He seemed a little hesitant to ask what was on his mind. "What happened the other night when you shook my hand and again yesterday at the aquarium?"

"I don't think you really want to know," she shook her head.

"Was it bad? Did you sense something wrong?" his eyebrows furrowed and studied her expression.

"No," she chuckled nervously. "It wasn't bad - quite the opposite."

"What then?" he coaxed.

"You ... you make me feel really ... good," she looked away sheepishly, a blush rising to her cheeks.

He took her chin in his hand and directed her gaze back to him. "You make *me* feel really good," he replied with a flirtatious grin and a raised eyebrow.

"No," she giggled nervously. "You have the complete opposite effect on me than I'm used to. Normally, people drain me. All the negative, bad things I encounter in people sap the energy from me. But whenever you touch me, I feel warm, wonderful and energized."

"Ah, I get it now," he shook his head dramatically. "You're just using me for my body! All that positive kinetic energy I'm emitting!" he teased with a laugh.

"Oh, it sounds so embarrassing when you say it that way!" she gritted her teeth and put her hands over her eyes as her face turned crimson.

"I'm just teasing you," he chuckled, "There's not a single person in the world that doesn't choose the person they're with based on how they make them feel. If I make you feel half as good as you make me feel, then we're both lucky to have each other."

He leaned forward and kissed her gently, but she took his cheeks firmly in her hands and pulled him into a warm, intoxicating exchange. With her secret safely shared, there was nothing standing between them, and she relished in his every touch, the feel of his arms about her, his warm, delicious mouth weaving its magic, healing every old wound and erasing every unpleasant memory. He was the long overdue cure she had searched for all these years, and to think she almost hadn't let him touch her!

Chapter 8

Gerard tossed his jacket on his bed, picked up the portable phone and dialed the precinct.

"Hey, Davis. It's me, McNally. What 'cha got for me?"

"I was wondering when you'd be calling in."

"I've been busy," Gerard answered and flopped down on his bed.

"Must be something awfully important. You're usually hounding me to death on your days off!" Davis observed.

"So what do you know?" Gerard steered Davis back to business.

"All three computers have been reset to factory settings, and all three women's instant messenger usernames were on that list you gave me from Roger Wesley's computer. So it looks like he knew all three women."

"I had a feeling," Gerard ran his hand through his blonde hair. "What about his alibis?"

"They all check out. He was nowhere near any of those women on the nights they were murdered," Davis answered.

"Dang it!" Gerard exclaimed and pounded his fist on the bed.

"But there's got to be a connection there. So I kept digging," Davis said.

"And..." Gerard prompted. Davis always liked to pause for suspense.

"They have a few more things in common." Again Davis halted for effect.

"Come on, Davis, I've got to shower and be somewhere in a little bit. I don't have all night for your dramatics." Gerard sighed.

"Hot date – eh? Is that what's keeping you occupied?" Davis teased.

"Stay on task, Davis. What did you find out?" Gerard rubbed a hand to this temple.

"If you're going to be that way, I just might make you wait until morning," Davis huffed.

"No, please, I'm sorry." Gerard tried to hide his exasperation behind a layer of apology.

Davis seemed satisfied. "Here's the deal. I went over their bank and phone records and all three women shop at the same grocery store, the same dry cleaner, same computer repair place, and the same video store. They all live alone, AND use the same online dating service!"

"Hmmm," Gerard rubbed the five o'clock shadow on his chin.

"Maybe they all just happen to be on Wesley's instant messenger, but there could be another man out there with all three on his list. I'm going to try to restore their instant message programs and get a complete view of their buddy lists. But it'll probably be tomorrow before I can do that because I'll need to crack their passwords and restore their accounts." Davis explained.

"How many guys in the Chattanooga area use that dating service?" Gerard asked.

"A hundred and thirty two," Davis said.

"Good grief. How many of those have filled out a profile?" Gerard stood up and went to the kitchen for a drink.

David paused, looking up the information. "Ninety-eight," he answered.

"What about who live in Northwest Georgia?" Gerard opened the refrigerator.

"Let me see here... yeah... twenty-four."

"Start with those and run background checks on them." Gerard popped the top on a can of soda.

"Did it already," Davis seemed proud of himself, and again paused for effect.

Gerard took a sip of soda, but when Davis still hadn't continued, he prompted, "And..." Gerard set his soda down on the table and reached for a notepad and pen in his pocket.

"Nineteen of them are clean; one has a string of traffic tickets; one's served time for DUI, and the other three have a few traffic citations," Davis recounted.

"All right, thanks. I'll be in first thing in the morning, and we'll take a look at what you've got." Gerard said.

"Okay, bye," Davis said.

Gerard interjected before he'd disconnected, "Oh, wait a minute... did you get anything back on the DNA tests?"

"Oh yeah," the officer replied. "There wasn't anything... no DNA from the killer on the victims' bodies. The autopsies don't indicate rape. It's almost like someone wanted to make it look like rape, but there's no medical evidence to substantiate it."

"Strange," Gerard rubbed his bristles again. "Put Roger Wesley under surveillance."

"Done," Davis answered.

"Thanks. I'll see you tomorrow," Gerard disconnected the call.

~*~

Sable showered and got ready for dinner with Gerard while Ellerie prepared for her own date.

"Where are you two off to tonight?" Ellerie leaned in the doorway watching Sable put on her makeup in front of her bedroom mirror.

"The Station House," Ellerie could see Sable's smile reflected in the mirror as she spoke.

"So you really like him?" Ellerie grinned.

Sable turned around and leaned against the dresser, facing her friend, "Oh, El, I owe you big time! He's fantastic!"

Ellerie stepped closer to her and took Sable's hands in hers, "I'm so happy for you two!" Sable could feel Ellerie's genuine joy charge through her hands and spread over her. It was the first time she'd experienced a good feeling from anyone other than Gerard. It was different than his touch, of course, but she could feel a positive friendly energy from Ellerie that she'd never noticed before. Wouldn't it always have been there?

"Thank you so much. I really do owe you one," Sable hugged her friend. "So where are you going tonight?"

"I've got a date with Roger," she smiled.

"Roger?"

"Yeah, ChattCowboy," Ellerie winked.

"Really? Did you have Gerard check him out?" Sable reminded, wanting Ellerie to be careful with a serial killer on the loose.

"No," Ellerie shrugged. "I'm not worried about it. I did a little snooping around myself, and he seems like a reputable business man. I'll be fine."

The doorbell rang and Ellerie spun around, "That's probably him." She went to the front door and opened it. Roger stood on the other side.

"Hi! Great to finally meet you in person," Ellerie grinned and extended her hand.

"You too," he smiled, shook her hand and came inside.

Sable stepped in the living room anxious to meet this cyber cowboy. He didn't look much like a cowboy. More like a regular businessman. He wore a navy suit, tie and shiny black shoes.

"Roger this is my friend, Sable," Ellerie introduced, and Sable extended her hand to him. She'd risk a stranger's touch to make certain Ellerie would be safe.

"So you're ChattCowboy?" Sable smiled and took his hand. She was surprised by by the sensation. Sable felt sadness, heartbreak and loneliness. It was as if her abilities had expanded somehow to include a greater range of emotions than only premonitions of disaster or criminal guilt.

"You've experienced a profound loss," the words came from Sable's mouth automatically and Ellerie's eyebrows furrowed when moisture pooled in Roger's eyes.

"Uh, yes," Roger nodded. "We buried one of my best friends this week."

"I'm so sorry!" Ellerie and Sable simultaneously sympathized.

"How – how did you know?" Roger's puzzled expression studied Sable.

"Sable's just sort of intuitive that way," Ellerie stepped between Roger and Sable. "So, I thought you'd turn up in a cowboy hat or something." Ellerie seemed determined to lighten the conversation with her chipper tone.

Roger smiled. "It's just a nickname my brother made up for me when he set up my instant messaging program. I like country music, and he's always teasing me about it and calling me cowboy."

The doorbell rang and Sable answered it, letting Gerard in. He'd showered, shaved and changed into a sport coat. He looked fantastic in his blue button up shirt and navy Dockers. She inhaled deeply of his aftershave as he leaned over and kissed her cheek.

"Hi Ellerie, Who's your –" Gerard stopped cold when Roger turned to face him. "Mr. Wesley?"

"Officer Reager?" Roger's eyes widened with surprise.

"McNally," Gerard corrected. "Reager's my partner."

"I'm sorry," Roger said as he shook Gerard's hand.

"Do you two know each other?" Ellerie's eyes darted from Gerard to Roger and back.

"Officer McNally is investigating my friend's murder," Roger explained.

"It was a murder?" Ellerie's eyebrows rose.

"It's that case I was telling y'all about – Jessica Honeycutt who was murdered in her home over on Gattis," Gerard clarified.

"The date rape?" Sable's eyes widened, and she looked at Roger. No wonder such profound sensations of sorrow and grief emanated from the man.

Roger rubbed the side of his face. "I just can't stand the thought of someone doing something like that to poor Jessica. To be murdered is bad enough, but to be violated first is more than I can stomach," Roger sat down on the couch and held his head in his hands.

Ellerie put a hand on his shoulder. "Roger, are you sure you're up to this? You've been through such a shock this week; I'm surprised you even asked me out."

"Why did you ask Ellerie out? I thought you said you didn't date women you met online?" Gerard's eyes narrowed with accusation.

"I don't. Ellerie's the first," Roger lifted his head from his hands and looked at Gerard.

"I'm flattered," Ellerie smiled.

"So why did you ask Ellerie out?" Gerard probed, coming to stand before Roger. Ellerie shot a perturbed expression toward Gerard. It was obvious she didn't like the idea of him interrogating her date.

Roger sighed, "I decided that life's too short to put things off."

"Ain't that the truth!" Ellerie patted Roger's back. "You and Sable have a reservation don't you?" Ellerie prodded, quirking one eyebrow at Gerard.

Gerard glanced at his watch. "We've got a couple minutes. So Roger, did I ask you the other day if you knew Melanie Roberts or Kathy Mentone?"

Roger looked up immediately, "No. Why?"

Sable came around and sat on a chair watching Gerard in action. He was definitely playing his homicide detective role.

"They were murdered in a similar fashion as your friend Jessica," Gerard had an accusatory expression on his face.

"I read about the murders. But I don't know them," Roger shrugged his shoulders.

"Maybe you know them as Melanie345 and ChattyKathy?" Gerard continued.

An expression of unmistakable fear washed over Roger's face. "Is – is that them? They were murdered too?"

"So, are you saying that you didn't know these two women's real names? Did you know that they were both murdered within the last month?" Gerard nearly barked at Roger.

"They stopped being online. I wondered where they went, but honestly I didn't know it was them or what happened to them!" Roger looked pale - a frightened ashen pale.

Sable rose from her seat and went to the refrigerator. She dispensed a glass of ice water, and carried it to Roger. "Here, sip this."

"Thank you." His grateful eyes met Sable's as he took the glass. Sable intentionally let her hand rest on his for a moment. Had she missed something earlier? She needed to double check.

"How did you meet them?" Gerard asked.

"I met Melanie in an AOL chat room and … let me think." Roger rubbed his chin. "Where did I meet ChattyKathy?" Roger scratched his head, "I think it was through that online dating service where I met Ellerie. Yeah, I think that was it." Roger pointed a finger at Gerard. "But come to think of it, she said her last name was Everett – Kathy Everett on her profile."

"Everett was her maiden name. She recently divorced Charles Mentone," Gerard answered.

"And both women are dead?" Roger's voice cracked a little with the question.

"Yes. Do you happen to have any rational explanation for why three women you knew have been murdered within the last month?" Gerard's stern stare scrutinized Roger's every move and expression.

Ellerie looked at Sable with wide-eyed trepidation.

"No, honestly, I don't. I know it looks really bad, but I don't have a clue." Roger's eyes pled with Ellerie as if he hoped she'd rein in her bulldog friend.

Ellerie didn't say anything, which was unusual for her. She looked at Gerard then Sable as if she were hoping for some clue about what she should do. Her eyes met Sable's, and she motioned for Sable to follow her into the bedroom while Gerard continued his interrogation.

"We did check out your alibis, Mr. Wesley, and it appears that you were nowhere near the three women on the nights in question. Do you know anything about what these women had in common besides the fact that they knew you?" Gerard asked.

Ellerie stepped into her bedroom, tugged Sable in, and shut the door behind them. "What do you think? Do I feel like I'm in danger?" Ellerie stared at her hands which clutched Sable's frantically. "I've enjoyed chatting with Roger. He seems like a really sweet guy. But this is getting a little frightening!" she whispered, her head darting in the direction of the living room.

"No," Sable shook her head. "I don't sense anything foreboding."

"What about when you shook Roger's hand? You felt something then. What was it? Do you think he's the killer?" Ellerie asked.

"He just felt profoundly sad, and when I handed him the glass, he was terrified. He's afraid he'll be blamed for those murders," Sable explained.

"I don't blame him!" Ellerie released Sable's hand and turned her back to her. "It doesn't look good."

"Gerard did say that Roger's alibis checked out. Maybe it's just a coincidence? Then again, do you really want to take the chance?" Sable wasn't one hundred percent certain about her impressions. There was something different about them lately. What if she was losing her ability to discern clearly?

Ellerie turned around with a resolute sigh, "You know me, Sable, I don't live my life this way." She shook her head side to side. "I don't live in fear. If you say I'm not in danger, and if you don't sense anything evil from him, then I'm going out with him tonight as planned."

Sable started to interject a word of caution, but Ellerie rushed on, "I've never let fear rule my life before, so why should I start now?" With a resolute nod, Ellerie stepped around Sable, opened the door and grabbed her purse. She marched straight to Roger. "Gerard, it's your day off, and we have somewhere to be. You and Sable need to get going too. You can pick up your investigation when you're back on duty."

With determination, she grabbed Roger's hand and pulled him from the couch. "Lock up when you leave, please."

Gerard looked dumbfounded. He watched Ellerie pull Roger out the door and shut it behind them.

"She's nuts. I always knew she was crazy, but I had no idea just how completely and utterly foolish she could be!" Gerard gaped at the closed door with a stunned expression.

"She's tough. She doesn't let fear rule her life," Sable observed. "You've got to say something for that kind of courage." Sable retrieved her own purse and extended her hand to Gerard. "I guess we should go." He laced his fingers with hers and shook his head. "I can't believe Ellerie would still go out with Roger after what she just heard."

As Sable locked the apartment door, Gerard stood behind her with his hands to her waist. He spoke softly in her ear, "What did you two talk about in the bedroom?"

She turned to face him, "She asked me if I felt she was in danger or if Roger was the killer."

"Because you touched him when you handed him the glass?" Gerard asked, still holding her waist.

"Yes."

"What did you tell her?" His eyes searched hers.

"I only feel friendship from Ellerie. Nothing is threatening her life – yet anyway. Roger is mourning and afraid, but he doesn't feel like a killer."

"So that's why she went out with him? Because you told her it was okay?" He looked upset.

"Gerard, I just told her what I felt. I didn't suggest she go out with him." Sable felt defensive. She stepped away from him and started down the corridor. Maybe he'd just pretended to believe her, but now that it came down to a real live situation, he wasn't so sure of her abilities. "Ellerie made that decision herself."

Gerard took her hand again, and they walked in silence through the corridor to the parking lot. She wondered what he was thinking. Was he doubting her? She didn't notice anything different in his touch. Then again, she wasn't a mind reader, and her abilities weren't that fine tuned.

Gerard opened the car door for her and let her in. He paused, standing there with his hand on the door, leaning over and looking into her eyes. "You really don't feel like he's the killer?"

"If he is, I can't sense it," Sable shook her head.

Gerard shut the door and came around to get in the car. After closing his door, he put the key in the ignition. Sable placed her hand on his wrist to stop him from turning it.

"Do you believe me?" She asked.

He let his hand drop to his thigh and looked at her, "Yes, I believe you."

"Why?" She really wanted to know why. How could he barely know her and trust her in a situation like this? For all he knew, she was a fake, and Ellerie was in danger.

"Premonitions aren't new to me, Sable. I've worked with gifted individuals in the past - on the force. I know there are some phonies out there, but I've learned to spot the genuine article."

"What makes you think I'm the genuine article?" she prompted.

He shrugged, "I just feel it in my gut." He turned the key in the ignition.

She chuckled at the irony. He used his intuition to spot someone with intuition.

After a few moments, she voiced her concerns, "But, I'm still nervous myself. What about Ellerie? What if I'm wrong?"

"She'll be all right," Gerard pulled out of the parking spot. "We've got a tail on Roger."

"Good," Sable breathed.

He drove onto the main street and then glanced at her with a smile. "I wish I could take you to work with me. It sure would save a lot of time barking up the wrong trees." He chuckled.

She didn't laugh. When she didn't say anything for some time he looked at her, "I'm sorry, Sable. I guess I shouldn't have said that."

"No," she shook her head. "It's okay. I was just thinking."

"About what?" He glanced at her and then back at the road.

"Do you want me to help you with this case?" She turned so that her back leaned against the Bronco door and faced him.

"No." He shook his head, "I couldn't ask you to do that. It wouldn't be right."

"I think I should. It could be my chance to atone for what I did to Dan," her eyes lit up with hope in the possibility of righting her wrong.

"You didn't do anything to Dan, Sable. It just happened. People die every day. You can't save the world," Gerard reasoned.

"But I can save Ellerie or whoever is next on that killer's list," Sable said, sincere in her offer.

He looked at her, "It's too risky. I know your insights could move things along faster, but you could get hurt. It's too dangerous."

"I want to do it," Sable insisted.

"Let's let it drop for now." He took her hand and squeezed it. "I want you to take some time and really think this through."

"Okay, but it's not going to change anything," she shrugged. She needed redemption and this was her perfect opportunity. Not to mention, she felt the need to protect Ellerie. Just because she didn't feel anything foreboding for Ellerie right now, didn't mean that couldn't change in the future. She knew from experience that her predictions only saw a day or two into the future while murderous residue lingered on a person like an incriminating fingerprint.

Chapter 9

Gerard and Sable met Bronson and Mandy Reilly outside the Station House restaurant at the Chattanooga Choo Choo.

"Hey Ger, how you doing?" Bronson greeted Gerard with a handshake and a slap on the back.

"Doing great. You?" Gerard smiled happily and introduced Sable to Bronson and Mandy. Sable shook both their hands and again, she felt a charge of positive emotion from each of them. She didn't even register the other three's chatty banter because she was too busy trying to figure out what was going on with her kinetic abilities. Why was she suddenly feeling positive charges of energy from ordinary people? Normally, all she picked up on were the intense negative vibrations from criminals or victims. With everyone else she felt nothing in particular. But now it was as if her powers had expanded somehow or reversed polarity. Otherwise, she should have felt positive energy from someone in her past besides Gerard. Certainly she would have felt it from Ellerie before tonight.

She thought back, trying to pinpoint when the changes first took place and decided it all started with her first handshake with Gerard. He was the first person to give her a positive feeling. Could the intense positive exhilaration she felt from Gerard have altered her in some way? Or perhaps opening up to him about her past had changed something?

"Sable, honey, are you all right?" Gerard put his hand on her back. She'd mindlessly followed the three of them into the restaurant and sat down when Gerard pulled out her chair, but she hadn't responded to the last comment directed at her.

"I'm sorry. Did you ask me something?" She looked at Gerard as he sat down across from her. Bronson pulled out the chair next to Sable's for Mandy and took his place across from his wife.

"Bronson asked if you were enjoying your visit to Chattanooga," Gerard said.

"Oh, yes, I'm thoroughly enjoying it," she grinned and winked at Gerard. "You'll have to forgive me. I get in my own world sometimes. Poor Gerard's been kind to put up with me."

"Yeah, she's such a chore to tolerate," Gerard quipped, grinned, and squeezed her hand across the table. He seemed to sense that she grappled with something perplexing and could use his touch. Her countenance conveyed her gratitude.

Sable forced herself out of her thoughts and actively engaged in a pleasant conversation with Gerard's friends. She enjoyed listening to the waiters and waitresses who each took a turn on stage to perform. They all particularly enjoyed their own waiter, who did a first rate imitation of Elvis. Then, Bronson spent at least thirty minutes trying to persuade Gerard to join him in his thriving business. Finally, Mandy insisted that Bronson stop hounding his friend. Gerard looked relieved when Bronson let it drop.

Over the course of the evening, Sable learned a lot about Gerard from his friends. For example, he evidently hadn't been serious with anyone over the last couple years after experiencing a breakup with a girl he'd dated for a year. Also, he never brought dates on his Saturday night dinners with Bronson and Mandy. This was a first, and Sable felt flattered. She enjoyed getting to know Mandy and thought that given the opportunity, they'd probably become good friends. After dinner, the two couples walked around the station and then went their separate ways for the remainder of the evening.

When they arrived back at Sable's apartment they could see through the window that Ellerie and Roger were sitting on the couch talking.

"You want to come back to my place?" Gerard asked as he peeked in the window.

"What? You mean you don't want to run in there and interrogate Roger some more?" Sable teased.

Gerard chuckled, "No, I'd like to selfishly enjoy my evening with you." He winked.

She leaned her back against the door. "I don't know," she fiddled with the lapel of his sport coat. "Maybe we should just call it a night."

Gerard looked at his watch, "But it's only nine o'clock, and who knows when I'll get another day off. We could watch a movie."

She thought for a moment and then caved. "Okay, one movie and then you better get some rest. I know you've got to be tired from all the sight seeing we've been doing. Not much of a relaxing two days off for you."

"These two days have been just what the doctor ordered," he winked and led her by the hand up the flight of stairs to his apartment. He opened the door and she stepped in. "You'll have to excuse the mess. I'm not the neatest guy in the world."

"It's not bad," Sable grinned as Gerard raked a stack of newspapers off his couch and let it drop to the floor. He flipped on his wide screen television and handed Sable a stack of DVD's.

"Look through these while I change," he said and crossed to his bedroom.

Sable kicked off her heels and sat down on the couch with the movies.

After a few minutes, Gerard returned in a pair of gray cotton sweatpants and a white t-shirt that accentuated every muscle in his chest and arms. Butterflies started in her stomach, and she handed him a DVD. "How about *Paycheck*?"

"Good choice. Have you seen it?" he asked.

"No."

"You'll like it," he said as he put the disc in the machine and started it.

He sat down on the couch beside her and she stood up. "Do you have any soda?" she asked.

"Sure, I'll get you one." He started to rise.

"That's okay, I'm up." Sable went to the kitchen.

"The glasses are in the cabinet to the right of the fridge," Gerard said.

"You want something?" she asked.

"Yeah, whatever you're having," he yawned.

As the previews rolled, Sable returned from the kitchen carrying two glasses of orange soda to find Gerard sprawled out the length of the couch with his hands resting behind his head. She stood over him holding the two drinks. She wasn't sure where he expected her to sit. The only other place available was a bean bag chair. He sat up a little, took a glass from her and shifted on his side. He took a sip of the drink, set it on the coffee table and motioned for her to lie down beside him.

She took a big anxious gulp from her soda and set it on the coffee table next to Gerard's. He started the movie with the remote and again motioned for her to join him. Nervously, she lay down beside him. He put his arm around her waist, and they both shifted to their sides so they could see the TV.

Gerard kissed her neck and pulled her close, snuggling up behind her to watch the movie. Soon the movie captured her attention and before she knew it the story enthralled her. About half way through the movie, she made a comment to Gerard and realized the poor man had passed out from exhaustion. She felt a twinge of guilt for keeping him so occupied that he hadn't been able to rest on his days off. Then she smiled, contented to be near him as she finished watching the movie. When it was over, he still slept. Unwilling to leave his embrace, she adjusted the pillow she lay on, flipped off the TV and closed her eyes.

~*~

Sable's eyes opened wide, her heart pounding rapidly and her breathing shallow. The only thing penetrating the darkness was the digital clock on Gerard's entertainment unit. It read 3:27. She flipped over, facing Gerard. His arm was draped across her waist, and she pushed her hands to his chest.

"Gerard, wake up!"

"Hmmm? What?" came his groggy mumble.

"Wake up. We need to check on Ellerie!" she insisted.

"Mmmm?" he groaned. "Why?"

"I think she could be in trouble!" Sable stood up, sliding her foot along the carpet in search of her shoes. She stepped into one and pushed his chest harder.

"What time is it?" he sat up, wiping the sleep from his eyes and blinking to focus on the clock.

"We fell asleep," she tugged at his hand as she put on her other shoe. "Walk me back to my apartment so we can check on Ellerie. I have a bad feeling."

"Really?" he stood up and his palm reached for the small of her back. "What's wrong?"

"I don't know for sure, but I think she could be in trouble! Hurry up and put on your shoes and a jacket. She flipped on a lamp, and he squinted. Within a few minutes, Sable and Gerard arrived at her apartment and Sable opened the door.

She turned on a lamp and went straight to Ellerie's room. Quietly she crept in, stood over Ellerie's bed and listened for breathing. From the light streaming into the room she could see that her roommate was sound asleep. Sable crept back out, shut Ellerie's door and sighed with relief.

Gerard waited for her in the hall with a puzzled expression on his face. "What was that about?" he whispered. She stepped back toward the kitchen, and he followed her.

"I just got to thinking. Ever since I met you I haven't felt any negative sensations from anyone. Everything has been positive – friendship from Ellerie, Mandy and Bronson. Even what I felt from Roger couldn't be described as negative. It was more a feeling of compassion and pity for someone who's profoundly sad and scared. I woke up a few minute ago with this thought that perhaps my abilities have shifted polarity somehow! I mean, I never felt positive feelings from anyone before you. It was always dark and sinister or nothing at all. But now, I feel goodness, compassion, friendship, and love. What if my senses aren't working like they used to, and I can't predict anything anymore? What if Ellerie's in danger or Roger's a killer and I'm just not sensing it?"

An expression of unsettling fear filled Sable's eyes. Gerard hugged her, letting her head rest on his shoulder while he stroked her hair. "Maybe you just weren't looking for the positive before and now you are. You must have encountered positive people before, but you weren't open to them. Now you are."

"What if I'm closed to the negative now? I could be useless in protecting Ellerie!" she whispered.

"Ellerie will be fine. You leave protection to me. That's my job," he smiled and kissed her cheek. "You're exhausted and you need some rest." Without warning, he scooped her up and carried her to her bedroom. He sat down on her full size bed with her on his lap, pulled down her covers, and shifted her on to her bed.

"You get some sleep, and we'll figure this out in the morning," he leaned over and kissed her forehead.

"Thanks for putting up with my bizarre, mysterious behavior," she let her hands rest at the back of his neck and her fingers lace through his hair.

"You should know something about me." He winked with a dimpled grin, "I have a thing for mysterious women." He was just too handsome, too irresistible in the middle of the night hovering over her. She pulled his lips to hers, lingering, tasting their soft hot sweetness. Her heart pounded in her throat and her breathing grew shallow. His arms slipped around her back, pulling her toward him. Sable's hands trembled and slipped under his t-shirt until her palms rested flush against his muscular chest. His mouth teased its way from her chin to the hollow of her throat.

He lay beside her now. The way his lips grazed her neck, the warmth of his hands on her face, and his fingertips caressing her shoulders sent a charge throughout her body unlike anything she'd experienced. Why did she care if she couldn't feel the negative anymore? It had always been a curse anyway! He was the intoxicating cure that healed her pain. With every caress, every kiss, the horrors of the past melted away, replaced with an indescribable sweetness, an innocence she'd long since abandoned and never dreamed she'd recover.

~*~

Innocence… the word intruded upon Gerard's thoughts in the midst of a breathless, deepening kiss. Ignoring the word, his fingertips played with the soft skin just beneath the waist of her sweater.

Innocence…the word repeated forcefully, and Gerard sat up on the bed.

"What?" she stared at him, the fluorescent bulb in her closet the only thing penetrating the darkness and illuminating his troubled face.

"We both need some rest," he breathed heavily, his heart pounding as if he'd run a footrace.

"Right, you have work in a few hours," she bit her lip and continued to breathe more heavily than normal.

He stood up, pulled the covers over her, and kissed her forehead. "I'll lock up" he whispered just before he shut her bedroom door.

Once inside his apartment, Gerard flopped down on his bed and tried to figure out what had just happened. He'd never wanted a woman the way he wanted Sable, but somehow he knew that taking her now would be wrong. Sure, he went to enough Sunday school to know it was morally wrong, but morality was the last thing on his mind at four in the morning. He cared for her too much. Gerard could picture spending the rest of his life with her, and he couldn't hurt her this way. He couldn't taint her newfound innocence; couldn't derail her quest for redemption. The right time and place would come, but it would be after the proper promises were made.

Chapter 10

Gerard hovered over his bathroom sink brushing his teeth, wearing nothing but a towel around his neck and a pair of shorts. The doorbell rang, and he quickly rinsed his mouth and swiped the towel to his face.

"Just a minute," he called as he shoved a pile of laundry into his room and shut the bedroom door.

Again the doorbell rang. He trotted toward it and turned the knob. Gerard's eyes brightened with his smile, "Hi!"

"Good morning," Sable greeted, stepping into the apartment, putting her hands to his waist and lifting onto her tiptoes to kiss his cheek. She took a moment to enjoy the sensation of Gerard's slightly damp, freshly-shaved cheek against her own.

He shut the door behind her. "I – uh – I'm just getting ready for work."

"I know," she sat on the edge of the couch. "I'm going with you."

"You are?" he chuckled.

"That's right. We need to solve this case." She nodded her head with determination.

"We?"

"Yes, we!" her hands gestured indicating her determination and readiness to get started. His eyes examined her from head to toe - from her blue silk blouse, down to her navy dress pants and loafers.

She glanced at her attire. "What? Am I not dressed appropriately to be a tag-along cop?"

Gerard shook his head with his eyes closed and sighed, "You're dressed fine. And you're going to be a distraction."

"A distraction? I take offense to that! You know good and well that I'll save you hours in needless investigation of innocent people," she defended.

"What you save me in investigation time, you'll lose me in focus. My mind'll be occupied on ditching Reager so we can lock ourselves away in a cloak closet somewhere." His face was serious, but there was a twinkle in his blue eyes.

Sable's jaw dropped slightly at his remark, and she smiled, "But I guarantee it'll be the most fun you've ever had at work!"

"You're really serious about this?" he stepped a little closer to her. "You want to tag along today?"

"I do." She gave a cheery nod.

He glanced at the clock on his entertainment unit and stepped closer still, his hands warm and strong against her face, "Then I have to get something out of my system first, or I'll be useless with you itchin' under my skin all day."

She inhaled the scent of his aftershave. His soft lips lowered to hers, tantalizing her and then enveloping her in a fiery, all-consuming kiss. Her hands caressed his chiseled physique, starting at his waist and sliding up his torso over the breadth of his broad shoulders. He gathered her up in his arms, and lifted her until only the tips of her toes managed to remain on the floor. Then as abruptly as he'd taken her, he lowered her feet to the earth, kissed her tenderly, and released her. She stumbled a little as she attempted to regain her footing and composure. He turned, and her eyes followed his brisk departure to the bedroom where he shut the door behind him.

"Oh my," she sighed, holding her hands to her cheeks to cool the flush. "*That* was supposed to keep us from getting under each other's skin today?" she muttered.

A few minutes later Gerard emerged in his uniform and placed his cap squarely on his head. The sensation of his skin on her fingertips still lingered, and knowing what his chest looked and felt like under that uniform made him even more irresistible. Combined with the remnant scent of his aftershave on her cheek and the tingling on her lips from his recent attentions, Sable knew he wouldn't be the only one with focus problems.

"You ready?" he winked and extended his hand toward her. She laced her fingers through his and basked in the glow of excitement and love she always felt in Gerard's touch.

As they drove to the precinct, Gerard explained a few things, "To make this easier, you're not my girlfriend."

"Okay," she nodded and chuckled lightly. Considering he'd never referred to her as his girlfriend, she found it comical that he felt the need to emphasize the point.

"I mean," Gerard waved his hand as he spoke, "You are, but for the sake of the Captain and Reager... we aren't seeing each other."

"I suppose it wouldn't be too professional bringing your girlfriend to work with you," she smiled.

"No," he shook his head. "So we'll just say you're a psychic consultant brought in to help with the case,"

"A psychic?" Sable rolled her eyes with a smirk. "I'm hardly a psychic!"

"You do have psychic abilities, or you wouldn't be tagging along with me today," he pointed out.

"But a psychic? Please. It makes me sound like one of those kooks on television at three in the morning!"

"What then? How am I going to explain you riding along with us today?" He lifted his palm with the question.

"Just tell them I have intuitive empathetic abilities which you feel would prove beneficial in researching this particular case," Sable suggested and then realized how strange that sounded.

"All right, but it's easier just to say psychic," he muttered as he turned into the parking lot.

He opened her car door, but did not hold her hand as they approached the building.

"I think it would be best if we don't tell people how you do what you do or exactly how it works," Gerard suggested as he opened the precinct door for her.

"I agree," she nodded as she entered.

She followed him to his office. He took a seat behind his desk and turned on his computer. Sable sat in a chair across from him wondering how she could possibly disguise the way she felt about him. She'd have to draw upon some of her legal experience – her ability to remain cool when inside opposing feelings raged.

"Hey, McNally," Officer Reager stepped into Gerard's office and plopped down in a chair next to Sable.

"Hi," Gerard smiled.

"Did you have a good break?" Reager asked.

"Fantastic," Gerard looked straight at Sable, and she averted her gaze toward his diploma which hung on the wall. "You?"

"Good. Slept a lot." Reager looked expectantly at Sable, waiting for Gerard to make an introduction.

"Reager, this is Sable Graham, she's a criminal lawyer and consultant who's going to be helping us on these murder investigations. Miss Graham, this is my partner, Allan Reager." Gerard gestured from Sable to Reager.

Reager's eyes brightened as he extended his hand and flashed a flirtatious smile at Sable, "Nice to meet you, *Miss* Graham." Gerard rolled his eyes and shot a warning glance at his partner.

"Nice to meet you, Officer Reager," she smiled at the dark-haired man whose pearly white grin must have cost him thousands of dollars in bridgework.

"You're not from around here," Reager noted.

"No, I'm visiting from D.C." she said.

"McNally brought you all the way from Washington for this? You must be good!" Reager leaned back in his chair and crossed one leg over the other.

"No, I was just in the neighborhood," she shrugged.

Gerard eyed Reager's hand which still held Sable's. "Uhumm," Gerard cleared his throat. "We've got a lot of work to do today. Davis has been busy while we were goofing off." Gerard tossed a manila folder full of papers on the desk near Reager.

Reager released Sable's hand, took the papers and thumbed through them. Gerard rose, carrying another manila folder to the doorway. He poked his head out and waved the folder in the air. "Davis, hey Davis, could you please make us another copy of this?" Gerard shut the door. He came to stand directly behind Sable and handed her the folder, "You can look through this one."

"Thank you." She tried not to look at him. If she did, she knew that Reager would see the infatuation in her eyes.

With great attention, Reager read over his copy of the documents while Gerard squatted down next to Sable. He braced his hand on the back of her folding chair and read along with her. Distracted by his close proximity, she forced herself to actually read instead of staring numbly at the report. Gerard nodded when he'd completed reading the first page, and she flipped it to the second. The slight eye contact it took for her to look at him and make sure he'd read a page before flipping it was all the interaction they had until she turned the third page. Gerard adjusted his stance and let his hand rest on her lower back. He moved it warmly from side to side in a gentle massage motion.

Surprised by his intimate behavior right in front of his partner, Sable's eyes darted over at Reager who still meticulously studied the report. Gerard's hand caressed her back, and then his index finger began tracing something along skin. The alluring tickle of his finger gliding on the silk caused her pulse to quicken. She was no longer reading the page in front of her. All thoughts were on Gerard and his daring attentions. It took a minute or so before she realized he was spelling out words on her back.

Y-O-U-R-E   B-E-A-U-T-I-F-U-L

He traced through the letters a couple times before she fully registered the phrase. Her smiling emerald eyes briefly caught his just before they darted up at Reager.

At that moment, Davis tapped at the door and poked his head into the office. Gerard stood up and received the folder. "Thanks Davis," he took his seat behind his desk leaving Sable staring at the report, trying to force herself to focus back on the case instead of Gerard's flirtatious antics.

"So," Reager broke the silence, "We've got three women all apparently murdered by someone who wanted to make it look like a rape, but there's no medical evidence to prove it. We've got three reset computers, three women who used instant messenger or dating sites and one man who knew all three women but who has an alibi for all three nights in question."

"Right" Gerard nodded at Reager's recap.

"Any chance he's the murderer, and we can punch holes in those alibis?" Reager looked at Gerard.

"What are you suggesting?" Gerard lifted an eyebrow.

"Roger's brother looks an awfully lot like him. What if his brother took his place on the nights in question while Roger murdered those women?" Reager suggested.

"Roger Wesley didn't murder anyone," Sable insisted.

Reager's attention shifted to Sable, giving her an incredulous stare. "Pardon me, Miss, but how do you know that?"

Gerard's lips curled into a slight smile.

"I just know he didn't do it. He's not a murderer. I don't sense anything like that from him," Sable defended Roger and just as the words left her mouth, she regretted them.

"You don't *sense* anything like that?" Reager sneered and pointed his thumb toward Sable as his attention turned toward Gerard.

"Miss Graham has intuitive empathetic abilities which will prove beneficial in researching this particular case," Gerard rattled off Sable's suggested job description.

"She's a psychic? You brought a psychic in on this case?" Reager sat forward in his seat, and looked at Gerard as if he'd lost his mind.

"Look," a dimpled grin formed at the corners of Gerard's lips, his eyes darted toward Sable's perturbed expression, and then the smile faded from his face. He gestured for Reager to settle down. "She's a criminal lawyer, and she has some intuitive abilities that are going to help us out here."

"Does the Captain know about this?" Reager asked.

Gerard stood up and cleared his throat, "We can't be sitting around here wasting time. We've got work to do." He motioned for Sable to rise, and he escorted her to the door. The three of them left the precinct together, and Gerard opened the front door of the squad car for Sable.

"She's sitting up front?" Reager grumbled in Gerard's ear.

"Come on, be a gentleman for once, Reager," Gerard scolded after he shut Sable's door. He went around to the driver's side and reluctantly Reager slid in the back seat. Gerard started the engine.

"I thought we'd drop by Joy Stablemeyer's office again." Gerard suggested. "She said she had lunch with Jessica the day of the murder. Maybe we can learn something more from her. But first, I think Reager might be right about one thing. Roger's brother does look an awful lot like him, and he lives in the same house. What if he's involved somehow? Let's stop by there and then go downtown."

"Good idea." Happy to have his suggestion given credence, Reager settled back in his seat.

After they arrived in front of the Wesley's condominium, Gerard turned to look at Reager in the back seat. "One thing… don't mention to anyone about Sable's abilities. As far as anyone's concerned, she's just a criminal consultant. We don't want to put her in danger."

"Fine by me," Reager agreed. Sable could tell by the tone in his voice that he wasn't eager to look like a fool for having a psychic for a sidekick.

They walked to the door, Gerard knocked and Derrick answered. "Hello. If you're here to see my brother, he's already gone to work."

"Actually, we just had a few questions for you, if you don't mind," Gerard replied.

"Me?" Derrick put a finger to his chest.

"Please, just a few," Gerard gestured that they wished to enter, and Derrick opened the door wider to let them inside.

"We'll need to make this quick because I have a presentation at ten," Derrick warned.

"It won't take long," Reager assured.

"Oh, this is Sable Graham. She's a consultant on the case," Gerard introduced, and Sable extended her hand in greeting to the man. He shook her hand and sat down, motioning for them to be seated as well.

"How can I help you?" Derrick asked.

"Roger mentioned that you set up his instant messenger program. Are you the technical one in the family?" Reager asked.

"I'm a technical consultant," Derrick nodded. Reager's knowing eyes met Gerard's.

"Did you ever do any work on Jessica Honeycutt's computer?" Reager inquired.

"No. I primarily work with businesses. Jessica took her computer over to Computer Geeks," Derrick leaned his back against his chair.

"Did you ever chat with the women that Roger chatted with online?" Gerard asked.

"No," he shrugged. "I don't fool with that stuff."

"So you don't use online dating services or instant messenger for chatting?" Gerard asked.

"No, I use my instant messenger for communicating with clients," Derrick said.

"Do you know a Melanie Roberts or Kathy Mentone?" Reager asked.

"No," he shook his head negatively.

"How well did you know Jessica Honeycutt?" Reager leaned forward.

"Pretty well. She was over a lot. She, Joy and Roger spent a lot of time together," Derrick explained.

"How would you describe her? I mean personality wise. Do you think she was stringing Roger along?" Gerard asked.

"Jessica knew Roger liked her. There's no way she couldn't have known it. It was obvious to everyone," Derrick rolled his eyes. Something about the question, or perhaps the answer, annoyed him.

"So you think she was stringing him along?" Gerard inquired.

Derrick grew more animated, waving his arms as he spoke. "Sure she was. She was a nice person and all, but Roger spent way too much money on those two women. They used him, flirted with him, and he's just too nice a guy to put a stop to it. He's too afraid of rejection to just come out and ask Jessica to make a commitment."

"Interesting," Reager nodded.

Derrick looked at his watch and lowered his foot to the floor. "I really need to get out of here if I'm going to make my appointment."

"Just one more question, and we'll leave," Gerard held up an index finger. "Where were you on the nights of Saturday January 8th, Friday January 21st, and Tuesday, January 25th?"

Derrick reached for his briefcase by his chair and pulled out his planner. "Can you please repeat those dates?

"January 8th " Gerard said, letting his pencil hover over his notepad.

"I was painting my bedroom."

"Friday the 21st," Gerard prompted.

Derrick flipped the page, "I went to a birthday party for one of my clients."

"What about Tuesday, January 25th?" Gerard added.

"Tuesday night I was home working on a programming project," Derrick said.

Gerard flipped to a new page in his pad and handed it and a pen to Derrick. "Would you please write down the names and numbers of anyone who can corroborate your whereabouts on the evenings in question?"

Derrick's eyebrows furrowed with annoyance and again he examined his watch. He quickly scribbled a few lines on the pad and rose from his seat. He lifted his briefcase and crossed to the front door. Gerard, Reager and Sable followed him, leaving when he did.

"So what do you think?" Gerard asked as he backed out of the driveway.

"I think he's our man," Reager replied. "Overprotective older brother, seeking revenge on all the women who've strung his brother along. Perhaps even jealous that Roger got more women than he did."

Gerard glanced expectantly at Sable, "What do you sense?"

Sable sighed and shook her head side-to-side slightly, "I don't know. I didn't feel anything."

"Nothing?" Gerard asked.

"No." Sable shrugged and tried not to let her anxiety show. What if she'd lost her ability to sense danger, and she was actually harming rather than helping Gerard's investigation? What if he leaned on her intuitive abilities and the killer got away because of her?

"Where is that Computer Geeks store?" Reager asked. "Maybe we should stop by there since all three women took their computers there."

"Good idea," Gerard agreed. "I think it's over on Ringgold Road."

Chapter 11

When they arrived at the computer store, a lanky man with curly red hair and freckles greeted them from behind the counter. "Welcome to Computer Geeks, Officers. How may I help you?"

"We'd just like to ask the owner a few questions." Gerard flashed his badge.

"I'm Mike Nagle, the owner," the man took a moment to shake Gerard's hand and then continued to tinker with the open computer that sat on the counter in front of him.

"Could you please pull your records on three of your customers for us?" Reager asked.

"Sure, just a second," the man finished inserting the sound card into the machine and then turned toward another computer. He opened his customer program and asked Reager for the names. He printed a sheet on each woman and handed them to Reager who spread them out on the counter for everyone to see.

"So Jessica Honeycutt's been bringing her computer here the longest?" Sable noted.

"Yes, she's a friend of the family," the man answered. "The other two are newer customers within the last couple months. They both came in with spyware on their computer in December. We get a lot of business from spyware and viruses. Nasty things, but they do keep us in business." The man grinned.

"Where did the other two women hear about your store? Do you keep records on that?" Gerard asked.

"Sure," he pointed to a box on the page. "Melanie Roberts came in with a coupon, and it looks like Kathy Mentone did the same."

"You said Jessica was a friend of the family?" Sable asked.

"Yes, she and my cousin are best friends," Mr. Nagle answered.

"Who's your cousin?" Gerard asked.

"Joy Stablemeyer."

"Really?" Reager's voice held a hint of surprise. "And what does Joy do around here?"

"Joy's great. She helps with marketing and fills in on weekends so I can get a break," Mike leaned his palms against the counter.

"That's nice of her," Reager replied and Gerard quickly made a note of the fact on his notepad.

"Could you please take a look at some dates for us and tell us who was working on these nights?" Gerard handed Mr. Nagle a piece of paper with the three dates written on it.

Mike pulled up the schedule on the computer. "Looks like Joy and Hank were working on the 8th. The 21st Joy and Hank were working again, and I worked here by myself on the 25th."

"Who is Hank?" Reager asked.

"Hank Abernathy. He's a teenager who helps out on nights and weekends. He's seventeen – a senior at Lakeview High." Mr. Nagle explained.

"When would we be able to ask him a few questions?" Reager tapped a finger on the counter.

"He'll be here today after school – around 4:30," Mr. Nagle answered.

Reager continued to tap his index finger on the counter. "Do you happen to know if these three women were having any computer trouble recently – perhaps something that would require resetting their computer to factory settings?"

"No, why?"

"These three women are part of an investigation, and all three had their computers reset to factory settings on these dates." Gerard explained.

"Hmmm…" Mike Nagle scratched his curly red head. "Could have been a virus. There's one going around that does that. It's the Doomsday Virus - one of those that tends to sneak past antivirus software – especially if the person isn't good about updating their definitions."

"Interesting," Gerard raised his eyebrows and looked to Reager.

"Very," Reager agreed.

"So did these women ever have this virus that you know of?" Gerard turned the paperwork around so Mike Nagle could see it.

Mike looked at the ladies' records closely. "No record of it here. Guess not. Doesn't mean they hadn't been recently infected though."

"How long does it take from the time of infection until the computer resets?" Reager asked.

"It'll usually have done its damage within twenty-four hours," Mike replied.

"So when someone has a virus like that, do you make them bring the computer here or do you make house calls?" Reager asked.

"Either. A lot of times we just send someone out." Mr. Nagle shrugged. "It's easier for the customer."

"Who usually makes house calls?" Gerard asked.

"Oh, any one of the three of us might take a house call," Mr. Nagle replied.

Gerard scribbled on his notepad and then extended his hand to the store owner, "Thank you very much for your time." Mike shook each of their hands and they left.

Once they were back inside the car, Reager asked, "What do you make of that?"

"Looks like we've got another connection to those three women," Gerard replied and looked at Sable, "Sense anything?"

"No, not a thing," she shook her head and looked out the window. Discerning her concern, Gerard squeezed her hand which rested on the seat between them. She smiled at him, grateful for the recharge. Reager eyed the gesture from the back seat but didn't say anything. Gerard's hand didn't linger there long.

99

"I think we need to pay Joy Stablemeyer another visit," Reager suggested.

"Definitely," Gerard and Sable agreed simultaneously.

~*~

Joy Stablemeyer sat at her computer typing in a family's details to calculate a group health premium. Reager tapped at her open door and she turned in her chair.

"Officers," she smiled. "Come in and have a seat." She motioned toward the empty chairs across from her.

"How are you doing today?" Gerard extended his hand in greeting. She shook it and Reager's. "This is Miss Graham; she's consulting on our investigation into Jessica's murder."

Joy extended her hand to Sable who took it. Gerard could tell by the spaced out expression on Sable's face that she felt something. When Sable didn't release Joy's hand, but simply stood there dazed, almost trance-like, Joy quirked an annoyed eyebrow at her and tugged her hand away.

Gerard stepped toward Sable and put his hands on her shoulders, looking into her eyes, "Do you happen to have some water?" Gerard asked Joy. "Miss Graham has a touch of epilepsy. She'll snap out of it in a minute and a sip of water always helps afterwards."

"Oh, my! Poor thing. Of course, I'll go get her some," Joy stepped around Sable and Gerard and out the door.

"Sable," Gerard put his hands to her cheeks and redirected her gaze toward his face. His touch pulled her back out of her daze and her eyes grew frightened.

"She did it," Sable whispered.

"What did she say?" Reager asked.

Sable repeated at a whisper, "She did it. She's the one."

A couple of seconds later, Joy re-entered the office carrying a bottle of mineral water and handed it to Gerard. "Thank you," he nodded at Joy, trying not to let his expression betray the knowledge he possessed. "Here, take a sip of this, it'll make you feel better." He unscrewed the top of the bottle and handed it to Sable. He directed her to a chair where she sat down. Gerard knelt down eye level with Sable with his back to Joy, "You had another one of your seizure episodes." He winked at her.

"Oh, I'm sorry. It's always so embarrassing when that happens." Sable apologized and nervously took a sip of her drink.

"Are you okay now?" Gerard asked.

"I'm fine, thanks."

Gerard stood and then he and Reager each took a chair to the left of Sable. Joy sat down behind her desk facing them.

"So have you had any luck locating the killer?" Joy asked.

"Possibly," Gerard shrugged. "It does appear that all three women knew your friend Roger. We don't know how he did it, but we suspect he's the murderer."

"Roger would never hurt anyone!" Joy insisted. "He's too kindhearted and timid to do anything like that!"

"Yet, we just can't get around the fact that he's the connection between them all. I'd say it's a matter of time before we pull him in." Reager replied.

"It's not Roger, You're barking up the wrong tree. Roger is the sweetest, most giving man on the planet. If anything, he's too kind, too sweet, and people take advantage of him."

"You sound as if you're a little infatuated with him," Sable noted.

"Me? Infatuated with Roger? No! We're just friends. He was in love with Jessica." Joy scoffed, but it was apparent Sable had hit a nerve.

"I see," Gerard nodded. "We just had a question or two for you that we forgot to ask the other day. You said that you had lunch with Jessica on the day of the murder. Where did you eat?"

"I got takeout at Formosa and we met at her office," she replied.

"That's a Chinese restaurant?" Reager jotted down the information on a notepad.

"Yes."

"Explains the soy sauce," Gerard noted. "Jessica had soy sauce on her blouse, and we thought perhaps she'd been out to dinner, but I guess it was just left over from lunch. Would Jessica leave a stain on her blouse all day?"

"Knowing Jessica she didn't even notice there was a stain. She could be oblivious sometimes," Joy replied.

"Oblivious to what?" Sable asked.

"Oblivious to anything – everything. She couldn't see how Roger felt about her. She couldn't see how I – She just didn't notice things. Too busy working and lost in her own world."

"Roger seems like he's bouncing back fine though," Gerard offered.

"How's that?" Joy asked.

"I ran into him the other night. He was out on a date with a girl in my building." Gerard ran across his chin. "Ellerie – yeah – Ellerie Tash is her name, I think." Gerard ignored Sable's annoyed expression. "Thank you for your time," Gerard rose from his seat and Reager and Sable followed suit.

"Let me know if you find out who really did it," Joy requested.

"Oh, we will, you'll be one of the first to know," Reager assured.

When they got back to the car and shut the doors, Sable tore into Gerard, "Why in the world did you give that woman Ellerie's name? Do you want her to be next? Why did you do that?"

"Because I know why she did it and how." Gerard started the engine. "And if I'm right, she'll try again, only this time we'll be waiting for her."

Chapter 12

Sable studied her steakhouse menu vacillating between shrimp or chicken. Reager, who sat across the booth from she and Gerard, debated between the porterhouse and the T-bone. Gerard knew what he wanted. He always ordered the T-bone, baked potato and a house salad. Sable's decision would have been much easier if she hadn't been so distracted by Gerard's hand resting on her thigh beneath the table, concealed from Reager's view.

The waitress appeared and Sable set down her menu.

"Will this be separate tickets?" the waitress' pencil waved from Reager to Gerard.

"Yes," Reager answered. "I'll have the porterhouse, French fries, a house salad with Ranch dressing and a large Coke," Reager handed the waitress his menu.

"You two are together?" the waitress deduced, probably because from the angle she was standing she could see Gerard's hand tracing along Sable's thigh.

"No," Sable replied.

"Yes," Gerard looked at Sable with a nod, "I've got it." Reager shot Gerard a suspicious glance. "She's helping us out today. I've got it."

The waitress looked at Sable expectantly and her eyes darted down at Gerard's hand which continued to spell something on Sable's leg. "I'll have the shrimp with pasta and a house salad with honey Dijon dressing and a Sprite," Sable said.

"I'll have the T-bone, baked potato, with house salad and honey Dijon dressing and a diet Coke," Gerard smiled at the waitress who giggled slightly, took the menus and left.

Reager leaned his interlaced fingers on the table and studied Gerard with expectant eyes. "So, tell us your theory."

Gerard still traced along Sable's leg, "Sable, why don't you tell us more about what you sensed back there?"

Sable's pulse had already set to palpitating and her face flushed from the phrase Gerard traced repeatedly on her thigh:

I L-O-V-E Y-O-U   I L-O-V-E Y-O-U
I L-O-V-E Y-O-U

Gerard and Reager waited patiently for her reply. She put her hand atop Gerard's to stop his distracting, yet thrilling, message. With him doing that, she kept envisioning late nights curled up on the couch, breakfast in bed, and a cozy home with toddlers jumping into the arms of their handsome father. She wasn't anywhere near the present murder investigation.

"Uh, well," she put her hand to her flushed cheek, wishing her heart would stop thumping so violently. "She's definitely the killer. It's a horribly cold feeling killer's convey. I saw violent encounters with the victims. Based on the pictures I saw of the three women in the file and what I saw when I shook Joy's hand, she hit Kathy over the head with some kind of sculpture while she sat at her computer. Melanie she struck with a lamp as she walked from one room to the other, and Jessica she stabbed in the back with a kitchen knife while Jessica leaned over looking for something in the refrigerator. "

"You got all of that from shaking her hand for less than a minute?" Reager's brown eyes widened.

"It was extremely vivid – probably because there were multiple recent murders." Sable swirled a straw in her water glass.

"Did you sense anything else – like why she did it or why the computers were reset to factory settings?" Gerard asked.

"I don't know about the computers. But the motive was jealousy – intense, raw jealousy," Sable replied.

"Of who?" Reager asked.

"Roger," Gerard laced his fingers with Sable's under the table.

"She's killing anyone who catches Roger's interest," Sable added.

"Right," Gerard nodded.

"So how do the computers fit in exactly? It obviously has something to do with the computer virus and her working at Computer Geeks on weekends – right?" Sable leaned her elbow on the table, looked at Gerard and waited for him to expound on his theory.

"Here's what I think happened. Joy wanted Roger for herself so she set out to eliminate all the women that stood in her way. Having been in Roger's house frequently, she could easily look at the usernames of the women with whom he chatted. She then set up her computer to simulate Roger's instant messenger account and sent them spyware. Next, she sent them a coupon which they used to get their computer fixed. "

"So that introduced them to Computer Geeks as the place to call when they had computer trouble," Reager interjected.

"Right, then she waited for a time when she knew she'd be working and sent the two women the Doomsday virus. They naturally called Computer Geeks, and Joy took the call. She didn't log it in the company computer, but went out under the pretense of fixing their computers and killed them instead." Gerard explained.

"We should get Davis to check the phone records for Computer Geeks and for each of the women," Reager suggested.

"Definitely," Gerard agreed.

"What about Jessica? They'd been friends for years. You really think she'd kill her best friend?" Reager looked as if he still wasn't convinced.

"Jessica was the last straw. Even with the other women out of the way, Roger was still too hung up on Jessica to notice Joy. So she had to kill her too. She could easily just show up at Jessica's whenever she wanted to," Gerard reasoned.

"That's why there was no date on her schedule for Tuesday night," Reager's eyes widened with understanding.

"Right. There was no date. Joy just stopped by and murdered her then." Gerard scratched his head, 'The only thing I can't figure out is why Jessica's computer was wiped clean. There's no reason to infect Jessica's computer as an excuse for being there."

"It could have been unintentional," Reager suggested.

"What if the other two women passed the virus to Roger and then Roger inadvertently passed it to Jessica?" Sable offered.

"Possibly, but wouldn't Roger's computer have been affected?" Gerard asked.

"Let's call him and find out," Reager pulled his cell phone from his pocket along with a suspect list and dialed Roger's work number. "Mr. Wesley? Hi, this is Officer Reager. We have a quick question we'd like to ask you. Has your computer recently been infected with a virus?" He listened for a few moments to Roger's reply. "Okay. Also, do you log on to your ChattCowboy account from work or only from home?" Reager nodded his head, thanked Roger for his time and disconnected the call.

"So?" Gerard prompted.

"He hasn't had a virus on his computer. Derrick keeps all his virus definitions updated and scans three times a week. He only gets on his chat account from home. So Joy could easily impersonate Roger by logging on with his chat username when she knows Roger's not home. But Jessica didn't get the virus from Roger."

"Maybe Jessica got the virus coincidentally?" Sable shrugged.

"Possibly. But I guess it really doesn't matter. We know Joy did it and that jealousy was her motive." Gerard said. "The problem is that your intuitive visions aren't going to stand up in court, nor will my theory without proof. So that leaves us only one alternative."

"Lure her into trying it again with Ellerie," Sable felt a sick foreboding feeling sweep over her.

"Don't worry," Gerard squeezed her hand. "I won't let anything happen to Ellerie."

"Who's Ellerie?" Reager glanced from Gerard to Sable.

"Ellerie Tash is a friend in my building – Sable's roommate – who is dating Roger Wesley."

"Oh," Reager's eyes widened. "And you're going to use her as bait? What if she doesn't want to cooperate?"

"I don't plan on using Ellerie as bait. We'll just get one of our female officers to impersonate Ellerie. She'll never be in danger," Gerard explained.

"But what if she comes after Ellerie at a time you don't suspect?" Sable worried.

"She won't change a system that works. I wouldn't be surprised if Ellerie turns up with a computer virus in the next few days and a coupon for Computer Geeks," Gerard said just as the waitress appeared with their meal.

~*~

Gerard accompanied Sable to her door while Reager waited in the squad car.

"And you'll see about getting Ellerie a computer to use over the next few days so hers isn't damaged?" Sable asked.

"Yeah, I'll call Davis and tell him to get one ready. I'll bring it by tonight."

"Thanks," Sable fiddled with her key chain. "You sure you don't want me to go with you to interview the teenager?"

"No, I think we can take it from here," Gerard took her keys from her and unlocked the door. "Now that we know Joy did it, I don't want to draw any more attention to you."

She nodded and started to enter the apartment, but Gerard leaned his back against the doorframe with one foot outside the apartment and the other inside, blocking her between them. Just as she looked down at his foot, he pulled her against him, holding her in his arms. The single dimple on his cheek deepened and his twinkling blue eyes communicated volumes.

"Thank you." His voice grew deep and sincere.

"For today? You're welcome. I enjoyed helping out."

"I meant thank you for making me love again. I didn't think I could." There was adoration in his eyes.

"Me either," she whispered just before his lips met hers. She loved his kisses. That first night she'd taken his hand, she'd seen and felt the possibilities between them, but nothing could compare with his kiss or his arms securely enfolding her. Each time they touched, her soul surged with an inexpressible, almost sacred poignancy. The sensation throughout her body was akin to the comforting relaxation of a hot shower on a cold morning or the sun's warming rays on a mild spring day. The visions that filled her heart and mind grew more vivid with each encounter - a home, a life together, children, laughter, long loving nights and precious blissful days.

He hugged her tight and whispered into her ear, "I've got to go, but I'll stop by this evening to explain things to Ellerie and bring her a computer."

"Okay."

He kissed her cheek and released her. He turned back and waved just as he walked down the stairwell.

~*~

Gerard hooked up the machine Davis had given him in the spot where Ellerie's computer had been. He'd moved hers to her bedroom with strict instructions not to go online with it until they solved the case.

"Davis says we just need to download your instant messenger program again and set up your account here, and we'll be good to go," Gerard said as he powered on the computer.

"I can do that," Ellerie slid onto the swivel chair by the computer.

"What do we do next?" Sable sat on the couch and Gerard took a seat next to her.

"We watch and wait," Gerard said. "Oh and Ellerie, never mention to anyone that you have a roommate. I don't know how much Joy knows about you, but we don't want to make it harder for her to do her thing."

"You mean, as in murder me?" came Ellerie's morbid retort.

"Ellerie!" Sable scolded. She didn't even want her friend joking about such things.

"We don't want to scare her off. We want it to be easy for her to do what she usually does. Once we get the coupon and the virus, we'll have one of the female officers with your same hair color and characteristics take your place in the apartment," Gerard explained.

"Where will we go?" Sable asked.

"We can stay at my mom's. She has room," Ellerie suggested. "She only lives about ten minutes from here."

"Good, that's perfect," Gerard looked at the computer monitor to see how the instant messenger installation progressed. "On second thought, maybe you both should go to your mother's now and let us handle things here."

"No way!" Ellerie's hand rose in a halting motion. "I love my mom and all, but I'm not staying there any more than I have to! Let's just wait until she makes a move and then we can leave."

"Then stay at my place. It would probably be best for our female officer to be here from the start so that if Joy is watching, she'll see her and assume she's you."

"I get it." Ellerie shook her index finger at Gerard, "You're just trying to steal my maid! This is all about getting Sable to come make your apartment sparkle!" Ellerie laughed.

"Yep, you caught me. That's it. I don't give a flip about your lives. I just want my floors clean enough to eat on," Gerard quipped.

"Now we know," Sable eyed him knowingly and pushed Gerard's chest. "That's what it's all been about. You saw Ellerie's apartment that night, found out I cleaned it, and everything since then has been an elaborate ploy to seduce me into becoming your housekeeper!"

"You've found me out," he chuckled and pulled her onto his lap. "But you don't know the half of it. I want a whole lot more than a maid!" he raised and lowered his eyebrows flirtatiously.

"Oh brother, you two really need to get a room," Ellerie droned and spun back around to the computer, fiddling with the installation program so she wouldn't have to watch the open display of affection.

A few minutes later, the software installation completed and Ellerie finished setting up her instant messenger account.

Gerard cleared his throat, "Seriously, you two should stay at my place. I have an extra room with two twin beds. You could stay there and I'll get Officer Johansen to stay here and deal with the computer situation."

"Poor woman. Does she know she's going to be used as shark bait?" Ellerie quipped.

"We talked with her today. We'll have other officers around for backup. Nothing will happen to her," Gerard assured.

~*~

That evening, Ellerie and Sable packed up a few things and settled into the spare room at Gerard's apartment. Officer Julie Johansen arrived to take Ellerie's place. She had the same auburn hair, similar build and could have passed as Ellerie's sister. Joy certainly wouldn't know the difference having never met Ellerie in person.

When Gerard kissed Sable goodnight outside her bedroom door, he felt grateful that Ellerie stayed in the apartment too. Otherwise he might forget his promise to himself. He slipped under the covers and tossed and turned for nearly an hour trying to get her off his mind. He'd known the woman for less than a week and thoughts of marriage were already congealing. As crazy as he'd been over Ally, he'd never seriously considered marrying her.

He tried to pinpoint what made him so completely head over heels for Sable. She was beautiful, no doubt about that. But he'd dated attractive women before. There was more to her than an outward beauty. He wasn't entirely certain if it was her intuitive abilities, but he loved the air of mystery about her and the way she genuinely cared for people.

Ironically enough, as much as she liked things neat and orderly, she was surprisingly low maintenance and easy to be with. Most orderly women he'd known were hard to handle. Nothing suited them. They were difficult to please, and he ended up running around in circles, yet never able to satisfy them. Not Sable. She didn't make demands. Yet, the relationship was new. Things could change in time.

Bottom line, Sable brought out the best in him. He wanted to protect her, care for her and provide for her. He liked how he felt about himself when he was with her. These were the thoughts that bounced through his mind like a ping pong ball in a Japanese tournament until he finally turned the television on and let the drone lull him to sleep.

Chapter 13

Wednesday evening Gerard, Ellerie and Sable sat around the kitchen table in Gerard's apartment playing UNO.

Sable tossed a red seven on the discard pile and asked Gerard, "So how's the investigation going?"

"We got the phone records back," he said, and threw down a red six. "They show that the first two victims made calls to Computer Geeks within twenty-four hours of their murders."

Sable's eyes widened, "That's good to hear - more proof mounting."

Gerard gritted his teeth and quirked his head to the side. "Still, that doesn't prove anything."

"How's my double doing?" Ellerie pointed her thumb over her shoulder, indicating the direction of her apartment.

"She's monitoring things, still no viruses or coupons for Computer Geeks," Gerard shook his head.

"As much as I know you and Sable love playing house together with me as your chaperone, I'd really like to go home to my own apartment," Ellerie grumbled and tossed down a card.

Gerard shook his head. "I'm sorry, El, but Joy is probably waiting and watching. As long as she is, you better stay here."

"Well, it's wearing on my nerves!" Ellerie's face puckered into a frown. Sable put down a card.

"What?" Gerard waved his hand toward the living room. "You mean you don't enjoy staying here and watching Sable turn my apartment into a showcase of cleanliness?"

Sable backhanded Gerard's shoulder with a playful tap.

"Oh, it's thrilling to behold," Ellerie rolled her eyes. After Gerard put down his card, Ellerie pronounced UNO and laid down a green six.

Sable grumbled and drew three cards. Gerard threw down a card, but it did not keep Ellerie from winning the game.

"Well, I'm off to bed," Ellerie stood up and stretched her hands high above her head with a yawn. "I'm going in to work early tomorrow. So if I don't see you two, have a good day."

"Why so early? You sure are spending a lot of time at the office lately." Sable stacked the cards and looked up at her friend.

"It's the next best thing to home," Ellerie shrugged and gave Gerard an accusatory glare. "Some people won't let me go home, so I may as well stay at the office where at least I have *some* of my things around me."

Gerard shook his head with a chuckle, "It'll all be over soon enough."

Ellerie walked toward her bedroom. "It better be!"

~*~

When Sable awoke Thursday morning, she looked over at Ellerie's unmade bed and glanced at the clock. Ellerie had already left for work On this particular morning, Ellerie had left her bed unmade as usual. Normally, Sable would have just shut the door and gone on, but since she shared the room with Ellerie, she couldn't tolerate the mess. After making her own bed, she went to Ellerie's. The moment she touched Ellerie's pillow a cold icy sensation seized her. No vision, no clue as to where or when it would happen, but Sable could not deny it. Ellerie was in danger – deep danger! Sable's heart raced and she ran to Gerard's room and flung open the door without knocking. He'd just gotten out of the shower and hurried to pull his bathrobe tighter around him.

He took one look at Sable's face and exclaimed, "What's wrong?"

"It's Ellerie! She's in danger. Get dressed, we have to go to her," Sable ordered.

"Where is she?" he asked.

"She got up early and went to work. She's in trouble!" Sable motioned for him to hurry.

He closed the door and finished dressing. "Call the precinct. The number's on the fridge!" he yelled through the door. "And tell them to send a car over to Ellerie's work. Then try to reach her on her cell."

"Good idea," Sable crossed to the kitchen to follow Gerard's orders.

He sat down on the bed to pull on his socks and shoes and then joined Sable in the kitchen. "Did you get Ellerie?"

"No, she's not picking up her cell and the office isn't routing her phone calls to her desk. I guess it's too early since they really aren't open yet."

"How do you know she's in danger?" Gerard asked.

"Her pillow. I touched it to make her bed and I just knew... she's in trouble, Gerard. We need to find her now!" Sable grew more anxious by the minute.

"All right... It's going to be all right." He put his hands on her shoulder. "You've had them send a car to her office – right?"

"They said they would, but I couldn't tell them exactly where she is in the building. I only know the company name and the company's number. I usually have to ask for her extension so I don't know where she is in the building. We've got to go now!" Sable started toward the front door. She pulled her coat from the rack.

"We will. It's going to be all right," Gerard soothed and helped Sable with her coat. They hurried from the apartment to his Bronco.

~*~

Ellerie sat at her computer developing a new company brochure. She heard a light tapping and looked up to see the woman from housekeeping at her office door.

"Come in. My basket's plenty full this morning. Been fighting with this stupid brochure for hours and still can't get it right," Ellerie sighed in frustration and turned back to her computer monitor. The cleaning woman stepped in and shut the door. Ellerie heard the door latch and glanced over her shoulder. "You're new, aren't you?'

"Yeah," the woman came around to the back of Ellerie's desk and stood by her. Ellerie reached beneath her desk to retrieve her waste basket. As she did so, Joy Stablemeyer pulled a telephone cord from her pocket and wrapped it around Ellerie's neck, and pulled it tightly. Ellerie fought back by rolling her chair backwards, pinning Joy between the chair and the wall. She slammed her so hard that a hanging picture jarred loose and fell, hitting Joy on the head. The unexpectedness of it caused Joy to turn, giving Ellerie a window of opportunity to yank the cord and pry it from her neck. It was enough to catch an agonizing breath and scream. Joy pulled harder, jerking the plastic against Ellerie's neck, asphyxiated her. Ellerie's fingers were caught between the cord and her own neck.

As Ellerie struggled to catch her breath, the excruciating, searing pain nearly forced her to lose consciousness. At that moment, she heard pounding at her door.

"Ellerie are you in there? Are you all right?" Gerard yelled from the other side.

The sound of his voice gave Ellerie the resurging energy she needed to fight harder. Again she slammed her chair into Joy, knocking the wind out of her. Ellerie could hear Gerard and Sable's voices yelling from the other side. The loud pounding continued as Gerard and two officers slammed their shoulders into the door.

Ellerie fought to maintain consciousness as time after time the men threw themselves against the heavy door. Unable to withstand the pain or lack of oxygen any longer Ellerie's eyes closed and her body relaxed into the darkness.

Finally the door broke and the men burst into the room to find Ellerie's head lying limp on her desk. Joy had shoved the phone cord in her pocket. "I just came in and found her this way," Joy panted her lame excuse.

"Yeah, right!" Gerard pointed his revolver at her, seizing the murderess as Sable ran to Ellerie in tears.

"Ellerie!" Sable cried. She put her hands on Ellerie's shoulders and tried to rouse her friend.

"Check for a pulse," Gerard ordered as he cuffed Joy and one of the other officers stated her rights.

"It's weak, but it's there," Sable replied. She hit the emergency number on her cell phone.

Soon an ambulance arrived and Sable watched them place Ellerie's weakened body on the stretcher. She buried her head against Gerard's shoulder as painful tears stung her eyes and caught in her throat. If only they'd gotten there sooner!

~*~

"I came as soon as I heard about it on the radio. I still can't believe Joy would do something like this!" Roger shook his head as he peeked through the window of Ellerie's hospital room. "How is Ellerie doing?"

"She's going to be fine. She put up a good fight and didn't lose that much oxygen," Gerard answered.

"We were able to talk with her about an hour ago, but she's resting comfortably now," Sable explained. "Well, as comfortably as you can when you've been cut and strangled by a plastic telephone cord!" Sable stared at Ellerie and brushed a tear from her cheek.

"I'm just sick about this. There was no call to do this to Ellerie. We were just friends. I even told Joy that a few nights ago. I told her that I enjoyed the date with Ellerie but that I didn't think it would go anywhere romantically," Roger leaned his fist against the wall and stared at Ellerie sleeping.

"I don't think she's mentally right," Gerard replied. "Reager called and said she cracked on the way to the police station and explained how she did it all. They warned her that she should wait for her lawyer, but she spilled it all anyway. She's so obsessed over you that she couldn't stand anyone else near you – even as your friend."

Roger shook his head, a sad expression on his face. "How did she do it?"

"It all happened the way we thought." Gerard's eyes met Sable's. He squeezed her hand, then he looked at Roger and explained how Joy had used the viruses and the coupons to reach the first two women and had snuck up on Jessica from behind during what should have been a casual visit. Evidently she never planned for the virus to make its way to Jessica's computer. The coincidental infection of her computer had been a turning point in the investigation that Joy had never planned on.

"Did she say why she attacked Ellerie at work instead of in her home like she did the others?" Sable asked.

"That's my fault," Roger interjected. "I told her about you interrogating me the other night and about Sable staying with Ellerie. She had to have known it wasn't safe to attack Ellerie at her apartment." Roger's countenance darkened with remorse. He ran his hand through his hair, then let it fall to his leg, "I even showed her a picture of Ellerie when she wanted to know what she looked like!"

"Guess we didn't cover that base too well," Gerard shook his head. "I should have told you we suspected Joy. I just wasn't sure we could trust you not to warn her."

"I understand," Roger nodded.

"But it's over now and Ellerie will be fine," Gerard put his arm around Sable and hugged her.

Epilogue

Sable sat next to Gerard in his Bronco as he drove toward their honeymoon cabin in Gatlinburg. He'd planned it all, wanting to surprise her. She looked at him, thinking of the road that had brought her here six months earlier. She smiled at his handsome face, and he glanced over to catch her eye.

"What?" he asked.

"I was just thinking of how different my life is now," she said. Adoration shimmered in her eyes.

He put his hand over hers and gave it a squeeze.

"To think that I used to only sense the darkness, only see the negative. Then I came to Georgia and found you. Everything's changed. You saved me." She let her finger trace along his cheek.

Gerard put his arm around her shoulder, and she snuggled against his side. Sable thought about Dan Vanderhoff and all the other people she'd worked with in D.C. She realized now that they were good people, but she'd been so afraid to feel that she hadn't allowed herself to sense the positive in others. Not until a profoundly good man touched her heart did she awaken to the beauty that had been there all along.

Gerard's voice broke into her thoughts, "Bronson said he didn't know how he was going to get by without you at the agency for a whole week."

Sable chuckled, "Well, he survived just fine before I came along."

119

"You've spoiled him with your gifts. He's getting lazy already - leaning on you to sense what's going on instead of using his investigative abilities," Gerard had a teasing tone to his voice.

"Oh, Bronson's investigative abilities are still intact. He's good at what he does," Sable defended her employer.

"So are you." Gerard kissed her forehead.

Within the hour, they reached the cabin Gerard had rented for their honeymoon. He parked the car and came around to open her door. The second she stepped out, he scooped her in his arms and carried her to the door. Gerard let her stand for only a moment while he unlocked the cabin and then lifted her once more.

She giggled as he carried her across the threshold, kicked the door closed with his foot, and crossed the room to a couch. He plopped down with her in his lap and pulled her into his kiss.

Sable sighed, feeling content as she nestled into Gerard's embrace. She thought back on the beautiful wedding they'd had earlier that morning. Bronson served as best man, and Ellerie as her maid of honor. It was a simple ceremony, only their closest friends and family. It unfolded just as they had envisioned it.

The fire crackled and popped in the rock fireplace, and a bouquet of two dozen red roses rested on the coffee table. Sable inhaled deeply of their aromatic scent.

She looked down at the arms that surrounded her and then up into her husband's handsome face. The firelight shimmered in his pale blue eyes. His hand caressed her cheek, and his fingers sifted through her raven locks. Gerard's dimple deepened as he admired his bride. Then, his face lowered to hers as it had a thousand times in her visions. She felt the sweet texture of his lips to hers and sensed the immensity of his love in the rhythm of his touch. With the fulfillment of her vision upon her, Sable's heart swelled with devotion for the man who had rescued her from the dark loneliness of night and delivered her to the light of a resplendent day.

About the Author

Marnie L. Pehrson was born and raised in the Chattanooga, Tennessee area. An avid enthusiast of family history, Marnie integrates elements of the places, people and events of her Southern family and heritage into her historical fiction romances. Marnie's life is steeped in Southern history from the little town of Daisy that she grew up in to the 24 acres bordering the famous Chickamauga Battlefield upon which her family resides.

Marnie and her husband Greg are the parents of six children. She is the founder of multi-denominational SheLovesGod.com which hosts the annual SheLovesGod Virtual Women's Conference the 3rd week of October each year.

Marnie works with talented individuals who have a message to share. Through writing and teaching she gives people the principles behind success - the laws that bring both personal and professional blessings. Then she offers them practical automated tools for creating their own WOW online. You may visit her projects through www.PWGroup.com.

You may also read more of her work at www.MarniePehrson.com and www.CleanRomanceClub.com. Marnie welcomes reader comments and may be reached at marnie@marniepehrson.com or by calling 706-866-2295.

Other Books by Marnie Pehrson

Angel and the Enemy - Best Seller!
Historical fiction, 287, pages, ISBN: 0-9729750-9-8
The War between the States is raging and Angelina Stone's world is falling apart. Her beloved father lies rotting in a Union prison and when her Georgia home is invaded by Yankee officers, Angelina knows she will never be the same again. Will Angelina be able to overcome her fears, lay prejudice aside, and learn to trust? When the stakes are high, will she risk losing everything? Only by doing so can she face the demons of the past and win the battle that rages in her own heart -- a heart that is eternally tethered to ... the enemy.

The Patriot Wore Petticoats
Historical fiction, 224, pages, ISBN: 0-9729750-4-7
Daring "Dicey" Langston, the bold and reckless rider and expert shot, saves her family and an entire village during the American Revolution. Having faced British soldiers, rushing swollen rivers, the "Bloody Scouts," and the barrel of a loaded pistol, nothing had quite prepared this valiant heroine for the heart-pounding exhilaration she'd find in the arms of one brave Patriot. Based on a true story about the author's fourth great-grandmother.

Beyond the Waterfall
Historical Fiction, 136 pages, paperback ISBN: 0-9729750-7-1
Jillian's feet were precariously planted in two worlds: the Cherokee nation on the brink of extermination, and the world where Jesse Whitmore belonged. On her first meeting with him, the charming and handsome merchant had set her young heart ablaze. Yet, could she trust him? Or was he just like all the other white men she'd encountered? Would he stand beside her while she witnessed her nation ripped apart, or would he join the ranks of the powerful greedy to betray her? Based on family history and local legend.

Hannah's Heart
Historical Fiction, 162 pages, paperback, ISBN: 1-59936-012-8
Hannah Jamison is ready to give her heart away. Unfortunately, the man she's falling for shows no indication of ever reciprocating her feelings. When Mother Nature intervenes in her behalf, all Hannah's dreams seem to be coming true . . . until she discovers that following her heart means losing the ones she loves. Is Hannah willing to pay the price?

Waltzing with the Light
LDS Historical Fiction, 268 pages, Paperback, ISBN: 0-9729750-6-3
Nestled within the valley of the Appalachian mountains, Daisy, Tennessee, seemed like a sleepy little town until depression-era drifter, Jake Elliot, entered it and knocked on the front door of the yellow farm house and met Mikalah, the oldest of the Ford children. Little did he know how his life and his heart would be affected from that moment forward.

Rebecca's Reveries
Historical Fiction, 224 pages, paperback, ISBN: 0-9729750-2-0
Rebecca Marchant had led a sheltered life until she found herself inexplicably drawn to the home of her father's youth. Surrounded by the historical landscape of the Chickamauga Battlefield in Georgia, Rebecca finds herself plagued by haunting dreams and vivid visions of Civil War events. As Rebecca walks a mile in another girl's moccasins through her visions and dreams she learns about compassion, forgiveness, temptation and the power of true love.

You Can't Fly If You're Still Clutching the Dirt:
How to Stop Worrying and Achieve Your God-given Potential
Inspirational Nonfiction, 148 pages, Paperback, ISBN 0-9729750-8-X
Deep down, you know God created you for a reason. He's told you that you're a child of God. You're made in His image, and He has a plan for you. You sense in your heart of hearts that you have wings to fly, but worries, fears, and insecurities drag you down to earth, preventing you from spreading your wings and taking flight.

This book will teach you how to quit worrying and trust God; easily distinguish between what you control and what God controls; find freedom to focus on the two decisions that are yours to make – What you want and Why you want it. Find deliverance from the worry-inducing questions of Who? When? How? and Where?

Lord, Are You Sure?
Inspirational, 152 pages, Paperback, ISBN 0-9729750-0-4
A roadmap for understanding how Heavenly Father works in your life, helping you understand why certain problems keep repeating themselves, how to break the cycle and unlock the mystery of why you encounter challenges and roadblocks on roads you felt inspired to travel.

Packets of Sunlight for Parents
Compiled by: Marnie L. Pehrson
Inspirational, 144 pages, ISBN 0-9676162-4-7
Brighten your day with inspiration for parents of tots to teens! Inspirational quote book.

Packets of Sunlight for American Patriots
Compiled by: Marnie L. Pehrson
Inspirational, 108 pages, ISBN 0-9676162-3-9
Let the founding fathers reignite your love for freedom! Inspirational quote book.

10 Steps to Fulfilling Your Divine Destiny:
A Christian Woman's Guide to
Learning & Living God's Plan for Her
Inspirational, 124 pages, Paperback, ISBN 0-9676162-1-2
Have you ever said to yourself, "I'd love to do great things with my life, but I'm just too busy, too untalented, too ordinary, too afraid, too anything but extraordinary"? Inside this book you'll learn how to reach your full God-given potential.

A Closer Walk with Him
SheLovesGod Study Lessons Volume 1
Inspiraitonal, 212 pages, paperback, ISBN 0-9729750-3-9
A collection of insights and ponderings on the scriptures and how we can apply them to our everyday lives. Great for the faith-lift you need in the morning, just before bed, or whenever you need a quick boost of inspiration. Each lesson is self-contained and independent. Read them in any order the Spirit moves you or read the 52 lessons in order as a yearly study guide - it's up to you.

To order call 800-524-2307 or visit
www.MarniePehrson.com

.

www.ingramcontent.com/pod-product-compliance
Lightning Source LLC
Chambersburg PA
CBHW050512260626
47157CB00004B/1295